Waltzing with an Echo

by

Dale Lovin

Aakenbaaken & Kent

Waltzing with an Echo

Aakenbaaken & Kent   New York

aakenbaakeneditor@gmail.com

ISBN: 978-1-938436-28-4

Dedication

Waltzing with an Echo is dedicated to my parents, my wife, Linda, and my children, Brandon, Amy and Brian.

Also

Mount Evans Home Health Care and Hospice of Evergreen, Colorado - Thank you for the mercy and compassion you offer to so many during their most difficult times. Because of you, walking the lonesome valley is not nearly so lonely. Oh, how our world needs more people like you.

Prologue

Empty desert and black night swallowed the speeding Ferrari. Hour after hour, the driver, with his shoulders hunched, applied relentless pressure on the accelerator. But no amount of speed or distance delivered escape from his memories - nor his demons.

After dawn and with the sun well above the horizon, the driver left the interstate for a two-lane road. Continuing a suicidal pace, he scanned the road ahead, looking for a specific landmark. Spotting what he sought, he slammed his brakes and wrenched the Ferrari from pavement onto an unmarked dirt road. An automobile that had been designed for cosmopolitan streets was now forced over rutted and precarious terrain as the road quickly narrowed into little more than a trail.

Undeterred, the driver jammed his foot even harder onto the accelerator and the Ferrari responded with a deafening roar and blinding velocity. A slight rise in the trail served as a catapult that propelled the Ferrari from the road. As though weightless, the engineering marvel traced an arc of pure grace through the air before slamming back onto the ground in a sickening thud. In a final torturous maneuver, the vehicle careened, totally out of control, slamming into a tree. Vapors spewing from crumpled destruction created the only remaining sound.

Repeated thrusts from the driver's shoulder managed to only partially open the door. With efforts of a contortionist, he squirmed, twisted his way clear, and stood quietly while taking in his surroundings. It had been years since he had been here. He bowed his head. So many memories. So many regrets.

Stooping to reach back through the restricted opening, the man extended his arm into the Ferrari and grasped a bag that he brought to his chest in a protective and loving gesture. Then, with a lowered head and a sense of determination, he began to walk.

He felt the air, marveling at how crisp and clean it was. In spite of his befuddled brain, memories found their way. He was young again, tasting the deliciousness of summer in an alpine paradise with his new wife. They had walked and talked, crafting dreams for their future. It had been fantasy become reality, all he had ever dreamed of.

They had hiked this very road. It had been their special daring adventure. And the birds, oh, how they had enjoyed the sounds of birds.

Where were the birds? The man halted, realizing that he had not heard a single sound since climbing from the Ferrari. Perhaps the noise of the crash had frightened the forest into silence. Bleary eyes searched the trees. No birds, no sounds. Moving on, he continued in a slow slog up the mountain until he reached the landmark he sought.

Nothing had changed, nothing at all. It was the same lush patch of grass, a small meadow with a mighty ponderosa pine in its center. The tree seemed to glare at him, asking why had it taken so long for him to return.

It was right there, beneath the ponderosa where the grass swayed. That was the enchanted spot. That was where they had spread their blanket. Sipping wine and speaking in soft tones, they had caressed - a brush of lips over eyebrows and fingertips soft as shadows. Kisses became fierce and passion fueled each new moment. It was not until afterwards that they had become aware of the singing birds. Lying together, enraptured by the rhapsody, they had whispered that their audience obviously approved of what they had seen. Why else would they offer such a musical ovation?

With moist eyes, the man made his way to the ponderosa. He leaned his back against the massive trunk and allowed his legs to collapse as his body slowly slid to the ground. Sitting at the base of the tree, he stared vacantly. Where were the birds? How he wanted to hear them again.

Finally, a sound reached him. But it was not the melodic birds he so craved. It was the rat-tat-tat of a woodpecker thirty feet above, shattering the forest's serenity. The bird hammered, its beak battering the ponderosa with determination. The man crooked his neck to watch the bird and listen to its rude clatter. Feeling cheated, he dropped his head and squeezed his eyes tightly closed. There would be no music today.

Rat-tat-tat.

The woodpecker's persistence prohibited any sense of peace or hope for introspection. The man sighed and then held a breath of resolve. He was ready. Upon opening the bag he had carried, a .357 magnum revolver captured the sun's rays.

Tears gushed. Cold, acidic metal slid over his tongue, lips clamped tightly over the barrel.

Rat-tat-tat.

Jaws set and eyes squeezed into sealed slits, he sucked hard through his nose, holding his last breath.

Rat-tat-tat.

Air burned within his lungs.

Rat-tat-tat.

A final command from brain to finger.

After the shattering explosion echoed and re-echoed across the mountain, haunting silence descended. The woodpecker did not return.

Within minutes, the first fly arrived.

Chapter One

Straight-up noon, no breeze and mid-June heat left no doubt that summer had arrived. Marshmallow puffs of clouds clustering in the west hinted of afternoon rain, but Brad Walker was skeptical. He had been paying attention to New Mexico skies for most of his life and recognized this charade for what it was. In all likelihood, today's clouds would congregate and morph from white to grey. Then, with a bit of boisterous rumbling, a few flashes of lightning and a thimble's worth of rain, they would simply whimper away.

Brad traced his foot over dry soil and unwittingly smiled. The best one could hope from these clouds was that they would linger long enough to spawn a classic New Mexico sunset. He had witnessed such firestorm spectacles countless times while growing up in this amazing land but still, he never took them for granted.

Silence was so absolute over the vast expanse of rangeland that his ears could almost feel a pressure. Brad ambled along the dirt road's edge, absently kicking his feet through weeds that thrived in the ditches on either side. An occasional startled grasshopper whirred, its clamor the only sound to break the silence. He turned to make his way back toward his vehicle, conflicting emotions stirring as he sauntered. He clearly felt pleasant anticipation but a stubborn hint of trepidation was growing worse.

Her ranch was less than two miles away. He could not help that the knot developing in his stomach had become so severe that he had to stop, walk and think. Brad needed a few minutes to sort out his thoughts and summon a measure of courage before seeing her again. Her telephone call had come as a surprise, and her voice had conveyed a sense of urgency. She was upset and faced a professional crisis. She asked for his help but wanted to speak face-to-face. That face-to-face was now only minutes away.

Brad reached his truck and stood beside the driver's door. How the heck could he have lost a wife to premature death and raised three children but feel what he felt every time he thought of Juanita? He shook his head in silence as he wondered about what was happening.

He thought back to last October when he had first met Juanita. It had been in Albuquerque where she was a federal prosecutor. A major part of her job was dealing with crimes stemming from hate groups. After his own close encounter with a group of white supremacists that had targeted him because of a case he had worked while an FBI Agent, Brad had been invited to attend a conference that she was directing. He recalled how upon first meeting Juanita, he had felt as if he entered the Twilight Zone, somewhere between a dream world and reality. Now, months later, his feelings remained turbulent as ever. But enough time had passed for him to realize that whatever he felt toward Juanita certainly was something that extended beyond her physical beauty.

How many times had he re-lived the night when a white supremacist had attempted to murder him by delivering a blow to his skull with a lead pipe? Brad had never spoken to a soul about this, but during that terrible experience, as he remained unconscious, a beguiling woman had entered his dreams. She had cared for him in some sort of transcendental world that seemed to Brad to be as real as anything that had ever happened in his life. All of his associates thought that a physician in a modern-day hospital had saved him but Brad wasn't so sure. He was not at all convinced that what he had experienced was a dream; a dream of a tiny cabin with no modern conveniences and a woman named Juanita who cared for him. Brad's heart never failed to beat a bit faster when he recalled how Juanita had nourished him with water and broth that were miraculous both in taste and their healing effect. What he recalled most clearly, though, was her face close to his. In faint candlelight she had smiled and touched him, her fingers lightly brushing his cheek.

He had initially tried to dismiss the dream episode with Juanita as no more than a result of the injury he had suffered in the assault to his head. But those efforts had evaporated when he met a real live Juanita at the conference in Albuquerque. He had felt it instantly when she first turned to face him. And when her extended hand had touched his, something totally inexplicable had transpired between them. Brad had no idea what to think. That first handshake had been so much more than simple physical contact. What had passed between their eyes bordered on something mystical.

The conference had passed as most conferences pass: endless talks, presentations and plans for the next conference. Juanita and he had been seated across from each other for much of the event, and Brad recalled her pleasant but efficient manner in coordinating speakers and presentations. They had spoken a few times during breaks. Each occasion had been brief and had consisted of typical small talk. But had he not caught her glancing at him? Each morning as the attendees gathered, he watched her mingle, her smile sparkling and personality effusive. But something had happened too often to be coincidental. While talking with others Brad saw her eyes seek him out. He grinned to himself. There was absolutely no doubt that she had noticed how he unabashedly stared at her. But it had all ended with nothing more than a proper and formal farewell. Brad recalled how he had driven home after the conference, unable to shake the image of her face and the sound of her voice.

After Albuquerque, his contact with Juanita had continued through a few email exchanges. They were mostly professional in nature as a follow-up to the conference but each message had held a few lines that timidly opened the door into the personal realm. At Christmas they had traded holiday greetings. Brad recalled how he held her card in his hand, mesmerized with a photograph of Juanita standing in front of her childhood ranch home. He had studied the card a dozen times each day, committing every detail of her face to memory. He had been thrilled to learn that she, like him, had been raised in New Mexico. Each time, after studying her card, he had concluded his introspection by closing his eyes and living again his dream in her tiny cabin. It was like it happened yesterday, her voice, her smile and the touch of her fingers.

In the dreary winter months following Christmas, they had continued with email communication that finally led to telephone calls. Their conversations had been light-hearted but each instance brought a slightly more intimate tone. Finally they spoke of Brad driving to Albuquerque so that they could share time together. But each time they had tried to schedule a meeting, Juanita found herself in a trial or conference and nothing had ever worked out.

Then her phone call of distress had come out of the blue. She was taking some time off work to be with her aging parents on their ranch. Would Brad consider a visit and a chance to talk? She hoped her request would not be an inconvenience but it was important to her. Brad shook his head as he inwardly smiled. It never crossed his mind to say no. The truth was that nothing could have stopped him from arranging his trip as quickly as possible.

The day had finally arrived and he had almost reached Juanita's ranch. Feeling foolish about being so apprehensive, he looked to the sky as if a solution to his nervousness might be floating somewhere above. He walked a bit to muster courage but he knew it was time to stop stalling. Brad slid behind the wheel of his old fishing rig, cranked the engine, took a deep breath and threw it into gear. As he headed down the road, he grunted, "Jesus H, I feel just like I did in eighth grade."

***

Reaching the crest of a hill, Brad slowed his vehicle to a crawl. He had a panoramic view of Juanita's childhood home, and he wanted to take a moment to absorb it. He wasn't sure why, but having a mental image of where she had spent her youth seemed important. A stone-capped mesa rose as a natural boundary, encompassing a sprawling valley where groves of cottonwood trees followed the meanderings of a creek. A tan-colored stucco house nestled comfortably within the shade of one such grove. That was where she lived. It was exactly as he recalled from her Christmas card. Outbuildings sprinkled the landscape and a corral of metal pipe held two horses, one solid black and the other a brown and white paint. Just beyond the perimeter of the corral, a windmill stood motionless, its fan blades reflecting sunlight. Along the creek an irrigated alfalfa field grew brilliantly green, its luminescence a stark contrast to the faded grass of the surrounding pastureland. Brad loved settings such as this, a blending of nature and man. He marveled at how time and space seemed inseparable in New Mexico.

With a deep breath and a mutter to himself, "Come on, Brad, you can do this," he eased his truck down the hill, turned a hard left and pulled to a stop in front of Juanita's house.

At the very moment he opened the door of his truck, he saw her. Juanita emerged from the front door and skipped lightly down two concrete steps to a stone pathway. As she made her way toward him, the first thing Brad saw was her smile, that beautiful smile. Wearing a white tee shirt, blue jeans and tennis shoes, she seemed to glide, her approach unfolding in slow motion. Brad held his breath. As she came closer, her brown eyes and coal-black ponytail mesmerized him. It was almost too much to take in. Juanita stood only feet away, expectancy on her face. The image crystalized, there was no way to escape it, he was back in his dream; injured and in pain, those eyes, the ponytail, her face over his, offering water. *Oh, my God. It's her, it's her.*

"Hello Brad. You're right on time so my directions must have been perfect." She cocked her head in a challenging gesture. "When we last talked, I remember that you told me that women simply could never know north from south or give accurate directions."

Brad opened his mouth to speak but a foolish grin and a shake of his head from side to side was the best he could do. Juanita tossed her head and laughed, but her unrelenting eyes held. She had him in a corner and expected a reply.

Gathering his wits, Brad summoned a comeback. "Just like a lawyer, you only hear what you wish to hear. What I said to you is that *most* women don't know north from south. But since you were a New Mexico ranch girl, I was certain your directions would be spot on."

She again laughed. "And you are just like a cop, full of hot air and baloney. Come on in. Mom has an incredible meal prepared, and I want you to meet her and my dad." With that, Juanita turned, and with an exaggerated motion of her head that said *follow me*, she led Brad into her house.

It was a step back into time. Brad sensed the decades of life that had passed in this humble home. Two reclining chairs, fabric worn thin, a table and lamp between them spoke of countless evenings where rest had come after another day of hard labor. A wood stove stood in the corner and small television sat on a simple stand. Photographs that Brad assumed were of family and a painting of cattle gathered beneath a windmill hung on a wall. A couch and few scattered magazines filled out the room.

Aromas drifting from the kitchen reminded Brad of days long past when he had been in his mother's kitchen. Breathing deeply, he let his senses fuel the memories. Knowing that houses tell much about the people who live within, Brad stood and methodically looked about, allowing the character of the house to speak. Understanding what was happening, Juanita remained silent and gave him time. Her evaluating eyes never left Brad's face and a slight smile turned her lips upward as she watched.

"So, this is that lawman you've been telling us about, the one who seems to have captured your fancy." A weathered figure with snow-white hair and brilliant eyes that scrutinized Brad from head to toe stepped from the kitchen. Walking with assistance from a cane, mischief beamed from the crinkles on the man's face. Brad was pleasantly aware that Juanita's brown skin could not hide the blush that crept into her cheeks in the wake of her father's impetuous pronouncement.

"Thanks a bunch, Dad." Her whisper went nowhere.

The man ignored his daughter and, with a wink directed to Brad, moved with force in spite of his cane and slight limp. He extended his arm and gripped Brad's hand with a calloused might that exuded confidence and physical strength. "Welcome, Brad Walker, welcome. My little girl here has told me quite a few things about you. We are happy to have you in our home. Now, I want you to come back here and meet the most beautiful bride in all of New Mexico."

Using his cane as a swivel, he spun with authority and Brad knew that he was expected to follow. The man turned his head back over his shoulder and with another wink announced, "By the way, my name's Otis. Now, for the love of heaven, don't ask me why any sane mother would curse a newborn male child with a name like Otis." He tapped his cane on the floor and twisted his face into part grimace and part smile. "Must've been her labor pains. Forget Otis. I'm Harv, just call me Harv." With another tap of his cane he turned and resumed his march into the kitchen.

"Thank you for having me, Harv. I'm pleased to be here." Brad glanced toward Juanita, raising his eyebrows and shoulders in a gesture of helplessness. But when he saw sheer mortification on her face and that her cheeks remained effervescent pink, he couldn't suppress a grin.

A round table was the centerpiece of the kitchen and commanded immediate attention. Blue dishes were set with precision on a white tablecloth and bowls overflowing with food covered every available inch. Brad saw roast beef, potatoes, gravy, salads, vegetables and a platter of sliced bread, steam still rising. He had no idea where to turn, what to say or do. Harv was leading like a general charging into battle, Juanita was nowhere to be seen and he suddenly felt abandoned. Events passing in a swirl, Brad stood before a table that was set with a feast deserving of royalty and he had no idea what to do or say.

He longed to seize Juanita and keep her close by for support and, as he tried to calculate how this could be gracefully accomplished, a woman seemed to simply materialize and suddenly stood directly before him. Swaths of grey rippled through her black hair, and magnificent brown eyes looked straight into his face. Juanita's mother held her penetrating gaze, offered her hand and smiled. Wrinkles about her eyes radiated life and brightened the entire room.

"Hello, Brad. Thank you for visiting our home. My name is Carmella." Her words were spoken softly, just loud enough to be heard but forcing one to actually listen.

As Brad took Carmella's hand into his own, he felt her warmth pass straight through, a soft magnetism within her grip. Brad glanced to Harv who was standing behind Carmella, his face beaming like the full moon. Managing to utter a greeting that he hoped was gracious, his eyes tried to absorb every feature of Carmella's open face. Brad quickly realized that he looked at a woman who was who she was, take it or leave it. He could not decide which was more expressive, her smile or her eyes. Lines of age that etched her mouth and face simply enhanced a striking beauty.

Thankfully, Juanita appeared next to her mother and placed an arm about her shoulders. The resemblance between mother and daughter was uncanny. Juanita and Carmella laughed simultaneously, their sparkling eyes defined the moment in a mockery of Brad's obviously stricken state. Realizing he was on the verge of looking foolish, Brad smiled, shook his head and raised his arms in a gesture of amazement. Moving his eyes from woman to woman, he spoke the only words he could think of. "Unbelievable! You ladies are absolutely unbelievable. I've never seen such resemblance."

Harv glowed as he moved toward the table and pulled back a chair for Carmella. "Come on now, we have to feed this man." Turning to Juanita he continued, "You've been telling us about Brad for weeks now but you failed to mention that he's a bit on the hungry side. For heaven's sake, let's get some food in this young man before he blows away." As he spoke, Harv tossed a glance to Brad, pure rascal gleaming in his eyes.

Carmella simply smiled and shook her head in hopelessness as she took her place and motioned for Brad to be seated. "Please forgive my husband, he's been too long under a New Mexico sun. His mind has suffered terribly over the years and I fear the damage is irreparable." Even in her humor, Carmella spoke with elegance and soft dignity.

As Brad took his seat, it was impossible to overlook the polar opposite images of Harv and Carmella. Harv's brash voice and mannerisms, white hair, fair skin and obvious Anglo descent cast a stark contrast to Carmella's refined voice, dark skin and Hispanic heritage. But as food was passed and conversation flowed, Brad soon recognized that he shared a table with people who lived life with deep and enduring love; love for each other and for the land on which they lived.

He learned that Juanita's two brothers lived on adjoining ranches and now handled the bulk of daily operations as their father had aged. Carmella spoke of how Juanita had been their only child to leave the ranch, determined to become a lawyer. As her story unfolded, pride in her daughter's accomplishments as a federal prosecutor was obvious, even as Harv leveled remarks about how much he missed having his daughter on the family ranch.

"You should see her on a horse," Harv proclaimed. "It's like she was born with reins in her hands and a saddle beneath her. The most beautiful thing you'll ever see. She's a vision straight from heaven." Juanita's eyes dropped but her smile could not be hidden.

Carmella and Harv peppered Brad with questions about the life and career he had known in the FBI. They listened with particular fascination to the story of his encounter with murderous white supremacists and how the episode had led to his meeting their daughter in Albuquerque. Through it all,

Juanita remained mostly silent, but her smile conceded pleasure in the relaxed back-and-forth that was transpiring between her parents and Brad. Harv's antics frequently prompted laughter from around the table but it was Juanita's laugh that so captivated Brad. Each time it happened, he felt his chest tighten. It was the same sound that had delivered such enchantment in his dreams after the assault; the laugh and dream that refused to go away.

After apple pie had been served, Harv looked directly to Juanita as he spoke. "Okay, Princess, I'm convinced that Brad here has enough sense not to go out and stir up a pissing contest with a skunk. Why don't you get going and have your talk with him." Harv then turned to Brad and, for the first time of the afternoon, spoke with no intention of being ornery or comical. "Thank you for coming, Brad. Juanita has something on her mind that sounds pretty darned serious to me. She said you were the only person she could think of who could possibly help her out. Carmella and I appreciate anything you can do." With that, Harv again turned to Juanita but the twinkle was right back in his eyes and pure rascal rang in his voice. "Now, that is the *only* reason you invited him down here, isn't it?"

Juanita abruptly stood from the table, crunched her napkin into a wad and tossed it straight into her father's face. "Please, Brad, take me away from here and this insufferable man. I prosecute people who have more manners and behave with more dignity than my own father." In spite of her mock scolding, Juanita's smile of adoration for her father simply radiated.

Harv threw his head back and laughed as Carmella looked on, shaking her head in sympathy for Juanita but her face reflecting absolute pleasure.

***

With the windows of Brad's truck lowered, fresh air and the vastness of the land brought a sense of freedom. Driving slowly, Brad followed the road to take them beside the alfalfa field that he had spotted earlier. Water spewed from a network of nickel-colored pipes and occasional rainbows reflected in the cascading mist. A fragrance of damp soil hung in the air and the purity of cold, life-giving water could almost be tasted as they passed. Juanita directed Brad beyond the field to a narrow road of wheeled ruts that followed the creek and cottonwood trees. Hereford cattle, with rust-colored bodies and white faces, stood behind strands of barbed wire fencing, curious as to the nature of the visitors.

Just before dropping into a shallow ravine, the road was blocked by a closed gate. Brad brought his truck to a halt and reached to open his door. Juanita beat him by a full second and gave him her laugh as she stepped out of the vehicle. "Chivalry may be alive and well in some places, but out here the passenger opens gates." She turned her body, lowering her face to speak through the cab's window. "Besides, I seriously doubt that all those years in the FBI taught you beans about opening gates. I'll bet dollars to donuts that even if you tried to open that gate, you wouldn't get the job done. And then, I would end up having to come to your rescue. Now, how embarrassing would that be?" With a lifting of eyebrows and still laughing, Juanita strutted to the gate. She wrapped a slender arm about the grey, cedar anchor post, snuggled her shoulder against the gatepost and, in a blink, flipped the wire loop free. Swinging the gate open, she cast a sassy "How about that" look to Brad and gave a mock bow as she waved him through.

Cool and unperturbed, Brad eased his fishing rig through the gate, ignoring Juanita's impertinent behavior. He watched through mirrors as she closed the gate and made her way back toward the vehicle. Just as she reached the door, Brad pressed the accelerator, leaving Juanita standing alone in the pasture looking like a lost child. He drove for several yards before stopping and backing up to gather his passenger. Juanita just stood, hands on hips and defiance on her face. Brad leaned across the seat and spoke through the passenger window. "Excuse me, Miss. I seemed to have taken a wrong turn. I'm looking for a coffee shop. I'm in desperate need of a latte. Can you help me?"

Juanita threw open the door and was back inside in a flash. With no change of expression, she stoically replied, "Absolutely, I will be glad to help you." Pointing with her finger, she continued. "See that big bull standing down there by the creek, all two thousand pounds of him? That just happens to be our ranch barista. Don't let the angry look on his face or those long, vicious horns bother you. He really is quite friendly. Why don't you just walk up to him and place your order? I'm absolutely positive he can give you a latte unlike any you've ever had before." Juanita turned sharply to face Brad, her eyes meeting his full on. Their gaze held, both aware of silent seconds ticking past. Juanita smiled first, then Brad. The laughter that followed was a sound of simple, long-awaited happiness.

***

Shade from cottonwoods caused the creek to appear as a subdued shadow. Juanita stirred tiny sandstorms in the current as she traced the bottom with gentle swirls of her bare toes. "This is where my brothers and I swam when we were kids." She shifted her weight on the log that stretched across the stream. "I think maybe I love this place more now than I did even then."

Brad sat cross-legged on the bank, watching her. "I can sure understand that," he replied as he tossed tiny stones into the water. "Why is it that we feel compelled to leave these wonderful places and go off into some crazy world and become whatever it is we become?" They were both quiet as they contemplated the question.

Brad spoke again. "Is this now so special only because you left it or, if you had stayed on the ranch, do you think you would still feel the same attraction?"

Juanita kicked her feet, flicking water into the air. "Oh, I don't know. I love my life in Albuquerque. I love being a prosecutor and all that goes with it. But every time I come home, this ranch just seems to cradle me. And, in the summer, this log right here is the first place I head for. My mom and dad always have so much they want me to do but they understand what's inside me. They know what I need. Dad just growls and tells me to get my little brown biscuits to the creek and don't come back until I'm good and ready." Juanita turned to Brad and gave him her laugh. "You were with Dad long enough today to know exactly how he would sound saying that to me."

With a nod and a grin, Brad acknowledged her assessment. "Oh yeah. I think I can hear him perfectly." But as he spoke, Brad's eyes were on the pendant that rested against Juanita's white shirt. Earlier, the stone had remained beneath her tee shirt, but after opening the gate it had swung free and now dangled over the creek as she bent to inspect her toes in the water. "That's a beautiful pendant. I love the colors."

"Thank you. It originally belonged to my grandmother and then my mom. The day I graduated from law school, Mom placed it around my neck." Juanita took the stone in her hand, caressing it between her fingers. She directed it in Brad's direction so that he could see it more clearly. "I was speechless and Mom just looked at me and cried. I've worn it every single day since then." She lifted her eyes from the pendant and shifted them to Brad. "When I'm in court, right in the middle of a really tough case, I can always feel this on my skin. It's like Mom is with me. I feel a piece of this ranch with me every day."

Breeze drifted through the cottonwoods. The old giants swayed, rustling leaves sounding like a sigh of contentment. Juanita and Brad did not speak, each savoring the peacefulness of the moment. When the breeze had passed and trees again stood motionless, Brad smiled at Juanita. "Okay, Miss Juanita, I have loved every minute of this day and I never want to leave. I wish to never set foot in a city again. But there is a reason you asked me to come here." And with a twinkle in his eyes he continued, "Even your Dad seemed to think you had a reason for inviting me."

"Oh, that man! He delights in embarrassing me." Juanita laughed as she brought her feet from the water to rest them on the log. Tucking her legs beneath her chin and wrapping her arms about her knees, she rocked back and forth, staring into the creek. After a few seconds she turned to Brad and, for the first time of the day, her face was not smiling. "Yes, Brad, I do want to talk with you about something." She paused, gathering her thoughts. "Something happened recently, something very tragic. But my instinct tells me that the tragedy may be only the tip of an iceberg." She looked straight at Brad for emphasis. "I have suspicions, a gut feeling, that's all. Not a single shred of evidence and I'm not sure what to think or what to do." She fell silent again, eyes focused on the water.

"I'm listening."

Lifting herself, Juanita nimbly stood on the log without again wetting her feet. "Come on, let's walk. I think better when I'm moving." She balanced herself against the trunk of a cottonwood as she slipped socks and shoes onto her feet. Brad never took his eyes from her pendant, swaying like a pendulum as she laced her shoes; the silver chain that held it remained obscured by her ponytail. Juanita stood, giving a quick smile as she spoke. "Okay, Mr. Brad Walker, it's payment time for that marvelous feast you enjoyed earlier. Let's go this way." She pointed to another clump of cottonwoods about a quarter mile downstream.

Stepping from the shade they had enjoyed, Brad felt afternoon heat that had intensified. He gave a quick glance to the sky, noticing the clouds that were building in the west. Brad let Juanita set the pace and she walked slowly, her eyes focused straight ahead. Walking beside her, he could sense that a million thoughts were spinning within her head. Anxiety that had suddenly developed was easily felt. They walked in silence for some distance before Juanita lifted her face in a quick glance to Brad and, with a sigh, began her story.

"This all started quite a long time ago when I was in law school at the University of New Mexico. I was one of the older students of my class because I had to take a break after college to work a while. It took a bit of time for me to save some money. Once I entered law school, I soon met a guy who was originally from California. He was also a little older than most of our class so maybe that's what brought us together. Other than the fact that we were the oldest people in our class, I'm not sure why we became friends because we were complete opposites. He was a fast-talking, slick operator from Los Angeles and I was just a very plain country girl. We were definitely the odd couple, with yours truly being the most odd. But for whatever the reasons, we became very good friends."

A shadow of a smile appeared on Brad's face but he made no comment.

"His name was Raymond but by the end of our first semester, everybody just called him Rapid Ray. He talked fast and had the quickest wit I've ever known. He seemed to always have a hundred things going at the same time. He loved to buy and sell cars, always at a profit, of course. He had ways to find a deal for anyone who wanted jewelry and he constantly had a line on a condo or vacation home for anyone interested. He was absolutely unbelievable. I have no idea how he made it through law school. All I ever did was study and squeak by. It seemed that Ray did nothing but joke around and have a good time. But somehow he passed every course, easy as pie." Juanita shook her head in wonder and looked up at Brad. "You ever know anyone like that?"

"Oh yeah. Some folks are just wired that way. That's just a certain type of an intellect I suppose. The other stuff you mention though, that's different. People who are always in a flashy deal of some sort, they cause my antennae to go up. There's usually more there than what meets the eye."

"You are so right." Juanita stopped walking and faced Brad. "I look back on things now and see them quite differently. But at the time, I simply found him fascinating. He never hit on me or tried to be anything other than a friend. He made me laugh and, with the stress of law school, I needed that." She paused, obviously in thought. "I suppose that more than anyone else in law school, Ray taught me that life does not always have to be so serious. He simply loved life and shared his gusto with everyone he associated with." Juanita resumed her slow walk.

Brad matched her pace as she sauntered, the next stand of cottonwoods growing closer. "Okay, what's the rest of the story?"

"Well, believe it or not, Ray fell head over heels in love with a nurse in Albuquerque and they married right after graduation.

I met her a few times but never felt that I really knew her well at all. Nobody could believe that Ray was so stuck on just one girl and that he actually committed to settle down so quickly. But regardless of what people thought, Ray seemed to be madly in love." Juanita looked to Brad and smiled. "Guess you never know, huh?"

"Yep, trying to predict or understand that kind of stuff is a fool's mission," Brad replied with a chuckle. "You'll lose every time."

Juanita gave a knowing smile and continued. "They had a crazy wedding at the top of Sandia Peak. The entire wedding party and heaven knows how many guests rode the gondola, drinking champagne and laughing all the way up to ten thousand feet. Then the ceremony took place under a tent with views over Albuquerque and all the way to eternity. The entire day was simply fun and happy like no other. We all rode the gondola back down and partied all night."

Reaching the cottonwoods, they once again stood in shade. Juanita sat on a rock and Brad leaned against a tree trunk. With a distant gaze, Juanita spoke softly, "And that's where the fairy tale ends."

Neither Juanita nor Brad said anything for seconds. From somewhere nearby, a dove cooed. Instinctively, they both turned their heads, looking for the unseen bird. "What a beautiful sound," Juanita whispered.

"My mom used to say that the cooing of a dove was the most beautiful lullaby in the world," Brad responded. They enjoyed silence for a few moments before Brad looked to Juanita with expectation for her to continue.

"After graduation, I really don't know all that much about what happened to Ray and his wife. They honeymooned in Colorado and then Ray took his new wife to Las Vegas, Nevada, of all places. To the best of my knowledge, he never practiced law or utilized his education in any way. I learned that he went to work for a big casino operation, doing what I had no idea. For as close as I thought we were, he never called or communicated with me or anyone in our class."

Almost imperceptibly, Juanita shook her head as if she still could not accept this behavior from a man she had considered to be a friend.

Her shoulders moved with a sigh as she continued. "Albuquerque is a small town, really, and I happened to pick up through a friend of a friend that their marriage lasted only about three years. His wife returned to her nursing career and those who knew her said she was a devastated woman. Apparently Ray made truckloads of money but along the way began using drugs and became a different person. I guess he had a different showgirl or hooker on his arm every night and was flying high as a kite. His wife would have no part of it and left him. I heard she didn't even try to get any of his money. She just wanted away from him and his life."

A twig that held a clump of cottonwood leaves lay on the ground and caught Juanita's attention. She bent to gather the twig, causing her pendant to dangle hypnotically. Brad felt helpless, completely captivated. As she twisted the twig in her fingers, contemplating its leaves, Brad's eyes were riveted. He had been with her all afternoon and, for the entire time, he had felt he was being transported through time. He was right back in his dream, injured, laying in a small cabin, a beautiful woman named Juanita caring for him. Brad felt his heart race. He had to deliberately force the thoughts from his mind and focus his attention back to the story she was relating. Juanita still was not speaking but remained focused on the leaves as if they held answers to her questions.

Tossing the leaves to the ground, Juanita stood and laughed. "Okay, Brad, I know what's happening here. You're standing there thinking that you drove all this distance just to listen to a crazy woman lawyer tell you a sad story of love gone bad." Her eyes had a sparkle again. "But you just remember that meal of roast beef and apple pie Mom fed you." She laughed her magical laugh. "So no matter about all of this nonsense, your trip was worth it."

Brad could not clear his mind or tear his eyes from Juanita but managed a reply. "The love gone bad story has been fascinating but I'm thinking that one of these days, you're going to get to the point of this whole thing."

"Don't be a wise guy. Zip it. I'm getting to the good stuff right now." Juanita gave Brad a look of exasperation and began pacing as she continued. "All that I've told you is years in the past. I had not heard from Ray since shortly after his wedding. Then, whammo, out of the big blue sky I'm sitting at my desk in Albuquerque one day about two weeks ago and my phone rings. It was Ray! I was flabbergasted to say the least. Once he had convinced me of his identity and my shock subsided, there was no small talk. He obviously had something on his mind and got right to the point." Juanita ceased pacing and looked at Brad, "I've replayed the conversation in my mind a hundred times. It's going to live with me forever." Doubt now clouded her eyes.

"Okay, Juanita, what's wrong?"

"I swear, Brad, it all happened so fast. Ray started talking and it sounded like he was about to crack wide open. The first thing he tells me is that he's done something terrible. He said he knew he should go to the police but was afraid to do so because he felt certain he would end up in prison." Juanita raised her eyebrows and gave a half grin. "Now, that got my attention! I immediately reminded him that I was a prosecutor and worked with police every day. He just shot right back that he wanted to retain me as his lawyer and whatever he told me would be privileged information. I was absolutely stunned. I tried to explain that I could not possibly be his lawyer, that I worked for the government as a prosecutor and could not represent private clients. Ray ignored every word I said. He told me that he visited Albuquerque frequently and had desperately wanted to see me for weeks but just had not had the courage to call." Juanita stopped speaking for a moment before raising her voice in exasperation. "Rapid Ray, afraid to call me? His dear friend from law school and he's afraid to call! Give me a break. I was trying to process what he was saying and what was happening but it wasn't making any sense."

"This is not exactly a typical reunion with an old friend." Brad spoke as he watched Juanita begin her nervous pacing again.

"Tell me about it! I continued to explain all the reasons that I could not possibly represent him and he started crying. I mean, Brad, this guy was broken up. I've never heard such heartbreaking sounds come from a grown man. I just sat there listening to him, feeling totally bewildered and stunned. I tried to wrap my head around the image of happy-go-lucky Rapid Ray and the sobbing mess that was talking to me on the telephone. It was all coming at me so fast and I couldn't make heads or tails of anything. Finally, I decided that the only thing I could do was set my lawyer mind on the shelf and let my human side take over." Juanita stood still again, self-analyzing. "I don't know if I was right or wrong, Brad, but I decided to simply shut up and let Ray talk."

Brad gave a nod of understanding.

Juanita returned to the rock and lowered her body to sit again. "Now, this is the crux of the whole story, Brad, and why I called you." She was silent and looked to Brad, a smile appearing. "Okay, you sure you really want to hear this? You can still back out."

"Lay it out, Juanita." Brad grinned. "I'm afraid of what your Dad might do to me if I decide to run now."

"Very good point. But, an important thing for you to remember is that my Mom is the one you should have concern about. Don't let that calm demeanor of hers fool you. She could be your worst nightmare." Juanita looked at Brad sternly, obviously trying not to laugh.

Raising his hands above his shoulders, Brad shook his head as he spoke. "Nothing more needs to be said. I absolutely hear you." They both smiled through their eyes.

"Alright, let me get this over with. I'm not at all comfortable with what I'm doing here but I can't figure another way to handle it." She exhaled hard. "So, here goes. Ray confirmed the stories I had heard. After law school he went to work for casino operations in Nevada. He had old friends there who brought him in to all kinds of matters related to casino business. He helped in research of merger deals, hired and fired staff, entertained high-roller clients, and all kinds of stuff. But then, Ray laid out some details that were not what I ever expected to hear. As an offshoot of entertaining big spenders and top clientele, he began to arrange hooker services for clients who paid huge money for anything they wanted beyond the gambling tables."

Juanita looked to Brad as if she needed to be certain he really wanted to hear more of her story. He returned her look with a nod that told her to continue.

"Ray admitted right up front that this quickly evolved into his own use of prostitutes and then he started using drugs. Before he realized what was happening, he found himself trapped in a vicious circle of money, drugs and sex. When he began to tell me this part of his story, he lost his composure again. He cried when he told of how he had lost his wife in the process." Juanita shook her head and lowered her voice. "Ray said his jet-setting lifestyle made him blind to what he was throwing away." Juanita looked to Brad. "All while he was telling me these things, I was thinking what a tragic way to live, but yet I wasn't all that surprised. Looking at it now, with some years under my belt, I suppose this was the real Rapid Ray that I had known in law school. I had just chosen not to recognize it."

Brad acknowledged her assessment with a slow shake of his head. "We all change as we grow. Mistakes in judgment are easy to see in hindsight."

"I suppose you're right. But, now comes the really sad part of the story where Ray's life unraveled into tragedy. Once he reached a point where his drug abuse could not be hidden and his hotshot casino associates recognized that he was no longer a legitimate or contributing partner, they flat out fired him, no second chances. So, still unwilling to face reality, Ray left Nevada but managed to wriggle his way into the gambling casinos on Indian reservations that have become so prevalent in the Southwest. Of course, it wasn't long before the same issues again surfaced and Ray found himself needing more and more money to sustain his lifestyle."

Juanita took a breath before continuing. "Ray told me that from that point on it was a screaming downhill slide. He finally said to hell with casinos and decided to operate on his own. From his few remaining connections, he managed to get himself involved with a group of people who made considerable money in the black market of stolen Native American artifacts. Drugs, prostitutes and stolen artifacts, these things became his life." Juanita's spoke to herself as much as to Brad. "And what was the most striking part of his story was how all of those things were traded so casually, just like a visit to the grocery store."

Juanita became quiet, her eyes focused on the ground before her. "And, it gets even worse. Ray said he turned to recruiting young girls, mostly Hispanic and Native American, and arranging sex for cash, drugs or artifacts, anything to make a deal." Disgust filled her voice. "Ray said what he was doing was so lucrative he couldn't make himself walk away." She paused. "God, this makes me sick. Ray admitted that as things progressed, he became desperate. His girls became younger and the men involved were absolute scum." She spoke with contempt. "Ray confessed that he had gone from a Nevada high-flyer to nothing more than a drug-using and drug-pushing pimp who also fenced stolen property; stolen property that should have been respected and regarded as sacred." Juanita lowered her head and was quiet.

After letting her words settle, Brad spoke. "You know, Juanita, I don't think it really matters whether Ray was dealing with high rollers in casinos or back-alley street slugs, the essence of what he was doing never changed."

"You are so right, Brad. Big money doesn't change a thing. No amount of glitzy, Las Vegas casino veneer can change how despicable so much of that world really is."

Brad simply nodded and Juanita was silent. The dove cooed again. This time neither of them turned to look. Juanita lifted her head upward, her brown eyes searching the sky.

"Now that I've had time to think about this, I realize that in all the years I knew Ray, the most down to earth I ever heard him sound, the only time he slowed down and talked like a normal person, was when he got to this next part of his story." Juanita looked straight at Brad. "Ray was crying again but this time it was a soft, heart-wrenching cry, not that terrible, uncontrolled sobbing. Ray told me that one-day he simply just woke up. He said that a realization of his wasted life hit like a freight train. He suddenly saw how much destruction he was bringing to himself and to innocent people. His failed marriage and the guilt he felt when he thought of his wife became unbearable. He said that he recognized that his only accomplishment in life had been to denigrate the human dignity of others."

Juanita swallowed. "Those were his exact words, Brad, that he had denigrated the human dignity of others." Juanita allowed a moment for the significance of the words to settle before continuing. "This confession came from a man with whom I had spent three years of my life. For three years, we studied how the law was crafted to protect people, especially the vulnerable. And, as lawyers, we were the designated guardians of that protection." Juanita paused, moving her head from side to side. "I don't know which is worse, that Ray became a traitor to something I so revere or the degradation that he imposed on young women and that he defiled the history and customs of Native Americans."

Juanita became quiet. Watching her shoulders scarcely move beneath her white shirt, Brad still did not speak. He chose to let the moment pass. Within seconds Juanita turned to face him again, speaking softly. "Now, are you ready for the last part of this story?"

"Go ahead, Juanita. Let's get this over with."

"Ray said that he had decided he had to get out of that horrible business and start over. He was going to walk away from everything, cold turkey, no looking back. But then unbelievable tragedy struck. One of the girls that Ray had brought into his business committed suicide. She was a young Hispanic girl. Apparently, several men had abused her. She lived in a trailer park and hung herself from the awning of her trailer." Juanita was silent and just looked at Brad.

With a sigh of defeat, Brad finally spoke. "I was afraid you were leading up to something like this." He shook his head in sadness. "What's Ray going to do?" He paused. "And just as importantly, what are you going to do?"

Forcing a bitter laugh, Juanita gave a hard look to Brad as she replied. "Ray isn't going to do anything, Brad, he's not going to do a thing." Her next words remained in her mouth, as if she couldn't decide whether to swallow or speak. Her voice was soft but heavy with irony when she finally continued. "You see, Brad, my old law school friend, Ray, he also committed suicide, just like that poor young girl."

"Jesus."

Juanita dropped her head and moved it slowly from side to side. "This is so sad but also terribly infuriating." She shut her eyes, pressing fingers on the bridge of her nose. "If only I could go back, do or say something different." She was silent, lost in her private thoughts.

Brad's mind raced, struggling for a proper response. What could he possibly say that would not sound hollow? He spoke softly. "Listen, Juanita, I have done my best to really hear and understand everything you have told me this afternoon. So help me, not one single thing here is remotely your fault. Ray's chosen way of life, all that he did and a final decision to end his own life, these are things over which you had no control."

"Well, that may be so but you have to know how our telephone conversation ended. You see, before Ray hung up, he lost it again. He was borderline incoherent. He kept repeating something and at first, I couldn't understand what he was saying. Then it dawned on me that he was muttering 'a life-for-a–life, a life-for-a-life'. He said it over and over again. Once I understood his words, I instantly knew that he was thinking suicide. I did my best. I promised to help. I assured him that something could be worked out. I didn't know exactly what to say but I just talked and talked. I did everything I could to reason with him."

"Was he listening? Do you think he heard anything at all that you said?"

Juanita gave a slight nod. "At the time, I thought he had listened. It seemed that he had processed things to an extent and was thinking rationally. He regained a degree of composure and we continued to talk. He asked if he could meet with me in Albuquerque." Juanita gave a look of bewilderment as she continued. "Brad, it was the way he asked. He was so shy, afraid to even talk about seeing me. It was so out of character from the Ray that I knew. When he asked for a meeting, it sounded like he was asking for a first date. I told him of course I would meet with him. I was emphatic that a meeting and an eye-to-eye conversation would be a logical first step to get things straightened out. I told him that I would help develop a plan for how he should move forward. He was perfectly agreeable and seemed relieved to have made a decision. He said he was calling from Salt Lake City but would be back in touch right away. He gave me his cell number and we agreed to talk every day."

"Juanita, you handled the situation perfectly. What else could you have done for heaven's sake? You can't keep second guessing yourself."

She spoke in little more than a whisper. "Brad, you didn't hear his voice. You just can't imagine how he sounded." The expression on Juanita's face spoke louder than her voice. "Let me tell you our last words. I want you to know how we ended our conversation."

Juanita's eyes bored straight into Brad's. Something inside was tearing her apart and Brad had no response. He simply nodded, waiting for what was coming.

"Ray's last words will haunt me until I die, Brad. His voice was so soft, he was no longer crying, just talking from his heart. I could feel him; I could literally feel his anguish. Ray told me had become nothing more than a street criminal and a pimp of young girls and he wanted to change his life." Juanita's voice became a whisper. Brad strained to hear her words. "He told me I was his only hope and that, of all the people in the world, he cared more for me than anyone else. He said I was the only person who he trusted to help him." Juanita lowered her head. "Then he told me that his life was in my hands and that he loved me." Juanita looked to Brad. "He said that he had always been in love with me."

"Oh, my gosh, Juanita, that's a terrible burden for you to carry."

She shook her head as she spoke. "I didn't know what to say. I told Ray that I loved him too. After I said that, there was silence for a few seconds and he just went away, ended the call without another word." Juanita looked straight into Brad's eyes. "His last words to me were that his life was in my hands and that he loved me."

"My God, Juanita, I am so sorry."

She placed her arms about her shoulders and held herself. Brad knew not to speak.

Shadows crossed the sky, obscuring the sun's light and darkening the afternoon. Brad glanced upward. Grey clouds tumbled and a restless breeze began to stir. Ignoring the weather, he held his voice, waiting for Juanita.

A faint smile crossed Juanita's face. "Okay, that's it. Now you know, Brad, Now you know. Thank you for listening."

"Juanita, of course I'll listen to you. Thank you for confiding in me. This is something that can't be kept inside. You have to talk, get it out or it will kill you. I will listen to you anytime. I hope you know that."

"Yes, I think I've known that all along." She gave Brad a penetrating look. "Otherwise, I would never have reached out for you."

Trying to decipher the meaning of her look and facial expression, Brad simply replied, "I'm glad you did."

They were quiet again, each looking away from the other.

Brad broke the silence. "Did you connect with him again after your conversation?"

"I called him multiple times. He never answered. A few days passed and I heard absolutely nothing. I had no idea what to think or do."

"How did you learn that he had killed himself?"

"About ten days ago, a phone call came in from a sheriff's investigator up in Gunnison, Colorado. Ray's body had been found near there. He blew his brains out."

"Jesus." Brad could not look at Juanita. He turned away as he whispered.

"That's when I called you."

Brad did not respond but the look on his face and a hint of a nod indicated that he understood.

"They found our law school alumni directory in his car. My name and number in the prosecutor's office were circled. That same number also popped up in his cell phone records. That's it. If not for a notation in the directory or cell phone records, it's possible that I would never have learned what happened."

Brad nodded his agreement. "What did the investigator ask you? How in the world did you respond?"

"All I told them was that we were law school friends and that he had recently called me. I explained that he was seemingly quite upset over a broken marriage from years past and that he was supposed to be on his way to Albuquerque to see me." A note of uncertainty tinged her voice. "I just wasn't ready to relate everything that Ray had told me. It didn't seem right." She shrugged. "I'm probably violating ethics by talking with you and not being absolutely honest with the investigators, but I'll just have to live with it." Juanita smiled. "I'm sure you figured out that I've also talked with my parents."

"Oh, heck yes and you did exactly right." Brad gave a dismissive wave of his hand as he stood up. Placing hands on hips, he twisted his body back and forth, a habit from years spent as a runner. He looked to Juanita, and held her gaze for a moment before asking the unspoken question. "Okay, Juanita, You've told me a sad story and I appreciate how difficult this is for you. But what's your plan and why me?"

Obviously pretending that she had not heard his question, Juanita allowed the question to dangle, refusing to meet his eyes. Finally, when she did acknowledge that he had spoken, she did so with a playful expression and tone in her voice. "My plan is quite simple and it has been executed. I have talked with you. That's it. That was my plan." With a soft laugh, she continued. "Mission accomplished you might say." She tilted her head and looked at his face as if she challenged him to respond before she gave a full smile.

In wake of the preceding somber moments, Juanita's changing expression brought a welcome sense of relief. With the shine returning to her eyes and humor once again in her voice, the air seemed to miraculously clear and oppression evaporated. Grateful for the shift and hoping to keep things more light-hearted, Brad fired right back. "Not so fast, young lady, you don't get off that easy. I'm pretty sure I'm reading the tea leaves correctly but I'm going to make you spell it out, word for word. After all, you're the lawyer here." Brad spoke in a devilish tone, letting Juanita know that he had no intention to make things easy for her. "I think I just might enjoy watching you squirm a bit."

Juanita's entire face smiled. "I was afraid you would be difficult to deal with so okay, I'm prepared. Here goes. I'll spell everything out for you just as you wish." She gathered her thoughts. "Honestly, I'm not positive about what may be in play here with issues of attorney-client privilege. Ray places a call to me, and who knows where he actually might have been when he called. He tells a New Mexico prosecutor a vague and disjointed story that probably involves several aspects of illegal activity." She glanced to Brad and raised her hands, palms upward as she shrugged. "And, all of this taking place over an unknown period of time. Plus, just consider the stuff Ray talked about: stolen artifacts, illegal drugs and sexual exploitation of young girls. You know perfectly well that, if any of that is validated, multiple states and jurisdictions will be involved."

"No doubt," Brad agreed.

"What Ray was rambling about is certainly vile and public safety or the safety of young girls is very much in play." Raising her voice in exasperation she concluded. "But I have not a shred of evidence of any kind to corroborate a single word he said."

Brad just looked at Juanita with a thoughtful expression but did not reply.

"I had clearly explained to Ray that I could not represent him. He just as clearly stated to me that he considered me to be his attorney. Once I realized he was suicidal, I promised to do anything I could to help him and I encouraged him to speak openly with me. Now, could that be interpreted to mean that I did in fact agree to represent him?" Juanita shrugged. "Beats me!" Cocking her head, she gave Brad a look that defied him to analyze the situation.

Brad grinned in bewilderment. "Thanks for clarifying things for me, counselor. I was a tad confused until you laid it out for me in those simple terms. Now, I see everything clear as mud."

Together, they shared a sad chuckle in mutual confession that neither knew what to think. "Come on, let's walk again." Juanita began walking in the direction of Brad's truck.

Moving in silence, Juanita let seconds pass before she continued. "Here's what I'm thinking. I'm not comfortable going straight to the police with all of the things that Ray said to me. Somehow that seems a betrayal of our conversation." She looked to Brad with raised eyebrows and a smile clearly meant to be conniving. "However, if I just happen to have a friend, who used to be in law enforcement but is no longer in law enforcement, and that friend happens to know a whole bunch of people in law enforcement, hmmm, I wonder if maybe I should talk with that friend?"

Juanita turned away, deliberately holding her focus straight ahead. She pretended to be in deep thought, but the conniving message in her words was clear.

"Hmmm, yourself! You are absolutely shameless. I'm guessing you want this friend to go snooping around the suicide investigation in Colorado and become a royal pest. You're thinking that if the pest becomes pesky enough, he might get a line on what Ray was up to that led him to commit suicide." After a pause, Brad concluded. "And, most importantly, you're also thinking that if all this works out, some poor New Mexico attorney, who is lost as night, just might be able to figure out what the heck she should do."

Juanita spun on her heels to face Brad, causing her turquoise pendant to arc through the air. "Why, Brad Walker, that is absolutely genius!" She slapped a hand across her forehead and appeared incredulous. "Why did I not think of that?" Her eyes dancing, she simply looked at Brad, waiting for his response.

"Before this nonsense goes any further, let's be clear that you are about as subtle as a train wreck. Your intention to manipulate me is totally transparent. A few pretty smiles along with an incredible meal from your mom and you think I will simply melt like Jell-O." Brad tried to invoke a scolding tone but knew it wasn't working and he couldn't keep a grin from breaking out. "Just so you know, this ain't my first rodeo, young lady. I know your kind and I am perfectly aware of what's happening here."

Juanita simply held her eyes on Brad with no reply, her smile saying more than a thousand words.

"Fair enough, Miss Juanita, I take your failure to respond and that smart-ass smirk on your face as an admission of guilt."

Juanita laughed, "Okay, I suppose you figured me out this time, but I have lots of tricks so don't get too relaxed." She winked. "I'll get you next time, don't you worry."

She again walked and Brad fell in beside her as he began speaking. "I do have a friend in that area who I can contact. His name is Sam Trathen. He's a police officer in Aspen and that's pretty close to Gunnison. We've known each other for years and Sam stays on top of what's going on throughout that whole part of the state." Brad took a deep breath. "In fact, not too long ago Sam and I found ourselves mixed up in a deal that involved kids who were being trafficked for sex. Sam's a good man and will help out if he can. My guess is that he will be able to come up with some answers." Brad turned to Juanita. "Okay, Miss Sneaky, happy now?"

"Delighted, Mr. Brad, absolutely delighted. Thank you." They had reached the same grove of cottonwoods where their walk and conversation had initially begun. Juanita turned to Brad. "I just ask that you help me take a peek behind the curtain. I want to know what Ray was involved with. If it's anything like what I suspect, there are other girls out there who are in danger and need help. Because of my position as a prosecutor, I feel a responsibility to at least look into things. I couldn't live with myself if something terrible turns up down the road because I failed to take some sort of action. But I also realize that I have to be careful about poking around in areas where I have no authority."

"I hear you and I understand exactly what you are saying. Let me talk with Sam and get a feel for what happened. I'm happy to help."

Juanita stooped to pluck a wildflower that sprouted beneath the trees. "Tell me about the case you mentioned, the one that involved children and sex trafficking."

Brad watched her hand as she traced her fingertips over petals of the flower. A chill ebbed down his spine as he imagined those fingers on his skin. He could not take his eyes from the sight or close his mind to the fantasy. Juanita glanced up, her eyes questioning as his lack of response to her question was taking way too long.

The moment was shattered as lightning sizzled over their heads with a near simultaneous crack of thunder. Brad thought back to the clouds that he had noticed just a few minutes earlier. Drops of rain, spectacular in size, began pelting and Juanita's laugh echoed the thunder as she bounded away, heading for Brad's truck. Within seconds of reaching the safety of his vehicle, the sky opened in a torrent.

Still laughing, Juanita looked to the sky. "I can't believe we didn't see this coming."

"It's completely your fault. This is your ranch. You were raised here and you should know better."

"Come on, city boy, this is nothing. The sun is shining just over there and this will be over before things even get good and wet." She pointed as she spoke. "Head for that mesa. Let me show you more of our ranch."

Juanita's prediction turned out to be accurate as the rainsquall vanished in only minutes and sunlight again poured into the valley. Juanita lowered her window and extended her face outside of the cab. "Isn't this beautiful? Even a brief storm makes everything so fresh. Can you smell the sage? I think that the scent sage after a rainstorm may be the sweetest aroma on earth." She held her face into the breeze and breathed deeply.

Brad merely nodded a response, unable to shake the feeling that he simultaneously occupied two places in time and space: the cab of his truck and a cabin from another age, with a woman named Juanita sharing both.

With a jab of her finger, Juanita directed Brad to drive a rugged road that twisted up the mesa she had earlier pointed out. He steered his truck between mounds of black *malpais* stone and Cedar trees that had somehow managed to root within the rockbound surface and now, they miraculously thrived. Brad shifted his truck into four-wheel-drive and inched up the incline. As they crested, cloud remnants of the failed storm stretched across the horizon and a sinking sun dipped toward evening.

"Follow the road over here," Juanita directed as she thrust her chin in the direction she wished him to follow. "It's pretty rough going but we are going to have a marvelous sunset and that's the way to get us just where we need to be." Juanita settled into her seat. "Now, tell me about that case you mentioned."

As he drove, Brad related the story of how shortly after his early retirement from the FBI to be with his terminally ill wife, he had accidentally stumbled into a case involving a wealthy woman who had been kidnapped. He explained that her abductors were people who dealt in trafficking children for sex and how his friend, Sam Trathen, had helped to unravel the tangled web. Juanita sat mesmerized as she listened to details of the harrowing conclusion that had taken place in the midst of a ferocious, nighttime mountain storm. Brad noticed that throughout his story, Juanita held her turquoise pendant, absently caressing the stone between thumb and fingers.

When the telling of his experience was finished, silence occupied the cab for several seconds before Juanita spoke softly. "Well, I certainly hope your encounter with Sam Trathen on my behalf will not turn out to be anything like that horrible ordeal."

With a laugh, Brad replied, "I think we are safe. I could live ten lifetimes and not have anything even close to that happen again."

Moving her head from side-to-side, Juanita's thoughts were clearly outside the cab of the truck as she spoke. "I don't know, Brad, I just don't know." Then, speaking more to herself than to Brad she whispered, "What in heaven's name can make people be so incredibly vile?"

They rode in silence for a few minutes before Juanita pointed the way to a windmill that stood like a lone centurion in the fading light. "Park right there. That will be perfect."

The second Brad brought his truck to a halt, Juanita threw open her door. "Let's get out." She walked in front of the truck to a metal stock tank that stood beneath the windmill. Brad watched as she circled the tank. Obviously well trained from a lifetime on the ranch, Juanita examined the water within the tank and cast an evaluative eye over the windmill. She sauntered back to the truck and propped herself against the hood. Brad joined her and together they faced the setting sun.

Evening breeze stirred. Little more than a delicate breath, it carried just enough strength to send blades of the windmill into rotation. Pumping mechanisms began to move, up down, up down, a gentle clanking of moving parts that probed beneath the earth in search of water. In a miniature fountain, water began to pour into the stock tank, its sound harmonizing with noises of the windmill. Cooling breeze of evening, cascading water and man-made machinery came together in easy stride, becoming a perfectly pitched musical instrument.

Orange and red ignited across the western horizon. Inhaling with all of her strength, Juanita lifted her face to the sky. "I love it here so much." She held her pose, eyes closed tightly.

Luminescence of sunset gave Juanita's skin the glow of copper and Brad held his breath. While her eyes were closed, he wanted to examine every detail of her face. Was it possible to comprehend the prescient feelings that she was the woman from his dreams and that he had been with her before. He forced himself to look away before she opened her eyes.

As sunset transformed the sky, the tragedy of Juanita's story seemed worlds removed and easy conversation flowed. The sky's fire gradually cooled into purple and stars began to dapple. As night descended, Juanita and Brad exchanged stories of events that had shaped their lives and the incredible coincidence that they both were raised in New Mexico. They spoke of their youth, their parents and how they had been raised. Brad told of the death of his wife, Elizabeth, and how much he cared for their three children. He related his love of rivers and the solitude of fly-fishing. Juanita spoke of a failed marriage to a man who had proved unfaithful. She admitted that in the wake of her heartbreak she had become withdrawn and shunned many aspects of a personal life, throwing everything she had into her life as an attorney. Juanita spoke softly, "I realize that such total devotion to my career has been nothing more than a defense mechanism but, that is what I chose to do. I've been happy,' she shook her head, "but I'm not so foolish that I fail to understand that some things have also been lost along the way."

Brad was unsure of how to respond so he remained silent.

With a sigh and a touch of reticence entering her voice, Juanita continued. "Usually, when I am lonely or when I think of how I may have chosen to live life differently, I've trained my mind bring me right back here to this ranch. I reminisce on how much I love the land, my family and all that goes with life out here." She paused. I loved riding a horse at sunset. I think of Mom and Dad, my brothers and how hard we all worked." Calving season was my favorite of all. Sometimes we worked twenty-four hours straight but it was magical. The miracle of new life never lost its wonder for me." She turned her face to look at Brad. "It was a lifestyle so far from what I do now but it's always in my heart." She absently reached for her pendant. "I love both worlds but out here on this ranch, this is where my heart really lives."

Juanita became quiet. Silence seemed appropriate considering the sky had become a black canvas, stretching across the horizon, shimmering with frosted crystals. As if on unspoken cue, they both raised their heads to view the heavens, and in doing so, their arms brushed. Warmth from Juanita's body took Brad's breath and he felt his heart quicken.

After several more moments of silence, Juanita spoke. A hint of embarrassment tinged her voice. "I have a confession to offer, wanna hear it?"

"Should I give you your rights first? I really have no interest in arresting you right now."

Juanita laughed. "I voluntarily waive my rights."

"Okay then, I suppose you can just confess away."

Even in darkness, Brad could feel that Juanita teetered, feeling herself on a tight rope between light-heartedness and something much more intimate. Taking a deep breath of courage, Juanita began. "All right, here's my soul, exposed for Brad Walker and all the world to see. After I met you last October at the Albuquerque conference, I made it a point to track down some FBI agents and police officers that knew you. It was just like I was a teenager again." She gave a soft laugh. "You have absolutely no idea how much I learned about Brad Walker!" Juanita looked up into his face with a smile. "Am I in trouble?"

Inwardly ecstatic, Brad managed to speak sternly. "Jury's still out. I suppose it depends on exactly what you learned, what you choose to believe and, on whether or not I get invited back for another meal at your parents' table."

Juanita laughed out loud. "Fair enough, I suppose." She threw her arms open wide to the sky and announced to the stars, "I have no more secrets, nothing more to confess." Juanita leaned forward from the truck's hood to stand straight. Turning to Brad with a smile she announced, "Just so you don't go around worried, everything I learned about you was absolutely wonderful. Now, I have a gift for you." She walked to the stock tank, her white shirt in contrast to the darkness. Brad strained to discern her motions as she lifted a cup that hung from the windmill and held it beneath the water stream that flowed into the tank. With a filled cup, she walked back to Brad. "My gift to you is water from the very heart of Mother Earth. Drink, my friend." Her face and eyes smiled as she extended the cup.

With only stars for light, Brad's eyes locked onto Juanita's as he accepted the cup, icy cold in his hand. Her gaze grew intense as he raised the cup. No detail escaped her scrutiny as she watched him tilt the cup and drink. When he had consumed half the cup, Brad handed it back to her. In an air of ceremony, their eyes still locked, Juanita lifted the cup and Brad watched her drink, his heart thundering. The water was exactly what had been given to him when the mysterious woman had nursed him after his assault. The cold taste of purity that he had been given that night would never leave his memory. Brad knew that he had just tasted it again.

When she finished, Juanita lowered the cup but her penetrating gaze remained. "You know, Brad, we met in Albuquerque at that conference. We scarcely spoke throughout the entire time. Until today, most of what I've known of you is what I managed to learn from the law enforcement grapevine." She moved her head back and forth. "But for some reason, from the first moment we met, I felt that I've known you all my life. Now, after our time today, I feel it even more strongly." She paused, continuing to look at him. "It's crazy, I can't explain it. But it is absolutely what I feel." She shook her head again.

Brad swallowed hard. What could he say? What should he say? How could he even begin to relate his presage that in some ethereal world, from another place and time, she had been an angel of mercy to him? He said nothing, their eyes holding in spite of the darkness. The windmill made music. "I know what you mean. I have the exact same feelings."

From somewhere in the distance, a coyote's howl floated across the prairie.

They stood in the night's quiet, neither able to think of what next to say. After lingering seconds and silence becoming awkward, Juanita gave a gentle jab into Brad's ribs with her finger. "There are three gates between here and home. Since I'm the official gate opener in this crowd and all you do is stay warm and cozy in your truck, you think maybe we should head for the barn?"

Brad moved his head from side to side and spoke in barely a whisper, "No, I don't think so. Not quite yet." Juanita came into his arms and, with no words spoken they simply held each other. Complete surrender passed in the slight sway of their bodies and the ecstasy of first touch. For the first time, Brad felt the beating of Juanita's heart. He knew it would not be the last. The kiss lingered, her hair in his hands, they clung desperately seeking each other. When the embrace finally eased, their eyes held. Silence was what they wanted. Neither could explain what had brought them together; neither wanted to try.

***

The ranch house was dark as Brad turned off the headlights just before pulling his truck to a stop. Juanita laughed. "Mom and Dad will tell me they were asleep. But don't think for a second that they aren't in there just watching the clock, waiting to hear the door open."

"Is there a shotgun pointed at me right now?"

"No, Dad prefers a rifle, not nearly as messy." Juanita's reply was matter-of-fact, but her smile was clear in dim light of the truck. "It's very late, Brad. You're welcome to stay here tonight. Dad would love to talk more with you and Mom's breakfasts are just as wonderful as her lunches."

Brad shook his head as he took her hand. "The last thing in this world that I want to do right now is to leave you, but I'm going to hit the road. If I'm going to help you figure things out about your friend, I have to get home, call Sam and head for Gunnison. Give me a day or two and I'll let you know what I learn about your friend, Ray."

Lifting his hand to her lips, she gave a squeeze and spoke with a sigh, "Okay, I understand. I thank you for this more than you can imagine." Juanita's face was reflective. "I'm not sure what you will learn but something inside me just has to know."

"If I were wearing your shoes, I would feel exactly the same. I'll do my best."

They sat, savoring last moments. Unspoken words dangled but the silence was comfortable, even soothing. Finally, his voice cautious, Brad spoke. "Let's see if I can survive your dad's rifle. Let me walk you to your door."

Without answering, Juanita opened her door and stepped out. Brad met her at the front of his truck and they sauntered, arms about each other's waist, not wanting the magic to end. Standing at her door, neither spoke in mutual understanding that words could not add to the moment. Finally, Juanita lifted her hand to Brad's cheek, her fingertips touching his skin softly. "Thank you for coming."

With her touch, white light seemed to burst within Brad's head. This had happened before. He was laying in her tiny cabin, injured, no electricity. She had brought her face so close to his as she touched his cheek and spoke to him in Spanish, her words still etched in his mind: *"Nuestro tiempo ya casi ha llegado"* (Our time is almost here), *"Hemos esperado tanto tiempo"* (We have waited so long), *"Se paciente, mi amor, se paciente"* (Be patient, my love, be patient). It was the same face, same voice and exact same touch.

Millions of stars from millions of miles throughout the firmament cast their glow. Seconds passed. Juanita's smile appeared and even the night's darkness could not obscure its illuminating effect. "Don't worry, Brad." She moved her head in a gesture of bewilderment. "I certainly do not understand what is happening here, not at all. I can't begin to explain this but I am certain of one thing." She paused, touching his cheek again as she spoke, "I am very happy that you came today and whatever is happening, I want it to keep happening."

Juanita held her gaze. Closing his eyes, mind spinning and heart hammering, Brad brought her close, wanting to drown in her warmth. So many things to say, so much to ask but he knew this was not the moment. Brushing his lips over hers in a final kiss, Brad whispered, "You have no idea what this day has meant to me."

With a feel of mutual understanding, the embrace dissolved. Their hands clasped in a final clutch before their fingertips slid over each other in reluctant farewell. Brad walked away.

***

Despite the darkness, Brad was aware of familiar landmarks slipping past as he drove north on Interstate 25: Fisher Peak above Trinidad, Spanish Peaks towering to the west. Greenhorn Mountain appeared as a gliding shadow and then, nestled beneath Pikes Peak, the silhouette of Cheyenne Mountain. As he passed through Colorado Springs, Brad glanced at his cell phone and realized that it indicated a missed call and voicemail. He hit the keypad and was surprised to hear Juanita's voice. Her tone was clearly distressed as she spoke, "Oh, Brad, I'm hoping you can help me. My pendant is gone. I didn't realize until long after you had left. I'm praying it's in your truck. Please, let me know if you have it. If you don't find it, all I know to do is retrace our night's drive. Maybe I lost it while opening a gate. Please let me know." The recording paused but Brad was certain he could hear soft breath before she spoke her farewell. "Thank you again, Brad. I have never felt so happy."

Taking the first available exit from the interstate, Brad parked and stepped to the passenger door, yanking it open. There it was, lying on the floor, trapped between the door and seat. Breathing a sigh of relief, he lifted the pendant closer to the overhead light of the cab. Smooth texture under his fingertips belied the embedded veins of copper that appeared as fractures within the blue stone.

Recognizing its striking beauty, Brad also felt an aura of intrigue. His mind went back to his time with Juanita as she dangled her feet in the creek. What he had not mentioned to her after she told the history of her mother presenting this treasure was that the pendant bore uncanny resemblance to a pendant that he had once given to his wife, Elizabeth. Stroking the stone, Brad felt its density and sensed the history of its creation. To Brad, turquoise was life itself. It held copper from within the earth and its blue the color of water and sky. His daughter, Meghan, now wore what he had given to Elizabeth.

Closing his fingers about Juanita's pendant, Brad contemplated the afternoon and evening. He felt warmth radiate and could not help but wonder: did his hand warm the stone or did the stone warm his hand? He simply did not know. What was he feeling within his hand? Was it the spirit of Juanita or the memory of Elizabeth? He dropped his head and closed his eyes to capture the image of Juanita, the creek and the ornament about her throat so mesmerizing. He held the stone tightly as he whispered, "What a day. What an absolutely unbelievable day!"

Walking back to the driver's door, he slipped the gem into the pocket of his jeans. A glance at his watch told him it was 2:30 in the morning, not exactly an appropriate time to place a call to Juanita. Brad lifted his phone and mumbled, "God I hate emailing on these damned things." Unable to manipulate his fingers over the tiny keypad, it required multiple attempts and a torrent of swear words to compose a message telling Juanita that her keepsake was not lost. Did she want it mailed or should he keep it for now? Hitting the send button, he took a hard inhale, threw his truck into gear and continued to drive.

***

The eastern sky glowed pink by the time Brad reached his home. He entered and, for once, had no interest in a Moosehead, the beer that he usually craved after stressful times.

Brad flung his exhausted body across his bed. He slept. Elizabeth came to him. She smiled, peace in her eyes. Juanita touched his cheek.

Chapter Two

A few hours of sleep and a workout were all that were necessary for Brad to re-energize after his all-night drive. While in the gym, he missed a call from Juanita. Her message said that she had been summoned back to Albuquerque to begin preparation for an upcoming trial. The defendant's attorney had promised a guilty plea but something had changed and he now demanded a day in court for his clearly guilty client. Preparation to take the case before a jury was now a last minute emergency. Brad replayed the message twice to listen to the part where she told him to keep the pendant. She saw it as an insurance policy that they would have to meet again soon.

Eager to get started, Brad made a call to Sam Trathen. His old friend told him that by pure coincidence he was already familiar with the suicide case and agreed to meet the next day in Gunnison. Pleasant anticipation fueled Brad as he gathered gear and packed his rig. A chance to enjoy the company of Sam was always a treat. The memories of experiences and stories they had shared over so many years never faded for either man. Added delight was the wild beauty of Gunnison and the surrounding land. That was why a fly rod and waders were tossed on top of his overnight bag.

Brad was at peace as he pulled away from his home and headed west. Easy thoughts filled his mind; take a drive, fish a bit, learn what he could about the suicide matter and arrange another visit with Juanita. Life was good.

Sam had suggested the best way to approach the matter would be to have lunch so they could tell a few lies before taking a trip out of Gunnison. A short hike would then be necessary so that they could visit the scene of the suicide. Sam readily acknowledged that many unanswered questions remained in his mind about the case and he welcomed an opportunity to go back to where it all started. Sam had chuckled when Brad mentioned that if he was just a few minutes late for lunch, it would be because he intended to grab a couple hours of morning fishing on Tomichi Creek. Just before terminating the call, Sam had growled, "Tell me something, Brad, how do you manage to cast a fly rod and hang on to your walker at the same time?" Sam's throaty laugh was the last thing Brad heard before his phone went silent.

***

After topping Kenosha Pass, South Park unfurled in an expanse of startling beauty. Brad crossed Michigan Creek and Four Mile Creek, which he knew brimmed with trout. Minutes and miles passed in fleeting reminisce of treasured memories with his children and Elizabeth. This was the land of fishing and campfire adventures. Massive and defiant, the Collegiate Peaks Wilderness appeared. Fourteen thousand foot mountains hovered over Buena Vista where Brad began his ascent of the Continental Divide over Cottonwood Pass. After crossing the snow-covered spine of the Divide, he descended into Taylor River Canyon. Afternoon light faded but Brad's faithful truck could have navigated the route without steering, so familiar was the road to the junction of the Taylor and the East Rivers, their confluence giving birth to the mighty Gunnison River.

Shortly before entering the hard-crust ranching community of Gunnison, Brad pulled to the side of the road, parked and stepped out of his truck. This country held a million memories and he needed a few moments to reflect. Looking northwest and up the valley, Brad saw Carbon Peak. The mountain stood guard over Ohio Creek as it ambled through soft soil of hay fields and grazing horses. The sun had long disappeared behind the silhouette of the Anthracite Range and the Evening Star hung in afterglow. So bright was the heavenly body that it seemed to bathe in its own silver light. Brad breathed easily, savoring the moment. It was here that he had ridden horses with his sons and brothers, camping beneath the cathedral-like stone formations known as the Castles. He could smell their campfire, hear their laughter and feel the tug of brook trout on his fly rod. He looked to the star. Was Elizabeth there? Could it be that she watched him? Did she feel him as he so clearly felt her?

Reaching into the pocket of his jeans, the turquoise of Juanita's pendant met his fingers. He grasped it, holding it tightly, aware that as he did so an inexplicable sensation seemed to radiate from the stone. His eyes remained fixed on galactic beauty while his hand was warmed by a miracle of minerals conceived within the soil of earth.

***

Tomichi Creek first breathes at thirteen thousand feet above the ocean, winding a course along the west side of the Sawatch Range until it spills into the Gunnison Valley. Brad felt the morning sun whisk away remnants of the chill he had felt when departing his motel shortly after dawn. He had arrived at the stream while the sun was still low and morning's shadows continued to streak hillsides and meadows. While waiting for sunlight, the water appeared grey and cold, not particularly welcoming. Relishing these quiet moments, Brad sat in his truck sipping coffee while the sun crept higher, illuminating the valley inch by inch. Brad was reminded once again of why he so loved this time of day. Early light seemed to bring a sense of anticipation and promise of new life. He watched it happen as Tomichi Creek transformed into a seam of sparkling blue. Draining his coffee he whispered, "Lord, this is beautiful."

With early sun to his back and his elongated shadow stretching before him, Brad approached the creek, fly rod in hand. To Brad, this was always the best part of a fishing experience, the virgin moments of first observing the water. This was why he fished. It was a time of listening, precious moments to feel the world about him. Brad heard poetry in eddies and vortices of streams. The relentless energy of river to ocean journey was something he could feel. Brad had taught his children that rivers were living beings, the very life-blood of the earth. Brad smiled to himself. He was perfectly aware that many people scoffed at his reverence for rivers. But then, why should he care? If folks were too dense to get it, then that was a choice on their part. The way Brad looked at things, if rivers can erode mountains or gouge canyons, why then should they not be able to also mold the personality of a person? One simply must take time to observe and listen. With a deep breath, he felt satisfaction. Brad knew that his children got it. They understood. Elizabeth and he had taught them well.

Standing on the creek's edge, Brad savored the moment, reflecting and remembering. He had walked away from his FBI career to be with Elizabeth in her last days. There had never been a regret. In those last days, while she had been out of the hospital and in their home, they had clung to each other knowing it was the end. He thought of how their children had been with him during that terrible time and how they had all become so close as Elizabeth slipped away. Now, they were grown, beginning their lives. That was the way it had to be. Brad inhaled hard, holding memories of his family within his body. With a final glance to the sky and the awakening valley, he pulled line from his reel and eased his feet into the water.

***

Thirty minutes late and casting a guilty glance at his watch, Brad rushed into the café. With an accusing squint, a knowing smile and a shrug of his shoulders, Sam Trathen insinuated that Brad's tardiness had been fully expected. Their handshake was solid. Years of working cases together and a sharing of life and families passed in the physical contact.

After a sandwich and time for easy, catch-up banter, Brad drove while Sam filled him in on the details of the suicide investigation. It had begun when a surveying crew, on a project for the Department of Wildlife, had discovered a Ferrari smashed to hell on a rugged dirt road. The empty wreckage was not far off the highway that led between Gunnison and Crested Butte and circling vultures had signaled the tragic story. When the call came in to the Gunnison County Sheriff's Department, it was by pure chance that Sam had been sitting right there. A missing person case out of Aspen had led him to Gunnison, so he was naturally invited to join the Gunnison investigators for the initial response.

Sam gave a sarcastic grunt. "I'm always looking for an excuse to get my ass out of Aspen and away from that phony, Hollywood glitter. Ain't nothing left in Aspen except pimple-faced trust fund kids and air-headed broads with dyed hair and silicone tits. Give me this any day." Sam gestured out the window to passing terrain that stretched to infinity. Brad simply grinned and nodded his head in agreement. "Anyway, I rode along with the responders from Gunnison County and was with them when they reached the body. I helped them process the scene and we've stayed in periodic contact. I know some parts of the story but certainly not everything that has developed since that first day."

Brad silently acknowledged his understanding with a shake of his head.

Soon after the mountains of Crested Butte came into view, Sam directed Brad to make a turn to the west. After only a short distance, he was forced to shift his rig into four-wheel drive. "Not exactly the kind of road I'll be driving my Ferrari over next Sunday afternoon."

"No shit, Sherlock." Sam laughed his agreement and pointed out exactly where the crashed Ferrari had been discovered. "From the looks of his demolished car, the guy didn't really care if he killed himself by destroying his car or by putting a bullet in his brain. He was obviously driving like a wild man and could easily have bought the farm in the wrecking of his car."

Brad continued to nudge his rig up the road until Sam told him to stop. "Okay, G-Man, hope your Hoover wing-tips can handle it cause this is where we walk."

Leaving Brad's truck, the two men set off. It was obvious that the trail had seen recent traffic and a well-beaten path made their walk relatively easy. Sam spoke, "When your boy, Ray, made this hike there was no trail at all here. We have the benefit of a bunch of investigators tramping in and out and a team of medical people that removed his body."

Another nod from Brad indicated he understood before he spoke. "The way it seems to me is that if there was no clearly marked trail, Ray must have had some reason to choose this specific place to hike. Otherwise, he could have shot himself back where he wrecked his car and saved a bunch of walking."

"Yep. I agree." Sam spoke matter-of-factly.

"There must be a reason why he didn't end it all right there after the crash." Brad's words were part statement and part question.

"I think you are absolutely correct and it turns out that the guy left a clue to verify just that point. We found a photo in his pocket. It was of a very attractive young woman posing beneath a tree. It was obvious from the surrounding background that the tree where she posed was the very same tree where Ray shot himself. You'll see the tree pretty soon. We don't have much further to hike and we'll be right where it all took place." Sam paused. "I don't know if the Gunnison folks have figured out the girl's identity or not. The day I was with them, there was no clue who she might be."

"It's just a hunch but I'm pretty sure marriage records in Albuquerque will give the girl's identity." Brad glanced at Sam. " So far, I've only told you that I'm interested in this matter because a prosecutor friend of mine in Albuquerque asked me to look into it. But you need to hear the whole background." As they walked, Brad related Juanita's story while Sam listened in silence.

After Brad had finished, Sam gave a low whistle. "Well, my friend, what you have just said throws a whole new light on what I know and what I've been thinking." Before Sam had time to explain further, he gave a thrust of his head as they entered a clearing. "This is it." Pointing his finger, he continued, "That's it right there. That ponderosa pine is where his body was found. He was on the ground, propped up against the trunk." Sam paused, "And that's exactly where the girl in the photo stood."

The place and the moment called for reverence and both men were silent. Brad slowly walked the clearing, coming to an outcrop of boulders where Crested Butte was visible in the distance. He walked back to where Sam continued to stand near the tree. Sam gave Brad time and remained silent.

Looking at the old giant, Brad ran his eyes along the tree's trunk from the ground to the top and then back again. It was impossible not to contemplate the life, love and tragedy that had apparently transpired here. Throughout his career, any time Brad had encountered tragedy it had caused him to contemplate his own life and the incredible good fortune he had enjoyed. He had never lost sight of the fact that life sometimes delivers a confluence of events that cataclysmic moments can turn upside down. Brad thought of Elizabeth's death.

Standing quietly beneath the tree, Brad looked inside his mind to see Juanita's eyes and hear the torment in her voice as she wrestled with thoughts of what she might have done differently. Even though his dear friend, Sam, was only a few feet away, Brad suddenly felt terribly lonely. For what or whom he wasn't certain. Without consciously thinking, Brad reached for Juanita's pendant. With a final glance at the tree and a deep breath, Brad turned to Sam. "Okay, my friend, tell me what you think."

They ambled to the rock outcropping and found seats within the boulders where they settled in for conversation. Sam took the lead. "Alright, Brad, here's what I know and what I don't know. Identification of the guy was pretty easy. Between what we found on the body and registration records on the Ferrari, we knew right away who he was. Everything matched up at the scene so there was no real concern about this being a homicide disguised as suicide." Brad nodded as Sam continued. "The first priority, of course, was to locate and notify next of kin. The Gunnison investigator told me that they found both parents had lived in California but have been deceased for years. There were no siblings or other relatives ever identified as far as I know."

Brad shook his head. Sam's words seemed to depict a rather sad life, devoid of family ties. He stared at the ground as Sam continued.

"The Ferrari was registered in Nevada so that's where they initially began searching for information on the guy. In a nutshell, they learned that in the past he had employment with some casino outfits in Vegas and Reno. Over years, he had several bank accounts and some were pretty significant. But beyond that, not too many threads tied him to any one place. He bounced around a good bit, living in rented apartments in various cities." Sam raised his eyebrows, "But I'm not talking just regular apartments. This guy spent his days in penthouses and high-end stuff. However, he must have pretty much supported his life by paying for everything with cash because there was precious little in the way of a financial paper trail."

With a skeptical look, Brad spoke. "For a guy driving a Ferrari, that smells bad right out of the gate."

"Now ain't that the painful truth." Sam chuckled his reply. "I guess that's why I miss your skinny ass. We always thought just alike. I only recall a couple of times when I had to clobber you over the head to make you see the obvious."

Letting the remark slide, Brad simply grinned at his old friend.

"There are a few things that bother me about this case," Sam continued. "But this is not my territory. This belongs to Gunnison and I was just along for the ride. And bothered or not, I sure can't fault the Gunnison folks. They have done a top-notch job in tracking down stuff from big city departments all over God's green earth. I don't have to tell you, but that isn't always easy. If this were a murder, it would be different. But an ordinary suicide in rural Colorado?" Sam shook his head, "I'm afraid that doesn't light up the radar screen in Los Angeles or Las Vegas."

"Oh yeah, I understand that. My only interest is in light of what my friend in Albuquerque had to say and I've told you about that. She asked a favor and I made a promise, so that's why I'm asking a few questions. I would appreciate your gut instincts on this and then I'll leave you alone and figure out what to do next."

Throwing his head back, Sam laughed out loud. "The last time you had just a few questions for me, we both ended up in one hell of a kidnapping case in Aspen and up to our eyeballs in human traffickers. I didn't just fall off the turnip truck, Mr. Hoover. If I had a hungry grizzly bear in my kitchen, I couldn't be any more leery than when you show up asking questions." Sam continued laughing.

It was impossible for Brad not to laugh along with Sam, conceding the truth of what had been said. "Okay, you old goat, you got me on that one. But if you can loosen your underwear one more time, I sure would love to know what your instinct tells you about this suicide business."

After a final chuckle, Sam became thoughtful before again speaking. "Well, there's nothing concrete here but I'm old and cynical enough to always see the suspicious side of things. When we went through what was left of the Ferrari we found a few things that just didn't smell right to me. Of course, when this first happened and my initial suspicions began to develop, I didn't have the benefit of what you had learned from your prosecutor friend in Albuquerque. Now, with her story tossed into the mix, things make a bunch more sense and I'm pretty certain that there's trouble somewhere in River City."

Brad pulled a stalk of grass from the ground, put it in his mouth and began rolling it with his tongue.

"At least as far as just the suicide is concerned, I think that what wasn't found in the Ferrari says every bit as much as much as what was found. There was no change of clothes or basic toiletries. There was no toothbrush, razor, nothing at all. Since gas receipts were scattered all about the car, we knew he had traveled a great distance. That tells me the guy had probably made his decision to commit suicide when he began his journey." Sam shrugged. "I had suspicions at the time but after talking with you and hearing the prosecutor's story, I'm even more convinced that there's more here than meets the eye." Sam was contemplative for a few seconds. "Now, don't accuse me of being a Sigmund Freud goof ball, but I think it is those very few things that he did carry that were what caused him to end his life." Sam added conviction to his voice. "I think he brought his demons with him."

"You mean the photograph of the woman under the tree?"

"Yeah, that photo for sure is critical. But we found other things in the car. He had a briefcase behind the driver's seat. In that briefcase were some newspaper articles about a series of burglaries of super high-end homes all over the Southwest. Every one of the cases involved theft of Native American artifacts, most of which were museum quality items. I'm talking the real stuff. Along with reports about individual burglaries, the articles speculated on an underground network that possibly linked them all together. Several law enforcement sources spoke of such a network that exists for marketing rare and valuable artifacts."

With a nod that he got the picture, Brad spoke softly. "Okay, I sure as hell understand. That would make anyone suspicious."

"There were also a bunch of other papers in the briefcase. Stuff with scribbled notes, a ton of names and figures that obviously were some sort of ledger-style documentation of financial transactions. There was no way to know what it all meant but the dollar amounts were damned sure significant. The deals ranged from a few thousand dollars to over a hundred thousand. Whatever Ray was up to, he was dealing in some tall cotton money."

"Wow."

"Some figures were circled in red and some in green. Lines connected dollar figures to names. Who the hell knows, but my guess is that the red circles with a line connecting them to a name represented money that Ray owed to someone. If I'm guessing right, our man Ray was in debt right up to the hairs in his nose."

"Anything in all that stuff to identify anyone?"

"Nope, nothing very helpful there. Just a bunch of first names or quite often nicknames. I'd say pretty much an equal mix of male and female names with dollar notations all over the place."

Removing the blade of grass from his mouth and twisting it between his fingers, Brad remained silent.

"I made copies of all the stuff that the Gunnison folks have given to me. When you called and said you wanted to talk about this, I figured you would want it so, I burned you a copy of everything. It's all back in my car."

Giving a toss to the stalk of grass, Brad stood up. "So, you thought Ray was involved in some sort of criminal enterprise involving stolen artifacts and Juanita's story confirms that. But she also says he talked about pushing prostitutes." Brad paused in thought. "If you're right about Ray being in financial trouble, could those female names in his records possibly be girls that he marketed as prostitutes, using their services in place of cash to pay off debt?"

"There you go again, thinking like a cop." Sam looked to the ground and shook his head slowly. "Maybe it's cause we've worked so many cases together, I don't know, but ain't it amazing how we see the world through the same filter?"

Both men were quiet, thinking of the countless hours they had spent together.

"Not that it means anything," Brad spoke, "but here is the way I see it. The photo was in his pocket. To me, that means the woman was close to his heart. The other stuff, that was all in a briefcase in the back of the vehicle. The photo was his heart, the briefcase was his demon." Brad looked straight at Sam. "Which do you think caused him to put a bullet in his head, his heart or the demon?"

The question seemed to have struck a nerve, as Sam's face became somber. After a long silence, he spoke, choosing his words with caution. "My friend, I have copies of everything for you when we get back to Gunnison. However, my rusty old brain and worn out instinct spoke to me this morning. They told me to bring something along on our hike today. I knew better than to leave it with the rest of all that mumbo-jumbo from his briefcase." Sam hesitated then reached into his shirt pocket. "This is a copy of the photo we found in Ray's shirt, the one that told us he had been to the same tree at some prior time in his life." Sam extended the photograph.

She was beautiful, her eyes young, sparkling and brimming with life. To see her standing in the exact place where Ray had taken his life jolted Brad, bringing the tragedy of whatever had happened to real life. When he looked up from the photo, he caught Sam staring at him. A degree of intensity in Sam's eyes suggested his friend was looking straight into his soul. Brad simply looked at Sam with a questioning face.

"That's not all we found in Ray's shirt pocket, Brad. We also found this, another photo." Sam again extended his hand. "I made a copy, just for you."

Brad accepted the photograph and, without realizing it, stopped breathing. The image in the photograph was small and had obviously been carefully cut and removed from a larger, group photograph. A tightening began in his chest as he looked at Juanita's face in the photograph. She was years younger but there was no doubt. It was her smile. Brad could hear her laugh simply by looking at her smile.

Brad looked to Sam.

"Both photos were in his pocket, Brad. And yes, I agree with you. The photos were Ray's heart, the briefcase held his demons." Sam paused. "I have no idea which it was that caused him to end his life."

Brad turned away. Juanita's words ran through his head, just as clear as when they had been together on her ranch. *He told me that his life was in my hands and that he loved me.*

Turning back to Sam, Brad lifted Juanita's photograph and spoke. "Sam, do you know who this is?"

With an unflinching gaze and an up and down shake of his head, Sam answered Brad's question without speaking a word. After a moment, Sam answered, his voice remaining low. "There is absolutely no logical explanation for how I know this, Brad. I can't begin to understand it. When we first found the photograph in his pocket, I had no idea of who the woman might be." Sam paused. "But from where we stand now, I'm willing to bet the farm that the photo is of your prosecutor friend from Albuquerque."

Brad shuffled his feet and gave a slight nod.

A hint of a smile now developed as Sam continued. "When you called me and told me that we needed to talk and said that you were doing a favor for a prosecutor friend in New Mexico, I heard something in your voice that sounded way different from the Brad I know. And then you show up for our lunch today," Sam's smile broadened as he paused, searching for his next words. "Every time your prosecutor *friend* is mentioned, a silly-assed grin is all over your face giving you away. You're trying to be casual about this. You want me to believe this is a simple favor for a prosecutor, nothing more than a casual helping hand for a lady lawyer who happens to be on the side of the good guys." Sam now openly smiled. "Come on, Brad. I can read you like a large-print book. We've known each other too long and I'm way too slippery for this stuff. You feel something for her, don't you?"

Looking again at the photograph, Brad kept his eyes down, unwilling to meet Sam's eyes but clearly feeling his friend's scrutiny. Then, summoning courage, he looked up to Sam and returned his gaze. "Sam, I hardly know her. I have no idea why or how this has happened, but you are absolutely right." Taking a breath and elevating the photograph slightly, Brad continued but his words were directed more to himself than to Sam. "Yes, Sam, I care for her. I care for her very deeply." Shaking his head in a manner that suggested he couldn't believe what he had just said, he repeated his statement, raising his voice. "I care for her very deeply." As if he had purged his soul, Brad exhaled, dropped his shoulders and gave Sam a crooked smile.

Sam's face brightened and his eyes beamed a smile that spoke volumes more than words. But as he replied, his voice remained cautious. "I'm not sure exactly where this conversation might be headed, but it's okay, Brad, it's okay. I'm thrilled for you. You have a lot of living to do and Elizabeth is gone. It's fine to open yourself up. I knew Elizabeth for years for heaven's sake. My wife and Elizabeth were the best of friends." Sam gave Brad a penetrating look. "I have no doubt that Elizabeth would want you to find some joy in life."

Brad remained silent. How could he even begin to respond? He could never explain the cabin from another world and how a woman named Juanita had nursed him to health. Brad thought of the pendant in his pocket. He didn't even know how to explain that to himself. With a slight nod, Brad spoke, "Thanks, Sam. You are right, as usual, and I appreciate you talking with me. I think it was good for me to openly admit what I'm feeling. I've had this all bottled up and no idea what to do."

"I can only imagine." Sam chuckled.

"How the hell do I resolve this? Elizabeth was the love of my life. I still think of her every day. She was who I was thinking of just a few moments ago when I stood under that damned tree and thought about someone blowing their brains out." Brad shifted his head from side to side. "Then, when I think of Juanita, I feel wonderful in a way I can't explain and never thought possible. But holy Christ, Sam, I'm oozing with guilt. Every time I think of Juanita, it's like I'm cheating on Elizabeth." Brad hesitated. "It's tearing me apart. I never want to let go of Elizabeth, never. But Juanita causes something to stir in my heart that I never dreamed could happen again. Holy shit, Sam, I am one screwed up guy!"

Sam's easy laugh was low and deep. "I've known for years that you're screwed up so we don't need to waste our time with that discussion. But what I'm hearing about your memory of Elizabeth and feelings for this lady, Juanita, are not even close to being screwed up. Give me a break, Brad. You gave Elizabeth everything you had and you continue to honor her in everything you say and do. That is something that will not change if you live another hundred years. I am absolutely certain of that. But wake up, Brad. If the big guy upstairs thinks enough of you to send someone else your way, you danged well better pay attention."

Brad's gaze remained focused on the ground but he gave a slight nod that he was listening.

"You and I have talked a million times about how quickly life passes and how all kinds of things happen to people that change life in a blink. God Almighty, Brad, blink, blink, blink and a whole life slips by. Don't blink and miss something that could literally transform your life, my friend. Keep your eyes open." Sam took a breath and was quiet before continuing.

"We've been partners for many years. I know damned well what makes you tick. I understand what's inside of you. If this prosecutor lady stirs you, then she is without a doubt a woman of substance. Don't blink and miss her, you idiot."

Lifting his eyes to look at Sam, Brad grinned. "Jesus, you are a pain in the ass but I'm listening and, as usual, you are probably right."

Laughing as he spoke, Sam drawled, "Of course I'm right. I'm right on two counts, you're screwed up and you need to give this lady a chance." Sam glanced at his watch. "My psychoanalysis clock is ticking. Any other aspects of your life I can straighten out for you or can we get on with why we came here in the first place?"

Returning Sam's laugh, Brad's body relaxed. "Okay, shitbird, since you're so damned wise and able to see through walls, how about you figure out what's going on with this case and help me score some points with Juanita."

A smile entered Sam's voice. "Knowing you and your abysmal skills in the social graces department, you're going to need all the help you can get. I find it hard to believe that anyone who doesn't work for the Humane Society would have any interest in you."

"Enough already. I can't handle any more of your nonsense." Brad began walking through the clearing, retracing their steps and heading back to the trail. "Thanks for coming up here with me. Let's head back so you can make it back to Aspen at a decent hour. Plus, I'm anxious to get my hands on those papers you have for me. Who knows, maybe something is there that makes sense in light of what Juanita has told me."

With a last glance at the tree where life, love and death had come together, the two men walked away.

His pizza was mediocre but at least Moosehead could be purchased in Gunnison so everything balanced out. Brad passed the evening in his motel room reviewing the materials that Sam had copied. He sorted through piles of papers, finding Ray's scribbled notes to be a complete hodgepodge of figures, names, circles and lines that were impossible to decipher. He stuck with his and Sam's initial instinct that it amounted to some form of financial record keeping but anything beyond that was sheer guesswork. In addition to the hand-written ledgers was an assortment of news articles from the *Albuquerque Journal* that laid out concerns of various law enforcement agencies regarding the trafficking of stolen Native American artifacts. Investigative agencies were questioning if a series of home burglaries across the Southwest, in which high-value artifacts had been stolen, could be related and part of a coordinated scheme.

In Brad's mind, the revelations Ray had offered to Juanita along with the suicide investigation and cryptic paper trail made it clear that Ray had been involved, directly or indirectly, in illegal activity of some sort. But Brad could see no clear path to resolution.

Thinking back to Juanita's story, it seemed that a pivotal point for Ray had been the suicide of a young girl. But the details of who, when, or where of that event were absolute unknowns. He shuffled through the stack of papers again. There were several female names scattered throughout the conglomeration of Ray's records and all seemed to be affiliated with a numerical or monetary notation, often with a line drawn to a male name. Feeling that he must be missing something, Brad scanned the pages again. He recalled something he had spotted earlier when he had first began sorting through Ray's papers. What he had seen now seemed out of place or context with the rest of Ray's notes. He flipped back through the pages methodically, trying to understand a system or rhythm to what Ray had recorded. He came to the sheet that he was looking for. It definitely was different from the others, a single page with only the name "Lucy" written in printed letters. The name was followed by three exclamation marks, all boldly circled in red. Brad shuffled the papers once again. All other names had been written in cursive. He found other entries for Lucy, written in cursive and followed by figures with a dollar sign and a line to a male name. He went back to the page with only the single entry of Lucy. It didn't take a laboratory examiner or handwriting expert to see that the letters had been printed with bold intention. Exclamation marks shouted the importance of the name and the circle around the name had been created with brashness. Obvious pressure on the writing instrument had resulted in a broad-bordered tracing of ink.

Spreading the assortment of papers across his bed, Brad sought to see the entire picture of what had been left in Ray's Ferrari. He lifted the sheet bearing only Lucy's name and held it. The materials on the table were totally haphazard, nothing more than hieroglyphics except to their creator. Brad again contemplated the paper inscribed with the single message of "Lucy." When viewed in context with everything else it was as if the one single sheet was a neon sign, screaming for attention.

"What the hell," Brad muttered as he reached for his computer. His first try utilizing key words came up empty for past articles in the *Salt Lake Tribune*. The second attempt paid off in a matter of minutes. Brad knew he had located what he was hoping to find in the *Albuquerque Journal*; a death notice, Lucy Hernandez, age 19, committed suicide by hanging, Bernalillo County authorities investigating. The article listed her only survivors as her mother, Victoria Hernandez, and father,

Alphonso Hernandez, of Cimarron, New Mexico. Another five minutes of searching and Brad had a photograph of Lucy Hernandez from her memorial service. It was her high school graduation photograph. Brad also had an address for Victoria and Alphonso Hernandez.

Sleeping alone in motel rooms was something Brad had detested for years. But since losing Elizabeth, the experience was practically unbearable. On this night, as he lay across the bed fully clothed, he closed his eyes and saw the school photograph of Lucy Hernandez, her eyes filled with anticipation of the life before her. What could possibly have happened that she would end that life after only nineteen years? Thinking of Juanita's story and all that he had learned during the day, Brad knew the very sad answer.

Sleep refused to come. He listened again in his mind to the words of wisdom Sam had delivered earlier in the day. Brad sought Elizabeth but her image was illusive. Frustration and loneliness permeated the darkness of his room. Brad reached for Juanita's pendant that now lay on the nightstand beside his bed. It was still in his hand when he awakened the next morning.

Chapter Three

Sunrise, coffee, sausage and eggs began his day. Brad loved the ambiance and spirit of Gunnison, a genuine western town. The life and energy of working people who appreciated each day and everything they had was apparent in the conversation and humor that filled the café. Sitting alone, he couldn't help but consider the contrast to large city coffee shops and the suits, ties and leather attaches they attracted. He felt perfectly at home among this morning's boots, jeans and pickup trucks. Brad was quite comfortable in both worlds but today he said a silent prayer of thanks that he was exactly where he was.

With a coffee to go, Brad drove straight into the glare of early morning sun before cutting south on 114 into Cochetopa Canyon. Mountains gradually gave way to the vast expanse of the San Luis Valley and a due south drive to Alamosa. Then it was east again, over La Vita Pass to Interstate 25 and then south to New Mexico.

As always, once over Raton Pass and in New Mexico, Brad had a sense of being home. He wouldn't trade his life in Colorado for the world but only New Mexico offered the quintessence of where he came from, the core of what made him who he was.

Highway 64 followed the Cimarron cut-off of the Santa Fe Trail. Imagining such vastness without roads or a hint of civilization, Brad was humbled at the courage and determination of the women and men who had dared to first venture into this land. Ancient volcanoes, now nothing more than sleeping mounds of rock and dirt, dotted the landscape. Prickly pear cactus and sunflowers blanketed the prairie beneath a dome of azure blue. But the dominant feature of the land was not really the land. What was most mesmerizing to Brad was the sheer immensity of all that surrounded him. The seemingly eternal expanse dwarfed all other life or existence.

Antelope looked up from their grazing as he drove by. The Sangre de Cristo Mountains materialized on the horizon, first appearing as soft blue shadows sprouting from the prairie. But upon entering the town of Cimarron, the true, rugged nature of the mountains was speaking their strength.

Brad was familiar with this town from brief visits in the past, as he had passed through while fishing in the mountains or on his way to visit the town of Taos. He also knew something of the violent and storied history of the late 1800's, when bar room brawls and gunfights in Cimarron were as ordinary as a west wind. Brad smiled with the memory of his high school history teacher who had talked at length about this village. The word Cimarron is Spanish for wild or unruly and the teacher had utilized a newspaper clipping to demonstrate the anarchic nature of early days in this region. The lesson had come from a mid 1800's article printed by the *Las Vegas Gazette*, which reported, *"Everything is quiet in Cimarron. Nobody has been killed for three days."*

With that bit of historical reference rolling within his mind, Brad drove to what he knew had been the very heart of Cimarron's lawless heyday, the St. James Hotel. Bullet holes in its walls and ceilings bore testament that the hotel had served as overnight respite for both the most famous of outlaws as well as legendary lawmen. Adding to the hotel's mystique, many believe that restless ghosts continue to haunt hallways and rooms of the elegantly refurbished inn. It had been years since Brad had visited this epicenter of early west bawdiness and, even though he was on a mission, Brad was delighted to have a perfect opportunity for re-acquaintance.

A lunch of iced tea served with a bowl of green chili and tortillas made the day worthwhile regardless of anything else. The aura of days past permeated the St. James Hotel dining room, with old walls holding photographs of the hotel's more famous patrons: Billy The Kid, Jesse James and lawmen such as Wyatt Earp. The atmosphere of the hotel was such that Brad would not have been all that surprised to see any one of them saunter through the door, spurs jangling and six–shooters hanging from their hips.

With a taste of New Mexico lingering pleasantly, Brad paid his bill but was reluctant to leave the beauty and the enigma of the hotel. Departing the restaurant, he walked through the hotel's lobby and stopped to admire a massive chandelier that hung as the centerpiece of the hotel. Brad stood beneath the myriad of shimmering crystals, his neck crooked upward. He considered the enormity of so much life that had transpired here: sordid behavior, treachery and cowardice for certain. But bravery, heroism and demands for a civilized existence had also flourished within these walls. Gazing into the maze of light and reflections of the chandelier, Brad wondered if the spirits of those early men perhaps did continue to breathe in some way. At least it was easy to understand how legends of ghosts could flourish here.

His moment of introspection was shattered by a woman's voice that Brad intuitively knew was directed at him. "Hey, mister, you intend to stand there all day or can I get you a room? The best night's sleep with a ghost you'll ever have. You have my personal guarantee. That is unless you happen to be afraid of a little old ghost." The voice came from behind the registration desk where, with eyes twinkling and humor in her face, a woman held a defiant pose, awaiting response to her challenge.

It was impossible for Brad not to smile back. He realized that he had been gawking and surely appeared as the consummate tourist. "I guess you caught me trying to communicate with the spirits," he grinned in embarrassment as he approached the grey-haired woman.

"Not to worry, go right ahead and communicate to your heart's desire." Laughing at Brad's obvious discomfort, she handed him a hotel brochure. "But just be sure to follow the rules." She pointed to the brochure. "No Ouija boards allowed, mister, they bring out the worst in our ghosts." She extended her hand to Brad, "Hi, I'm Louise, the friendly hotel clerk who just happens to be on duty at the moment. I promise that I'm here to serve you, not haunt you." Louise laughed again and Brad joined in as he shook her hand, taking note of her firm grip and a face that reflected decades of life but an ever-present expression of humor.

"Ghosts or no ghosts, this is a fascinating place," Brad said as he swept an arm to encompass the entire hotel.

"Oh, yes, interesting indeed but I'm happy to see you return from that trance you were in. I was getting worried about you. I was afraid you might just float like a vapor right up into that chandelier, lost forever. You could become one of our resident ghosts." Louise leaned forward, extending her body over the desk. "But for all of the characters that used to drop by here to sleep, gamble or fight, and as famous as they made this old hotel, I swear we still get just as many interesting folks in here today as they did in the 1800s." She lifted her eyebrows and lowered her voice to a whisper. "The only difference is today they aren't carrying guns, thank God." She paused. "And, most of them wear red shorts that don't even begin to hide their skinny white legs. And what they wear for shoes! Little plastic flip-flops or fancy leather sandals." She lowered her voice even more. "They look like a cross between Jesus Christ and Elton John." Louise spoke loudly again. "Can you imagine John Wayne walking in here wearing shorts and sandals?" As Louise mimicked her vision, her voice dropped to an artificial base tone. "Howdy, Miss. The name's Rooster Cogburn, any chance of a nice feather bed and some sushi? " Louise stood in silence, her sun-browned wrinkles radiating pure mirth.

Brad looked down, examining his blue jeans and tennis shoes. "No shorts or sandals here and I don't eat sushi, I swear."

Louise let loose with an open laugh. "The way you were staring up into that chandelier, like you were about to start levitating, I thought for sure you were going to be one of the loony ones. I apologize. Now that I've known you for at least thirty seconds and since I approve of your dress code, I'm pretty sure you're only half crazy. That makes you perfectly normal in my book."

They both laughed before Louise fired again. "Okay, you shook my hand, listened to my philosophy and laughed at my jokes but you didn't tell me your name." She shook her head. "Come on now, you don't really think that a salty old broad like me is going to let you off that easy?" Louise held the moment, expecting a wisecrack retort.

Brad hesitated before replying. "Let's start this all over from square one." He walked to the chandelier, turned on his heel and strode back to the desk with purpose. As he approached Louise, he extended his hand over the counter, gripped her hand and spoke with exaggerated seriousness. "Hello, my name is Brad Walker. I'm visiting from Colorado and admiring this magnificent old hotel. Since you obviously enjoy employment here and are most certainly familiar with the history of this region, please give me historical background of this building and its past clientele."

Louise brushed her hand through the air in a dismissive gesture. "Gimme a break. I like the other guy better, you know, the goofy one whose face turns red when he realizes he was caught acting like a nerd."

They both laughed before Brad replied, "If I turned red every time I screwed up or did something stupid, I'd be walking around like a traffic light stuck on stop."

"Alright, Mr. Brad Walker from Colorado, now that we have been formally introduced, I shall give you the privilege of treating me." Louise pointed to coffee carafes at the end of the registration desk. "Let's have some coffee while business is slow and I can sit right here in this beautiful lobby, talk to you and keep an eye on my job at the same time. I like mine black if you don't mind." Louise stepped from behind the registration desk and moved to a pair of Victorian chairs positioned only a few feet away. She seated herself and gave Brad a 'what are you waiting for' look.

After drawing two cups of coffee, Brad bowed in submission as he handed a cup to Louise, "At your service, madam." He took a seat next to her, rolling his eyes in exasperation.

"Thank you so much, handsome stranger." Louise breathed her words. "I thought you would never ask." She closed her eyes, sipping with an exaggerated sigh of contentment.

Placing elbows on knees, Brad held his coffee in both hands, sitting quietly for a few moments and looking straight ahead before addressing Louise. "I can tell from listening to you speak that you aren't from the South and you sure as heck aren't from Boston, so my money says that you are from right around here, probably most of your life." Brad turned to face her. "How am I doing?"

"Somebody up in that chandelier told you that. Damn those ghosts! There is absolutely nothing private or sacred with those guys around."

After a sip of coffee, Brad replied with authority. "I don't need a ghost to tell me what I can see with my own eyes and hear with my own ears. You're wearing jeans with a big silver belt buckle, a squash blossom necklace and New Mexico jewelry on both hands. Now, lots of women from Miami or St. Louis dress like you are dressed but they just can't pull it off. You know, obvious phonies trying to be something they can never be." Brad paused. "You were born wearing just what you have on right now. You are New Mexico born and bred. This is easy as pie for someone who pays attention." Brad looked straight at Louise, cocking his head forward as he spoke, "And I pay attention, young lady."

"Well, well, I guess you might be a hair brighter than what I first thought. Yes, I've lived all of my sixty-two years within fifty miles of Cimarron. I raised my family here and now I've got myself three little grandbabies that keep me pretty busy, at least when I'm not behind that desk there." Louise nodded in the direction of the registration counter. "I wouldn't have it any other way. Life's not always easy here but I can't imagine living it anywhere else."

"I absolutely understand."

Louise placed her coffee on a table beside her chair. "I only work here part-time but sometimes I have to work an all-night shift. I'm getting too old for that kind of craziness so I'm thinking it may be time to retire and enjoy those grandbabies." She smiled at Brad. "You honestly think this place can manage without me? Who's going to harass folks like you once I'm gone?"

Brad grinned. "What worries me is who's going to keep track of the ghosts."

Louise retrieved her coffee and gave Brad a serious look. "It's fun to joke about that stuff, but believe me, lots of crazy and spooky things really do happen around here. I used to blow everything off as nonsense." Louise shook her head. "But not anymore. I'm a cynical old grandma but this place has made a believer out of me." She looked straight at Brad. "If you ever spend a night here, just don't you be surprised at what might happen." The implied meaning of her words dangled as Louise lifted her coffee and peered at Brad over the rim of her cup as she drank.

Before Brad could reply, a man and woman stepped up to the registration desk. Louise took a last sip of coffee, lightly touched Brad's arm and whispered, "Gotta run. Hope you come back soon cause I didn't learn a thing about you." Louise gave Brad another quick up and down appraisal as she lowered her voice. "I think I might like you. We need to talk some more." With that, Louise hustled to her position behind the counter and Brad saw her smile re-appear as she greeted the arriving guests.

Louise and Brad enjoyed one last interval of eye contact and unspoken communication. They both noted the large man at the counter, his shorts bright red.

***

After a glance at a map, Brad made a stop to fuel his rig. Afternoon light was beginning to lean across the hills and shadowed fingers crept into arroyos. Following a dirt road out of town and driving slowly, Brad tried to be mindful of the beauty of his surroundings, but beauty was not coming easily. A sense of loneliness prevailed and with every bump in the road Brad simply felt isolation. He had grown up in terrain and environment practically identical to what he saw, but this evening's drive was haunting rather than nostalgic. Brad could not fathom the feelings that the parents of Lucy Hernandez must experience each time they drove this road, knowing that their daughter would never travel it again. Lucy Hernandez was never coming home.

The house was pretty much what Brad had anticipated. Faded stucco that had endured decades of New Mexico sun, wilting west winds and periodic blizzards stood beneath wooden shingles that curled upward at their edges. A sagging wire fence encompassed the house and the patches of scraggly weeds that passed for a yard. Several of the fence posts leaned precariously and a weary-looking gate with inoperable hinges hung permanently open. Beside the gate, what appeared to be an old roofing shingle hung for dear life, a rusted wire its lifeline. Faded but still discernable, a wood burning upon the shingle spelled out the name "Hernandez."

The rusted hull of an antique pick-up truck sat perched upon cement blocks to one side of the house. Another pick-up truck that was obviously in running condition sat parked by the front gate. Its tailgate was opened and carelessly strewn about the bed of the truck were bales of hay, scattered tools and empty oilcans.

Brad pulled his truck to a halt and sat for a moment. He understood that whoever was within the house had almost certainly scrutinized his arrival and would be following his every movement. After a few seconds, he stepped from his truck and moved toward the gate, walking slowly and glancing to the sky, as if more interested in the weather than the house. With perfect timing, his ideal entree appeared from around the corner of the house. A dog that looked as ancient as the Pyramids and hobbling on a crippled leg came toward him, tail wagging but caution in his eyes. Brad dropped to one knee and slowly extended his hand. The dog held his position for a moment before inching forward, his olfactory senses working overtime to evaluate the unexpected guest. Remaining motionless, Brad allowed the dog's cold wet nose to explore his fingers before finally shifting his hand to scratch behind the old mongrel's ear. Within seconds, they were on their way to a fast friendship. As Brad caressed the dog's head, he heard the opening of the house door and knew that he was being watched. Pretending not to have heard the door, he ignored whoever was there and remained focused on the dog. Speaking softly, he stroked the animal's matted fur as if the dog and he were the only living creatures for miles.

Not until the dog became comfortable enough to squirm closer did Brad shift his attention to the front door of the house. Her eyes were what captivated him. Brad had never seen such intensity. The woman standing in the half-opened screen door concentrated in such a manner that Brad felt she could see right through him, observing his actions but also able to peer straight into his soul.

Standing slowly, Brad held her gaze as he stepped toward the house. "Good afternoon, Mrs. Hernandez. I hope I'm not intruding."

She remained silent, her eyes apprising the man who approached her.

"Mrs. Hernandez, my name is Brad Walker. I'm here because a friend of mine in Albuquerque, a lawyer, asked if I could help learn more about your daughter, Lucy." Brad let his statement settle before continuing. "My friend wants to know because she thinks there may be people who broke the law and caused Lucy harm. She wants to punish those people if possible." Brad paused again. "My friend is hoping that if she can learn more about what happened to Lucy, she might be able to help other young women."

Only a few feet now separated Brad from the door where Victoria Hernandez stood, her penetrating scrutiny continuing. Brad remained fascinated by the depth of her eyes. But once up close and after a few moments, he saw that veiled within the pools of brown lay a sadness that she could not obscure.

With a movement of her head that was barely perceptible, Victoria Hernandez spoke. "Are you a policeman?"

Brad stood still and waited a moment before replying, giving Victoria Hernandez time to process what was happening. "No ma'am, I'm not. I used to be a policeman. I was an FBI Agent for many years." He paused. "My lawyer friend in Albuquerque knows that I understand law enforcement and that I care about people like Lucy. That's why she asked me to visit with you."

Seconds passed before she retreated back inside her house, closing the screen door. A filmy barrier now separated them as she spoke, "Please wait, I will get my husband."

Brad gave a subtle nod, indicating he understood and squatted to stroke the old dog that had followed and now sniffed about his shoes. By the time the screen door again opened, the dog lay on his back, eyes closed, savoring a tummy rub and soft words from his new best friend.

Alphonso Hernandez stood in the doorway. He was not a tall man but, with obviously powerful shoulders, he exuded a large appearance. Alphonso wiped his hands on a red, grease-stained rag. Victoria stood just behind her husband. Neither of them spoke.

Brad stood and the dog opened his eyes in silent protest that his tummy rub had ended way too soon. "Quite the watch dog you have here." Brad gave a slight nod toward the dog that lay relaxed on the ground. "Reminds me of most of the dogs I've had in my life."

With a cautious smile, Alphonso extended his hand to Brad. "You're just lucky. He ate the last person who stopped by here. I guess he must've gotten all that meanness out of his system. Give him a few hours and he'll be a whole new beast, snarling and slobbering like he was Lucifer himself."

Brad felt the grip of a man who was no stranger to manual labor and who relied on physical strength for his daily existence. But Brad also saw that Alphonso carried the same sadness in his eyes as Victoria. Physical strength was no match for the anguish that simmered within Alphonso and his wife. "Thanks for the warning. I promise to be brief and be on my way before things turn bad." Brad smiled as he returned Alphonso's grip. "Mr. Hernandez, my name is Brad Walker. Did your wife tell you why I am here?"

Stepping aside to make room, Alphonso motioned for Brad to enter his house. "Yes, Mr. Walker, she told me." With a questioning look at Brad he continued, "You seem to already know our names, but I'm Alphonso and this is my wife, Victoria. Welcome to our home."

Victoria Hernandez offered her hand to Brad, her face now relaxing a bit as she spoke. "Please, come and sit." Victoria led the way into a small living room and motioned Brad to a chair, its fabric worn to a shine. A crucifix hung on the wall directly behind the chair and dominated the ambiance of the room. Victoria and her husband took seats on a couch that placed them directly facing Brad. Their hands automatically clasped as they looked at him, nervousness making their bodies rigid.

Alphonso spoke. "Mr. Walker, what can we do for you?" He hesitated. "The matter of our daughter is difficult for us. We have suffered very much." Alphonso took a breath, intending to say more but something failed and his eyes dropped. No other words followed.

Brad saw Victoria's hand tighten within her husband's as silence suddenly created its own sound. Alphonso stared at the floor, unable to speak. Victoria placed both of her hands over her husband's and looked to Brad, her eyes pleading for comfort, mercy or a possibly a shred of hope.

After a hard swallow, Brad leaned forward, placing elbows on his knees. "Before we begin, please let me tell you something about me. I'm a father. I have three children and I cannot imagine your loss." Brad shook his head as he spoke softly. "I honestly do not know what I would do if I were in your shoes." He waited a moment before continuing." But it is important that you know something else about me. I do understand loss. I lost my wife. Her name was Elizabeth. She died way too young." With a deep breath, Brad continued. "I don't know how my heart managed to keep beating. The loss you endure is different from mine but we both know pain. We know how it never really goes away."

Alphonso lifted his eyes to look at Brad.

Shifting uneasily, Brad continued. "Alright, now you know something about me. I have one more thing to say before we talk about what brought me here today. This is a favor for me. I'm not that much older than the two of you. Please, call me Brad. No more Mr. Walker and I will be honored if I may call you Victoria and Alphonso."

Tension in Alphonso's face seemed to ease as he tilted his head up and down. After moments of reflection, he found his voice and spoke softly, "Of course, Brad, of course."

Victoria's hands remained securely folded over her husband's but, as she spoke, Brad sensed a glimmer in her eyes that had not existed moments before. "Thank you, Brad. I am very sorry to learn of your wife." Her eyes wandered to the crucifix as she searched for the words she needed. "Many shadows surround our hearts, sometimes they become quite dark. I will pray for sunshine on your heart to take the shadows away." Victoria was quiet and she and Alphonso looked to Brad, their faces telling him it was time to proceed.

Brad nodded, gathering his thoughts. "My lawyer friend in Albuquerque is a prosecutor. When most people think of a prosecutor they see a person who works within the legal system to punish people and to deliver justice to those who do evil deeds. My friend certainly does just that. She works very hard to punish people who deserve to be punished. But punishment is not really what my friend is all about, not at all. What really makes her who she is and creates what's inside her heart is that she is a protector. My friend is a protector first, a punisher after that."

Victoria and Alphonso Hernandez remained still, their eyes never leaving Brad.

"My friend, her name is Juanita, just happened to learn that a girl had committed suicide after becoming involved with some bad people. That's all she knows. She has nothing else to go on except her instincts as a prosecutor and her heart as a protector. That is why she called me. She asked if I could use my experience in law enforcement to help find out what happened." Brad was quiet for a moment. "There is one more thing you should know about me. My wife was a prosecutor." Brad looked with earnestness at the couple seated before him. "I can promise you that the heart that beat within my wife, a heart that yearned to protect, is the same heart that beats within my friend, Juanita. Whatever happened to your daughter, Juanita wants to prevent from happening again to other girls. I cherish that kind of heart in a person and that is why I agreed to help her."

Victoria released the grip she had maintained on her husband's hand and brought her hands into her lap. Alphonso's eyes softened as he spoke. "Thank you, Brad. Lucy was the light of our life and what happened to her should never happen to anyone. We are willing to talk with you." He took a breath. "What do you want to know?"

With a soft exhale that released much more than air, Brad straightened his back and sat straight. "Okay, I don't have many facts to go on so please bear with me. My friend, Juanita, had some very strange information come her way that indicated a girl had committed suicide after becoming involved with some vile people. But everything she heard was without details or any corroboration. However, what Juanita learned led me to a police officer in Colorado who is involved in an investigation of a man who is deceased. This man left some jumbled records that mentioned someone named Lucy. But once again, nothing specific and lots of speculation is involved. All I know for sure is from a news article that I found in the paper. It gave the bare facts of Lucy's death. Simply from piecing together a few bits and scraps of information, I have strong suspicions that your daughter's tragedy is related to people who are involved in criminal activity." Brad shifted his eyes from Victoria to Alphonso and back again. "But it is important that you know I have not talked to any other law enforcement agency about this. I have not seen any police reports dealing with Lucy's death. I came to you first. I want to hear your story, in your own words, about what happened." Brad stopped speaking.

With a questioning glance at each other, Victoria and Alphonso absorbed what they had heard. Victoria gave a nod to her husband that he should speak. Alphonso adjusted his body on the couch and rubbed fingers over his brow. After gathering his thoughts he began to speak. "Lucy was our only child. We wanted more children but God did not grant us that wish." Alphonso made the sign of the cross. "She grew up in this house, the three of us together. Lucy was happy, loved school and had many friends. But from a young age, Lucy had stars in her eyes, she wanted more than this small house and small town. Her talk was always of a city. She wanted bright lights, traffic, people and noise, all of the things she did not have here."

Victoria unconsciously nodded her head in agreement as she listened to her husband.

"We wanted Lucy to go to college but she knew that we had no money. I told her we would find a way and that she could go, study, learn and find her place in a new world." Alphonso hung his head for a moment as his voice lowered. "But Lucy had a heart also, Brad. She refused to see herself as a burden." Alphonso clearly was finding it difficult to continue. He became quiet, just shaking his head.

Victoria again reached for her husband's hand as she began speaking on his behalf. "Lucy was so sure of herself. She thought that she could work for a while to save money before starting college. My daughter was very beautiful, Brad. She and her girlfriends spent hours learning about how to become a model and Lucy was certain that she had what it took to be a famous model and make lots of money. She had a vision of living the city life, that was what she dreamed for and then she would go to college."

Brad acknowledged Victoria's story with a sad drop of his eyes. He was pretty sure that he knew what was coming.

"It broke our hearts but we could not change her mind. Shortly after graduation from high school, Lucy left for Albuquerque to live with friends. She was so excited, so sure that she would make her life away from this small place. It was her dream finally coming true. For a while, everything seemed fine. She found a job waiting tables but that was only until she could get her break as a model. Her letters and phone calls were happy and we were beginning to think that maybe we had been wrong to doubt her." Victoria glanced to Alphonso. "We wanted so much for her to be happy. We even had thoughts that we had been wrong and she would make it on her own."

It was now Alphonso who subtly nodded his head in agreement as he listened to his wife.

"But as the months passed, we knew that things were changing. Lucy quit her job as a waitress. She began to speak of going out on dates. She said she had boyfriends who treated her well and took her to expensive places. She sent us photographs that showed her with one of these so-called dates." Victoria's face scowled. "This was not a date. The photographs showed Lucy with an older man and his car was very fancy. When she called on the phone, her voice began to sound different and it was easy for us to know that she was with the wrong crowd. She even told us that she went to Las Vegas, Nevada for a weekend."

Brad spoke in a low voice, "I'm so sorry."

Alphonso drug his shirtsleeve across his face as he again spoke. "I drove to Albuquerque to see her. I didn't even know how to find her since she had moved and never given us an address. When I got her on the phone, she was very upset that I was in town. It took some arguing but she finally agreed to meet me at a coffee shop. The second I saw her, my heart just died. She was not my little girl. It was easy to see that she had just wiped makeup from her face and everything about her was different from the daughter I knew. She talked with me for a while and I begged her to come home with me right then. Just get in the car, I said, and let's go home." Alphonso held his breath, seeking composure. Placing his hands over his face, a pitiful moan escaped before his choking voice continued. "Lucy started to cry. Huge tears were falling from her face. I was crying too and I begged her. She started sobbing but said she could not come home again. She said it was too late, too much had happened. Then she ran out of the coffee shop and left me sitting there all alone." Alphonso's shoulders shuddered. "I never saw my Lucy again."

Through closed eyes, tears streaked Victoria's face and her body gently swayed back and forth. Brad closed his own eyes. It seemed intrusive that he was even in the room with them. To be a witness to their suffering suddenly struck as sacrilege.

For what seemed eternity, the only sound was that of Alphonso crying. Victoria enduring her torment in silence seemed even louder. Feeling horribly out of place, Brad rose from his chair and walked into the kitchen. He stood over the sink, staring through a window that framed the fading light of dusk. Another day was ending for Victoria and Alphonso Hernandez. Tomorrow would be just the same as today. The days would never end. Brad felt sick.

A soft touch of a hand on his shoulder ended his introspection. He turned to Victoria who stood close beside him. Through grief-stricken eyes, she looked to Brad with a smile. "We are glad that you are here. Do not feel yourself a stranger in our house." Placing her hand on his arm, Victoria led Brad back into the room where Alphonso remained seated, his composure returning. She again sat by her husband as she spoke, "This is very hard but something good is going to happen because you have come to see us." Victoria looked to the crucifix. "God will not continue to turn his face away from us." Her hands moved, making the sign of the cross.

As Brad settled again in his seat, Alphonso nodded agreement with Victoria and looked to Brad with an expression that said he was ready to continue.

"Okay, what I hope to learn is who were the people that Lucy became involved with in Albuquerque. Who was she seeing, how was she living, who paid her bills? Can you help me with this?"

Victoria and Alphonso exchanged looks before Victoria answered. "Lucy was very quiet about those things. When she talked of having dates, she would never mention a name. She knew that we did not approve of how she was living. If we asked anything about her personal life, she shut us down. That was a part of why we were so worried. We did not know and she would not tell."

"You mentioned letters and photographs. Did you keep anything like that?"

"We have every letter that she mailed to us. She never gave a name of a friend or anything specific at all. We noticed that there was never a return address on anything she mailed. She was very careful not to give us too much information."

Brad nodded that he understood. "What about the photographs she sent? Do you still have those?"

"Yes, I kept them. There were only three or four. She sent them to me on my phone." Victoria smiled. "I learned how to use the phone just to be able to keep up with my daughter." She cast a friendly but mocking look to her husband. "Lucy knew Alphonso would never bother with learning how to look at photographs on a little electric box so she sent them to me and asked that I share them with her father."

"I understand perfectly. I like the old fashioned paper stuff myself." Brad grinned knowingly and Alphonso responded with a shrug of his shoulders and a sheepish smile.

"Let me get my phone for you." Victoria stood and made her way to the kitchen. "And by the way, Brad, you will be having dinner with us tonight. I hope you like pintos and cornbread."

"Oh, my gosh, I knew that's what I was smelling. I grew up on pintos and cornbread. I would love to join you."

Victoria returned with phone in hand. "The beans have simmered all day and the cornbread will be out of the oven soon. When we finish here, let the feast begin." Victoria gave a full smile that struck Brad to be incredibly beautiful in the wake of the afternoon's sadness.

With a flick of her fingers, Victoria located the photographs and extended her phone to Brad, scrolling quickly. "Let me take a closer look here." Brad pulled cheater glasses from his shirt pocket and scrutinized the photos as Victoria repeated the process more slowly. It was hard not to focus on Lucy, the same face he had seen in the news clipping, a beautiful and younger image of Victoria. Brad had to force his eyes to scrutinize other aspects of the photographs: a Mercedes Benz and a man. He looked closely at the man, trying to see behind his sunglasses and flowered shirt. Brad longed to see beneath the leather hat that cocked sideways and rested low over the man's face. Flashy, but indistinguishable jewelry was apparent on the man's hands. There was nothing else to see. An average sized man that exuded an appearance of being much older than Lucy. It was impossible for Brad to articulate within his mind exactly why the man seemed grotesquely out of place with Lucy but something was clearly wrong.

As Victoria scrolled to the last photograph, Brad's heart skipped. It was a shot of Lucy; the smile on her face seemed unnatural and forced. Brad guessed she was unhappy with the man's arm about her shoulder holding her close as they stood behind the Mercedes. Nothing of substance could be seen of the man but clear as a bell and in perfect focus was the New Mexico license plate of the Mercedes.

"Would you mind sending these to my phone?"

"Of course. Is there anything there to help you?"

"Maybe, I'm not sure but I sure would like to have those photos." Brad gave Victoria his email address and in seconds he had what he needed.

After the photo exchange, Alphonso seemed to read Brad's mind. "You are welcome to look at the letters Lucy mailed home to us. I don't think they will help but we will show them to you if you wish."

"If you don't mind, I would like to just glance at them. Are there any other personal items that belonged to Lucy while she lived in Albuquerque?"

Alphonso's voice quivered but he did not break down. "Yes, that was a terrible day. We had to identify Lucy's body. After it was over, they just handed us a big bag. They told us this was all they found in her residence. It was some clothing, purses, makeup and stuff like that. It had her high school yearbooks and," Alphonso took a deep breath, "the dress she wore to her senior prom."

No one spoke for a few seconds. Victoria rose and stated, "I'll get the letters."

Brad looked at Alphonso. "You are a strong man. I don't know that I could have done what you have done."

Alphonso looked to the ceiling. "We do what we have to do."

Victoria returned and placed envelopes in Brad's lap. "Go ahead, Brad. Take a look for anything that will help. I'm going to the kitchen and get our dinner ready."

"Yes, Brad, take your time. Come to join us in the kitchen when you are ready." Alphonso stood and followed his wife.

It was easy for Brad to determine that Lucy's letters had been crafted with deliberate intent to avoid sharing personal details with her parents. She had written in a generic manner that revealed nothing of her life. Brad found nothing of significance.

He replaced each letter into its envelope and sat quietly, looking about the house and reflecting on his time with Victoria and Alphonso. The Crucifix cast a spell over the room and Brad found it difficult not to fixate upon it. Many questions remained concerning the events that surrounded Lucy's suicide and what the police investigation had determined. More questions needed to be asked and he knew that he should look through Lucy's personal belongings. But every instinct within Brad told him that enough painful memories had been stirred for one sitting. Should he press on this evening or should he return at another time? Brad wasn't sure if his reluctance to continue was because of concern for Victoria and Alphonso or was it that he had endured enough heartache himself for today.

Interrupting his thoughts, Victoria came back into the room. She handed a folded paper to Brad as she sat on the couch again. "There is one person in Albuquerque that may have known what was in Lucy's heart." With a tilt of her head she indicated the paper she had just given to Brad. "His real name is Manuel Lujan but, to all who know him, *Abuelo*, Grandfather, is the only name ever used." Victoria was quiet while Brad looked at the name and address written on the paper. "Alphonso and I have thought of going to Albuquerque to visit with *Abuelo* but we have not had the courage to hear what we are afraid he will tell us."

Brad looked to Victoria with question on his face but remaining silent.

"*Abuelo* lived around here for years. He was originally from Pueblo de San Ildefonso, down close to Espanola. He split his time between his pueblo home and here in Cimarron. *Abuelo* lost his wife years ago and lived alone ever since. Everyone loved him. He was devout in the Catholic Church but yet he never let go of the traditional beliefs of his native pueblo teachings. That happens a lot around here."

A slight shift of his head indicated that Brad understood. "I know the pueblo. I visited there quite some time ago. The countryside around there is magnificent. Black Mesa is a gift from God."

Victoria smiled. "Yes, it is beautiful country. I think that is the reason he returned there so often. He said it was good for his soul." Victoria lightly patted her hand over her heart.

"I can understand that."

"*Abuelo* was seen as part medicine man, part religious teacher, who knows for sure? But we all loved him, including the young kids in school. *Abuelo* seemed to always have answers. No one could ever explain it, but that old man was always predicting the future. What he could see and understand was amazing. We all learned that if *Abuelo* said something was going to happen, it was best to pay attention." Victoria shook her head in wonder. "He had a way of knowing the future but he could also look into the past." Victoria paused, choosing her words carefully. "Yes, *Abuelo* was able to see into the future and to understand the past. But it was more than that." Victoria lowered her voice and her eyes bore straight into Brad. "*Abuelo* could see inside a person, he knew exactly what was in a person's heart." She moved her head ever so slightly. "Sometimes that was wonderful, other times it was very frightening."

"Yes, I can see how that would be." Brad's face told Victoria to continue.

"*Abuelo* used to visit our home often. I cooked for him and he spent hours with Lucy. They took walks together all over our land and Lucy shared her deepest secrets with him." Victoria paused. "We never asked *Abuelo* to break the secrecy of their bond."

"You were wise," Brad nodded as he spoke.

Lowering her voice, Victoria continued. "*Abuelo* had a daughter who went off to school and became someone important. She lives in Santa Fe and Albuquerque, always doing big things with big people." Victoria dropped her eyes but not before Brad detected sadness, perhaps disapproval. "*Abuelo* loved her dearly but never accepted her modern ways. He felt she had become lost. He feared that she no longer remembered the things that matter most in life."

The room was silent while Victoria's eyes shifted about the room. After moments, she continued with her story. "When *Abuelo* grew very old and lost his health, his daughter moved him to Albuquerque. She put him in one of those homes for old people. Everyone knew that it broke *Abuelo*'s heart, but what could we do?" Victoria paused. "Lucy loved *Abuelo* and missed him terribly when he left. There was something special in the love she had for him and he returned her feelings. When she called us, she often mentioned that she had gone to visit *Abuelo*." Victoria paused again and looked straight at Brad. "Alphonso and I think that Lucy may have told things to *Abuelo* that she would never have spoken about to us."

"So you think I should talk to *Abuelo*?" Brad lifted the paper. "Will he even talk with me?"

"I don't know. Alphonso and I talked about it just now in the kitchen. We're not even certain that he would speak with us. Many people went to *Abuelo* with their troubles but their secrets always remained safe with him." Victoria looked to the Crucifix. "*Abuelo* will be with God very soon." Victoria smiled. "I think even God may not learn everything that old man carried in his heart."

Brad's decision about whether to continue questioning Victoria and Alphonso was now easy. He tucked the paper into his shirt pocket as he looked at Victoria and declared, "I'll be there tomorrow. If he loved Lucy, maybe he will talk with me. It's worth a shot."

Brad wasn't sure if Victoria's face reflected gratitude or relief but he knew that it was the right thing to do to call it a day. Victoria and Alphonso had suffered enough for today.

Victoria's smile brightened the room. "Come now, Brad. Cornbread and pintos await us."

***

When Victoria and Alphonso learned that Brad had stopped at the St. James Hotel for a green chili lunch and had met Louise, they laughed with delight. "Everyone knows Louise," Alphonso informed Brad. "She keeps that place running. I suppose you will be staying there tonight, won't you?"

"Nope. With this marvelous meal under my belt, I'm heading straight on to Albuquerque. I want to start tracking things down right away."

Victoria threw her head back and laughed out loud. "Don't try to fool us, Brad, you are afraid to sleep in that haunted place." Her eyes twinkled. "Big time policeman afraid of the ghost stories he heard from Louise. Come on, tell the truth now." Victoria and Alphonso continued laughing at Brad's inability to think of a quick response.

After a dessert of cornbread drenched with warm honey, Brad made preparations to leave. No one spoke as Victoria and Alphonso walked with Brad to his truck. Light from the house cast a subdued glow as they stood together, feeling gratitude for the bond that had grown so quickly. Alphonso gripped Brad's hand, "*Gracias*, my friend. Thank you for coming. We are always here for you." Brad did not respond but simply placed a hand on Alphonso's shoulder.

Victoria looked up to Brad's face, her penetrating eyes barely visible. "I have a question for you, Brad. You know us. You see that we have little. We have a few cows. Alphonso mostly works for others to make our living." She paused and swallowed hard. "In your life, you have seen much of the world. You have lived in many places and known many kinds of people. Tonight, you saw the photographs of Lucy with that man and his fancy car." With a deep breath and anguish in her voice Victoria asked her question, "Why do people who have so much live the way they live? Why do people who could change the world for good instead choose to make it so much worse?" Victoria was quiet. "Why do people choose to make their mark on the world with an ugly scar instead of a beautiful rainbow?" Her voice ached with her next words. "Why would someone with so much take my daughter?"

Brad held his breath. He could think of nothing to say. Finally, he replied, his voice also in a whisper, "I do not know, Victoria, I simply do not know."

Victoria wrapped her arms about Brad and spoke softly, "*Vaya con Dios. Vaya con Dios.*"

Hand in hand, Victoria and Alphonso walked to their front door, and stood watching as Brad's truck disappeared into the night.

*****

Headlights guided Brad over the twisting and rutted road away from the home of Victoria and Alphonso. Victoria's question echoed within his mind, her voice haunting. Once away from the house and alone on the road, he had to stop. He needed to feel the air and breathe. With lights and engine turned off, he stepped out of his truck and stood in the absolute quiet of the night. He lifted his face to look into the night sky. What silence. What glory. What tragedy. Where was the answer to Victoria's question; *why do people choose to make their mark on the world an ugly scar instead of a beautiful rainbow*? Eyes searching the indigo sky, swirling with millions of stars, Brad listened for an answer. None came.

He reached into his pocket seeking Juanita's pendant. To simply touch it was not adequate. He clutched it tightly. Standing in the silence of night, Brad contemplated the ageless mysteries of the sky above and the countless questions that swirled within his mind.

With a sigh, he climbed into his truck, fired the engine and began his night drive to Albuquerque.

Chapter Four

The only clothing he had removed before sleeping had been his shoes. Brad rolled from his bed and stretched remnants of the night's drive out of his body. Making Albuquerque shortly before dawn, he had slept only a little but there was nothing restful about the motel room and he was anxious to get started. He sat on the edge of his bed. What to do first, call Juanita or call Sam? He opted for Juanita. Upon reaching her message recording, the sound of her voice stirred all of the emotions he had come to expect when thinking of her. The image of her face caused a skip in his heart as he considered how his unexpected trip to Albuquerque meant they would soon be sharing a lunch or dinner together.

After leaving a message for Juanita telling her that he was in Albuquerque, his next call also failed to reach the person he sought. Sam Trathen's voice told him that he was unavailable but promised to call back as soon as possible. Brad left a message providing the license plate of the Mercedes from Victoria's photograph and gave Sam a quick summary of what had happened the previous day in Cimarron.

With a shower and shave out of the way, Brad located a café that offered huevos rancheros and hot coffee for an early lunch. Feeling human again, he asked for a coffee to go and pulled up directions on his cell phone to *Abuelo*'s nursing home. Cranking his engine and feeling Albuquerque's desert heat building, he headed out to begin his day.

***

Sitting in the parking lot, Brad finished his coffee as he evaluated the exterior of the facility where *Abuelo* lived. The grounds were immaculately landscaped with trimmed grass and manicured flowerbeds. At the entrance, a fountain spewed water with the sounds of a mountain brook. But Brad saw the landscaping for what it was. The grass, flowers and gurgling water were nothing more than a diversion from the cruel reality that this building was life's last stop, end of the road.

Brad recalled Victoria's words that *Abuelo*'s daughter had become a person of importance. He wondered what had transpired in the lives of *Abuelo* and his daughter that led to this place? What must go through the mind of a man who had lived a life where the power of weather and the beauty of nature shaped each day, faced his final days trapped in such a sterile world? How would it feel to have sunrise announced by a nurse switching on a television instead of a brightening sky, the wind or the song of a bird? What if traffic and sirens were the only outside sounds to hear? A shudder traveled through his spine. "Holy Jesus, I hate these places."

As he approached the reception area, Brad was aware that his every step was being scrutinized. Two young women sat behind a desk, one wore a headset and was obviously occupied with a telephone call. The other eyed Brad's approach as if he carried an infectious disease. She watched as he came closer and incessant motion of her jaws went into high speed. Fascinated, Brad witnessed expert tongue utilization that wrapped chewing gum over her right molars and then in a singular motion deftly dispatched the glob to the left.

Thinking that this was a Juicy Fruit lady if ever there was one, Brad tried to meet her gaze but his eyes refused to obey what his brain commanded. As if magnetized, his vision locked on her pink sweater and how it stretched so tightly over bulging breasts that the fabric practically quivered. A nametag dangled from the left protrusion identifying the woman as "Raylene." Unfortunately, by the time this fact registered with Brad, it was too late. When he finally managed to force his dilating eyes away from Raylene's breasts to meet her gaze, Brad had lost his opportunity for a congenial encounter. The woman coolly wrapped chewing gum around the tip of her tongue, slid it beneath her upper lip to lodge it safely in the opposite side of her mouth. Then, with an exaggerated smile, Raylene greeted her visitor. "Well, sweetie, now that you've learned to spell my name frontwards and backwards, how 'bout you just tell me what you need this morning." Her artificial smile remained frozen as her eyes opened and closed in an exaggerated blink.

From the way she stretched each syllable halfway to tomorrow, Brad instantly knew that Juicy Fruit Raylene was from the Deep South. His mind raced, calculating how best to recover from his blunder of ogling her voluptuousness. "Good morning, ma'am. I'm guessing Alabama or Georgia. Am I close?"

Raylene's mouth and tongue moved in perfect synchronization, her gum popping like small firecrackers as she rolled her eyes. "Well now, bless your heart, you're standing there thinking you can just charm me to death with a little fast talk and a cute smile." The tip of her tongue peeped from between her lips and held, as if sniffing the air. Then, in slow motion, Raylene fully protruded her tongue, stretching the gum into a thin sheet. Brad stood dumbfounded as Raylene somehow managed to twirl her morsel of pink flesh between her lips in a maneuver of blinding speed. When completed, multiple threads of Juicy Fruit wrapped about her extended tongue like strands of cotton candy.

Thinking to himself that Raylene belonged in the Cirque du Soleil of gum chewing, Brad forced a stone face and spoke evenly. "I'm sorry to bother you this morning, but I am looking for Mr. Manuel Lujan. Could you please help me?"

Raylene leaned back in her chair, her breasts thrusting. "Now, didn't I know it would be something like this?" A broad smile and a gum transfer over bleached teeth transpired as she spoke. "The very second I saw you heading over to this desk, I had you figured out. Anybody that belongs here knows right where to go and they make their way down the hall and go straight to where they have their business." Adding emphasis to her words, Raylene pointed a manicured fingernail in the direction that Brad assumed led to where residents lived. Raylene shook her head as if she had just encountered a revelation of life. "But, you come strutting your stuff over here, all fancy and friendly, and announce that you want to see Mr. Lujan." She leaned forward, bringing her body closer to Brad. Her intent had been to garner Brad's full attention to her stern message. However, all that registered was that her breasts now rested on a stack of papers that lie strewn about her desk. In a flash Brad considered that they were the most gorgeous paperweights he had ever seen. Perfectly aware of where Brad's attention was focused, Raylene's voice assumed a tone of self-righteousness. "I think you are probably a lawyer or some other sort of flim-flam slickster that wants to try and swindle poor Mr. Lujan out of something." Another gum roll and tuck over the molars. "That's what I think Mister whoever you are."

Wondering how things could have gone so badly so fast, Brad noticed that the lady seated next to Raylene was no longer on a telephone call and was watching Raylene with a look of sheer mortification. Taking heart that he had done nothing to deserve such scorn and not knowing whether to laugh or become angry, he directed a response to both women. "Sorry, ladies, I'm not a lawyer or flim-flam slickster. I'm here at the request of friends from Mr. Lujan's hometown. They have asked me to stop by and visit with him."

The lady with a headset looked in Raylene's direction, her eyes and face clearly expressing that Raylene was out of line. Oblivious to her desk mate, Raylene again leaned back; the mounds beneath her sweater bulging like twin volcanoes on the verge of eruption. "Well, here's what's about to happen, Precious. You are going to sign your name right here on our visitor log, and then you and me are going to walk down that hall." She gave another jab in the air with a painted fingernail. "And you can explain to Mr. Lujan all about these dear friends that are just so concerned." Gum roll and a spectacular pop. "Then, if Mr. Lujan says he never heard of those folks or doesn't care to spend his time with the likes of you." She shook her head and double-popped her gum. "Me and you will enjoy another walk down the hall, side-by-side, right to that door you just came through and you can take your snake oil straight on to your next stop." Raylene's tongue once again poked out from between her lips, treating Brad to another display of acrobatic gum art.

Still managing a straight face, Brad shifted his gaze between the two women as he calculated a response. "Sounds fine to me. I appreciate you showing me the way."

"Sorry, mister, nobody is showing nobody nowhere until you sign this book." The fingernail that had earlier pointed down the hallway now rapped with authority indicating the exact spot where Raylene demanded a signature. "Signature and printed!" Her face beamed with pleasure at how she had taken command of the situation.

"Happy to oblige." Brad pulled a pen from his shirt pocket and followed Raylene's instructions.

Lifting the register from her desk and holding it aloft as if she hoisted the Holy Grail itself, Raylene examined Brad's signature. When satisfied, her voice became pompous as she proclaimed, "Well, it appears we have Mister Brad Walker with us this fine day." Eyelashes fluttering and accomplishing another shift of gum, Raylene ceremoniously replaced the register and stepped from behind her desk. "All right, Mister Bradley Walker, it is okay if I call you Bradley, I hope. Please follow me." With that, Raylene gave a spin and began to march.

Brad managed a quick glance to the headset lady as he prepared to follow. She burst into a huge smile and gave a thumbs-up gesture of support. Brad winked and returned the overture with his own upturned thumb.

Spiked heels pounded an echoing cadence as Raylene made a determined advance across the lobby. Brad's tennis shoes silently kept pace, now realizing that her slacks clung to her buttocks in the same manner as did her sweater over breasts. Dutifully following a few steps behind Raylene's left-right, left-right jiggle, Brad was now free to gawk as licentiously as he pleased.

Raylene led Brad to a nursing station that separated two hallways where a left or right turn was necessary. Without breaking stride, she tossed a quick glance over her shoulder to be certain her subjugate still followed and, with military precision, spun her body to the right. The rhythmic clanking of Raylene's spiked heels and her jiggling buttocks instantly seemed obscene and out of place. Wheelchairs lined the hallway and age-ravaged bodies, little more than sticks covered with clothing or a blanket, stared like skeletons through vacant eyes. Brad tried to look beyond the wasted bodies, women's mouths smeared with lipstick and false teeth slipping from shrunken gums. Heads with disheveled strands of hair mechanically swiveled as curious faces silently tracked the two people who moved with such purpose within their midst. The acrid odor of disinfectant and urine found a way into his nostrils. Closing his eyes, Brad whispered silently, "Please, God, please don't let it end like this."

***

From the doorway, the figure of Manuel Lujan was a picture of frailty. Even though supported by pillows, he still leaned precariously to one side of his wheelchair. His head drooped over his chest in sound sleep and his mouth hung open. White hair, deliberately grown to shoulder length, could not obscure a neck so thin that it resembled a discarded pencil, brittle and brown. Bones of his shoulders protruded through a faded shirt and the blanket over his legs formed the outline of an emaciated body. No movement came from Manuel Lujan, nothing to indicate awareness that people had entered his room.

While Brad remained in the doorway, Raylene stepped quietly as she approached the sleeping man. To Brad's relief, her movements and entire demeanor dramatically softened as she gently touched the man's shoulder and leaned close to speak. "Mr. Lujan, someone is here to see you." She stroked his upper arm as the old man sucked a startled breath in response. His head rose from his chest, eyes blinking in bewilderment. He looked to Raylene's face, struggling to focus. She spoke again, her face only inches from the man. "Mr. Lujan, a man is here to see you. His name is Brad Walker. I'm not sure that you know him or if you even want to see him. If you don't want to be disturbed, I will take Mr. Walker away and you can go back to sleep."

Manuel Lujan stared vacantly.

"Mr. Lujan, would you like for me to tell Mr. Walker to leave?"

A face devoid of expression gaped at Raylene.

"Wouldn't you like to just go back to sleep, Mr. Lujan? Doesn't a nap sound very nice?"

Raylene was silent as she gave Manuel Lujan time to respond. The only sound was from a garbage truck somewhere outside, screaming hydraulics and banging dumpsters reverberated. The movement of Manuel Lujan's head was scarcely perceptible but the up and down gesture was exactly what Raylene had hoped to see. Re-energized and with a triumphant look of 'I told you so' she stepped toward Brad motioning that his time had expired. "Mr. Lujan does not wish to speak with you. It's time for you to leave."

At wit's end with her insolence, Brad brushed past the painted woman, practically snarling his contempt and forcing her to take a step back. Startled with this sudden personality transformation, Raylene froze in uncertainty. Even her jaws ceased movement. Brad dropped to one knee directly in front of Manuel Lujan and placed a hand over the old man's arm. "Mr. Lujan, last night I was with Victoria and Alphonso Hernandez in Cimarron." Brad paused. "They send their love to you, *Abuelo*. They asked that I speak with you about Lucy."

Embedded in folds of brown skin that reminded Brad of wind-blown New Mexico soil, the eyes of Manuel Lujan were enshrouded in a milky film. Brad watched him blink several times, struggling to comprehend. Brad held his position, aware that Raylene remained just behind his shoulder, a dutiful centurion standing guard. He saw the man's eyes shift, looking toward Raylene and then back again, blinking repeatedly. "Mr. Lujan, Lucy loved you very much. Victoria and Alphonso told me that she visited with you frequently until something bad happened. They are hoping you can help them and me understand about Lucy's life."

Like a metronome, the man's eyes shifted from Brad to Raylene, back and forth, searching.

With light pressure on a fragile arm and looking directly into the eyes of Manuel Lujan, Brad made his plea, "Mr. Lujan, Victoria and Alphonso need your help. I am asking for help." A delicate pause. "Mr. Lujan, Lucy Hernandez is also is asking for your help."

Silence of a graveyard, seconds ticked.

From within Manuel Lujan's eyes, Brad saw something register, a glimmer of comprehension forged through cloudy mist. The old man made another look toward Raylene, his eyes now clearing as seconds passed. Brad remained motionless and silent. Raylene simmered.

Manuel Lujan now shifted more than his eyes. His entire head turned, neck muscles straining, until he looked directly at Raylene. With a voice of gravel he spoke in words that were barely audible but enunciated with authority. "I wish to speak with this man. Leave us now."

Her face deflating like a leaking balloon, Raylene caught her breath and ice formed in her eyes. The glare directed at Brad was palpable with contempt as she hoarsely whispered, "Don't forget to sign out, Mr. Walker." Rigid with anger, she stormed from the room.

Manuel Lujan looked at Brad, a mischievous grin now spreading across his wrinkled skin. Lifting both hands to his chest and curling bony fingers into the shape of cups, he made a gesture of holding breasts. With a toothless smile he whispered, "Nice sweater!"

Open laughter filled the room as Brad threw his head back in sheer delight. In his own quiet mirth, the shoulders of Manuel Lujan quaked uncontrollably.

Looking around the room, Brad saw a single chair. A nightstand stood beside the bed and a small television perched on a chest of drawers that served as a closet. The walls were starkly bare and blinds over a single window obscured outdoor sunlight.

Rising from his knee, Brad drug the chair across a linoleum floor, bringing it close to the wheelchair. He seated himself and leaned toward the aging man. "Thank you for your kindness and for talking with me."

Still enjoying the moment of humor, Manuel Lujan's pink gums remained visible behind a smile. Stubble sprouted about his face in irregular patches but the milky film over his eyes had disappeared. His aged eyes were now clear and perception registered as he focused his gaze upon Brad. Seconds seemed suspended as Manuel Lujan scrutinized Brad, clearly evaluating the man seated before him. Finally, he spoke. Struggling to project and his voice cracking, the old man moved his lips. "I knew you would come." His eyes never left Brad's. "Yes, I knew you were coming." His wrinkled face expanded into a full smile as Brad's only response was a mystified expression.

"I am an old man. I am sure many say I am an old goat." His shoulders shook again as he chuckled. "But I know many things. No one can deny that I know many things." His face became serious as he paused. "It is not always easy to know. Sometimes it is very hard." His eyes drifted, looking about his room, wall to wall and ceiling to floor. "It is hard to know things from inside this place. Answers are found in the stars, moon and wind." He shook his head sadly. "I no longer can see the stars. The moon does not shine in this room and my skin never feels the wind." He paused. "I am very sad." He brought a long breath into his lungs before continuing. "After Lucy died, I had to close my eyes and try very hard. But that is what I did. I tried very hard to see and to listen." He shifted his head up and down, smiling, obviously pleased with himself. "Yes, I knew you would come."

Brad simply nodded as he thought back to how Victoria Hernandez had spoken of how uncannily *Abuelo* could predict the future.

"May I call you *Abuelo*?"

"Of course, that is my name."

"I know that something very bad happened to Lucy. It is too late to change the terrible things that she endured, and that breaks my heart. But, *Abuelo*, if you can help me know what happened, who caused her such pain, it is possible that something can be done to prevent such awful things from happening again."

Shifting within his wheelchair, *Abuelo* grimaced, pain reflecting in his eyes. Once situated, he pointed to his throat and whispered, *"Agua."*

Brad rose and poured water from a pitcher on the bedside table. *Abuelo* accepted a plastic cup from Brad with a trembling hand. As he lifted the water to his lips, the tremors became worse and liquid spilled out onto his chin, dripping down his chest. After a moment of realization, the old man' eyes found Brad's and another grin creased his brown face as he spoke, "Son-of-a-bitch."

Reaching to help steady the cup, Brad again laughed out loud. "Not a problem. I suspect you were thinking about that lady's sweater and got yourself all excited."

Abuelo showed his gums again as his shoulders moved. "Maybe someone should spill water on her. She has a big fire."

Brad continued to laugh as he helped Abuelo tilt water into his mouth.

After swallowing and wiping a shirtsleeve across his wet chin, *Abuelo* looked straight at Brad. "I do not have much time. My day is almost here. I have been waiting for you and I am glad that you are with me." A deep breath followed before he continued. "Lucy did not tell me her secrets but she knew that I could see inside her heart. She sat right where you are now seated and let me look into her heart." He raised his hand, pointing a twisted finger in Brad's direction. "I am no longer able to speak clearly with my voice but I can tell you what you need to know." He became silent, looking at Brad.

"I'm listening, *Abuelo*."

Straining to project, his voice quivered. "Lucy kept a book. She wrote in it every day. That book, it will tell you all you need to know. That is how Lucy will talk to you. Read the words of her book." *Abuelo* said nothing more and closed his eyes.

Leaning back as if he had been shoved, Brad whispered to himself, "Jesus H, a diary. Lucy kept a diary!" He heard Alphonso's voice telling of a bag that contained Lucy's personal items. That was exactly where Lucy's diary would be found. Thinking back, Brad realized that he had been too overcome with the emotion-charged moments with Victoria and Alphonso to grasp how significant those things might be. "Thank you, *Abuelo*. I know where to find the book."

"Good, that is where you must start." *Abuelo* slowly moved his head from side to side, a knowing look in his eyes. "But, that will be only the beginning." Lifting his arms, he extended both hands toward Brad. Understanding exactly what was wanted, Brad offered his own hand and *Abuelo* took it, wrapping brown, leathered fingers over Brad's. Strength from decades of life streamed from *Abuelo* and, in their physical contact, Brad felt a flow of energy. After seconds, *Abuelo* again spoke. "I have listened but have not yet heard the answers." He paused. "The answers will come but you must pay attention to the wind. You must look into the night sky. Among the stars, that is where the ancient ones live. The ancients have been wronged and they are angry. You must go to them, look to the stars, stand in their home and listen to their voices. They have the answers you seek." *Abuelo* was quiet. Brad did not move. Holding tightly to the man, he dared not even blink.

Abuelo's breath was becoming labored and his voice more strained. With a nod toward the stand beside his bed he spoke, "In the drawer, I have prepared a message for you." He managed a weak smile. "I told you that I knew you would come. Read my words, they are for you."

Brad gently pulled his hand away from *Abuelo's* grasp. He stood and moved to the bedside stand that held a single drawer. Having no idea what to expect, he slid open the drawer. Body lotion, aspirin, a box of tissues and a small crucifix on a leather necklace were all that he saw. He looked closer. Beneath the tissues lay an envelope. He lifted the envelope, closed the drawer and returned to *Abuelo*. "Is this what you mean?"

With a nod *Abuelo* answered and again extended his hands to Brad. With the envelope in Brad's lap and their fingers again interlocked, intense concentration caused *Abuelo's* brow to furrow and his eyes narrowed. "Read my words later, they can wait. Read when you are alone." He paused and sadness fell over his face. "You will be tested. This will not be easy." Brad felt increased pressure on his hand. "Dark shadows will take you beneath the earth." With another side-to-side movement of his head, ominous premonition clouded *Abuelo's* face. "The sun will not go with you." *Abuelo's* eyes opened fully again as he repeated, "The sun will not be with you when you step below the ground." *Abuelo* was silent. "My prayers are for you."

Abuelo held his breath and with final excruciating effort, he leaned forward, close to Brad's face. "Listen to the ancient ones. Be strong and be brave. The serpent you must face is evil."

The grip of *Abuelo's* hands eased. A deep exhale and relaxing shoulders indicated that a tremendous burden had been taken away. *Abuelo* leaned back, nodded toward his bed and whispered, "Sleep." His eyes blinked heavily.

Brad eased his hand away, swallowed hard and, with heart racing, rose and walked to the bed where he pressed the call button for assistance. Within seconds a nurse appeared and wheeled *Abuelo* to his bed. Brad watched as she gently helped the man to stand and then ease him into his mattress. She tucked sheets about the frail body, stroked his forehead and whispered, "You can sleep now, Mr. Lujan, sleep for as long as you wish." The nurse turned to Brad and gave a smile as she softly spoke, "He is a special man." She left the room, leaving the two men alone.

Brad stood over *Abuelo*, examining his fissured face. It was impossible not to wonder about the years of life within this man. What secrets were buried within those canyons of aged skin? *Abuelo* returned Brad's gaze, weariness showing in his eyes. After moments of silence, Brad stooped close to *Abuelo* and, placing a hand on his shoulder, breathed a farewell. "Thank you, *Abuelo*. I will always remember you."

A smile and the knowing look between two people who share a special secret was *Abuelo*'s only response.

***

Brad walked back through the lobby, his mind spinning with what he had just experienced. Lost in thought, he almost missed the Headset Lady who now sat alone at her desk. He made a dash to see her before the Juicy Fruit Queen reappeared. Upon seeing Brad approach, Headset Lady burst out laughing, "I'm so happy to see you. No tar and feathers, no broken bones or daggers stuck in your back!"

"Good heavens, what was that all about? I deserve combat pay for that ordeal."

Headset Lady continued to laugh. "Well, I hate to tell you this, but that little scene was worth a whole lot more than I'm going to get paid today. I mean, seriously, that was entertainment!" She extended her hand. "Hi, I'm Samantha and I promise not to pour gasoline on you."

Taking her hand, Brad returned her smile. "Gasoline and matches would be welcome after what that lady put me through. I think I'll send her a truckload of gum for Christmas this year, maybe sneak in a little laxative to boot."

Samantha's face beamed. "I'm so sorry Mr. Walker. Not that it's any excuse, but last week we did have some guy, claiming to be a lawyer, sneak in here and try to hoodwink a poor resident into signing some baloney documents. Management is obviously concerned so they put out a notice, asking everyone to be diligent and cautious for people who don't belong here." Samantha shook her head in bewilderment. "Raylene now sees herself as the first line of defense against all swindlers and horse thieves. You just happened to show up at the wrong place and the wrong time."

"Well, you can go to the bank with this. The second I walk out of here, I plan to contact every swindler and horse thief I know. I'll tell them to peddle their wares anywhere but here! Whatever they have to gain, it sure ain't worth it." Samantha and Brad laughed together for a moment before Samantha slid the register toward Brad. "Sign out right here and you are a free man."

With a second's hesitation, Brad winked. "What happens if I don't sign out? Any chance that Miss Congeniality might catch a little heat for not following the rules?"

With a poker face to be proud of, Samantha pulled the register away. "You are free to go, Mr. Walker. Have a wonderful day." Her eyes twinkled as Brad waved and walked away.

***

Back in his truck, Brad sat for a moment, reflecting on what had just happened in his talk with *Abuelo*. He had no idea what to think about how the old man spoke in riddles and seemed to look into the future. However, there was no question that he had to examine the contents of Lucy's diary. He was equally certain that the diary was with her personal belongings back in Cimarron. He remembered how he had deliberately chosen not to extend the evening for Victoria and Alphonso by asking to see her personal effects. "Guess I'm going back to Cimarron sooner than I thought," he muttered softly.

***

Holding the envelope that Abuelo had given him, Brad felt both anticipation and bewilderment. He could not imagine anything more bizarre than the encounter he had just experienced, but something told him that whatever was within the envelope was going to add to the mystery of *Abuelo*. He slid a finger beneath the seal and extracted a sheet of plain white paper that was folded within. Without realizing that he did so, Brad held his breath, laying flat the creased note that was *Abuelo's* message. It was written in pencil, the writer's hand had obviously been shaky and the lines angled from left to right in a downward slant across the paper, but every word was perfectly legible.

Brad ran his eyes over the letter. Unconsciously moving his head in mystification, he read the words a second time. Then he read them again.

I have asked but answers were not given
Only you can do this

The people of the Pajarito await you
They will speak but you must go to them
They are angry
Listen for their voices
Only at night can they be heard
You have tasted their water before
It always flows
Drink it again
You will be alone when you face the serpent
He lives near the fire

"What in the name of heaven?" Brad muttered his exasperation. Under any other circumstances he would have dismissed the note as sheer gibberish and given it a toss. But today, his head and gut spoke differently. After reading *Abuelo's* words again, he replaced the letter into its envelope and folded it to fit inside his shirt pocket. "Good God Almighty, what the hell is going on here?"

Checking his phone for messages, the two calls he was hoping for popped up on his screen, Juanita and Sam. Brad was anxious for both but which message to select first was an easy decision. His finger hit the keypad for Juanita's voice. "Oh, Brad, I'm so sorry I missed your call. I'm dying to hear what you've learned and why you are in Albuquerque. I can't believe how terrible our timing is though. I'm in the middle of trial prep and am totally buried with witness interviews. I'm still negotiating with an absolutely incompetent defense counsel. I'm desperately trying to work some sort of last minute deal but I have no idea if I can make it happen. Lunch is out I'm afraid but let's shoot for a late dinner. I'm hoping to be free by eight o'clock or so. Let's stay in touch." Brad listened as Juanita paused. "Thank you for helping me." Another pause. "Later tonight?" A longer pause. "I've missed you." Brad heard Juanita's breath. "Bye."

Clicking off her message, Brad rubbed his brow and felt his heart pound. He was so wanting to see Juanita. But now, after hearing her voice, it was like he had been kicked in the chest. He allowed his mind to replay her words, "I've missed you." Placing both hands over his eyes, Brad whispered to himself, "I miss you too, Juanita. I miss you more than you can imagine.

After gathering himself and with a sigh, Brad punched in to retrieve Sam's message. "Hey there, Mr. J. Edgar." Brad grinned at the gruff sound of his friend's voice. "That New Mexico tag comes back to a joker named Edmond Knapp. I can give you the boring details about his date of birth, height, weight and all of that stuff if you wish. But I think the main thing you need to know is that he's a forty-five year old white guy with several arrests. However, thanks to lawyers and cream cheese on the moon, nothing's ever managed to stick. Also, being the ace investigator that I am and knowing how you need all the help you can get, I made a call to a guy I know in the Albuquerque PD. I'm glad I did cause there's more to your boy, Edmond, than what initially meets the eye. I think you better call me. This guy sounds like he could be bad news. Let's talk right away."

Once he had replaced the phone in his lap, Brad softly swore, "Jesus H." Leaning his head back, Brad closed his eyes. *Abuelo's* words and demeanor had rattled him even before the mysterious letter. Hearing Juanita's voice but now facing a delay before he could actually see her, left him somewhere between euphoria and depression. Then Sam had topped everything off with a message of a character that might be trouble. Brad's mind filled with thoughts of how this was exactly the way things had begun with Sam as a lead-up to ultimately finding himself in the middle of human traffickers. It was also a repeat of his stumbling into the midst of white supremacists that had tried to murder him. In each instance, one thing kept leading to other things and before he knew what happened, he had ended up in quicksand up to his nose. Releasing a soft swear under his breath, he hit the re-dial button for Sam and listened to his own whispered words, "My aching ass, I'm too old for this."

After the second ring, Sam picked up and barked into the phone. "Ain't no trout in the Rio Grande that far downstream. You're in the land of lizards and cactus." Without offering opportunity for response, Sam continued. "I should know better than to ask, but just what kind of pickle juice are you getting yourself into this time?" Sam's trademark throaty chuckle followed his jab at Brad.

"You tell me, wise-ass. You're the one who called in a panic, Remember?"

Sam was still laughing as he responded. "Don't get all stirred up now. Keep your pretty panties dry. I'm trying to help you out."

A groan preceded what came out as statement of fact rather than a question. "Are you a pain in the ass or what."

Sam's chuckle again set the tone. "I'll take that as a compliment. Now, I'm going to take charge here and help you along. The Mercedes tag and Mr. Edmond Knapp are very interesting items. I talked with that friend I mentioned from Albuquerque PD and found that the good Mr. Edmond Knapp bounces around between third-rate gift shops and has his fingers in trading post operations all over the Southwest. He buys, sells and trades pottery, Native American blankets and artifacts. Some of his stuff is junk but some is the real deal, honest to gosh pieces of antiquity."

Brad's grunt was sarcastic, "Sounds like a line straight from Juanita's story."

"Absolutely. However, there appears to be a bit more to the story than a poor retail clerk scratching out a living. He's been popped on drug charges for dealing out the back door of his various business establishments. He pled a couple down and others got dropped for whatever reason, so he's never taken a hard hit."

"Okay."

"It's from about two years ago that things get really interesting. My guy tells me that the Albuquerque PD has watched this bonehead transform practically overnight from a hand-to-mouth pretend businessman and small potatoes dope dealer to major gentleman status. He started driving top-of-the-line cars, moved into a fancy condo out toward the mountains and just in general began living the good life." Sam took a breath and was silent.

"I'm listening."

"A couple of things are important here, Brad. First, Albuquerque PD has a snitch that tells them Edmond Knapp has graduated from selling grams of snort to moving sizeable quantities. But, that ain't all. The guy has managed to get involved with some high rollers in the world of artifacts and is up to his ears in making deals to move pretty pricey stuff in under the table deals." Sam stopped speaking and Brad heard the sound of Sam shuffling through papers.

"Alright, Sam, something tells me you haven't made it to the good stuff yet."

"Not even close, not even close. Where Knapp makes his real money these days is in arranging deals where drugs, pottery and various artifacts are traded for sex"

"Holy shit. This is just what Juanita talked about and precisely what we suspected after looking at those records that came out of the Ferrari."

"Yep." Sam laughed. "So help me, Brad, I wish I could forget I ever knew you. You've been nothing but trouble since you left the Bureau."

"Come on, let's get this over with. Do you have anything more worthwhile to say?"

"Well yes, as a matter of fact I do have more to tell you and it may be important so listen closely." Brad detected a somber tone creeping into Sam's voice. "If you ever find yourself face-to-face with Mr. Knapp, you should keep in mind that about six months ago, a well-known art and artifacts dealer from Arizona turned up dead as a doornail in Albuquerque. The informant that is talking to Albuquerque PD says it was the work of Knapp and that he pulled the job as a contract executioner for some big boys after a deal for pottery, drugs and sex went bad."

"Jesus. I doubt that I'll ever meet Knapp but thanks for telling me anyway. That puts an even more serious twist on this whole thing."

"No kidding. The PD has no evidence beyond the word of their informant so they have no case at this point.

"I understand. Brad was quiet for a moment before continuing. "Since I'm here in Albuquerque, would your friend at the PD be willing to meet with me? I'd like a chance to talk things over. Maybe he could tell me where Knapp lives, works or hangs out. All the regular stuff."

"Oh hell yes he will talk with you. He's a great guy and a heck of an investigator. His name is Sid Pruitt, been with the PD for years. I'll call him and tell him to give you a ring."

"Okay, thanks Sam. I have a few hours to kill before I hopefully will see a certain female prosecutor tonight for dinner. Maybe some cop talk will help me get my mind off of that beautiful woman for a while. Never can tell, something useful might even pop up about Edmond Knapp that will help figure out what to do next." Brad then gave Sam a summary of what he had learned from Grandfather about Lucy's diary and told him he would be heading back to Cimarron after some time with Juanita.

It was the old Sam that Brad loved to hear as his friend literally barked into the phone. "You simple-minded shit, make sure that you see that lady tonight an let this cop stuff take its proper place. In the name of heaven, get your priorities straight. You're retired, in case you've forgotten, just an old faded-glory has been. Give your whole story to Sid and let him run with things as a real, on-duty cop." Sam took a breath. "Sometimes I think you must have been dropped on your head the day you were born."

"Okay, okay, I hear you. Don't go and blow a gasket. Just give me a call after you talk with Sid. I'll take it from there and set up a meeting to give him all I know. I even promise not to tell him that you are a complete horse's ass."

Sam laughed his laugh. "Sid has known me for a long time so you are way too late in breaking that bit of news."

***

After a quick drive south on Interstate 25 and negotiating traffic to cross town on Central Avenue, Brad jumped on Rio Grande Boulevard, heading to a delicatessen that he had visited in the past with Elizabeth. He loved this place for two reasons. First, it had great food but an added attraction was that a wonderful bookstore was located right next door. Brad needed time to think about his visit with *Abuelo*, the mystifying letter and what he had just learned from Sam. A little time to dine in peace on a beautiful outdoor patio sounded like the perfect medicine for the moment. Then, while waiting to hear from either Sid or Juanita, he would browse the bookstore and savor the moment.

Settled with an iced tea, Brad relished shade from the canopy of trees that draped over the café's patio. Elizabeth and he had enjoyed the very table where he now sat when they had stayed in a unique inn that was located just a bit further up Rio Grande Boulevard. The inn with lush gardens and fields of lavender, peacocks roaming about and roosters crowing each morning had an ambiance that Elizabeth and he had found wonderfully romantic.

Smiling to himself in the pleasant memory, Brad leaned back, wanting to replay the time with *Abuelo*. The old man's sense of humor would cause anyone to love him instantly but the rest of their time and conversation had not left Brad feeling especially tranquil. In fact, a sense of unease was stirring. Brad closed his eyes to envision the look on *Abuelo's* face and to listen again to the murky words he had spoken. The ominous warning of danger issued by *Abuelo* carried a mystical aura that Brad was innately inclined to dismiss. But Brad found that dismissal was not coming easily. In spite of his determination to be analytical, he felt a chill prickle his skin as he recalled the words of *Abuelo*. What was it about that old man? Was it his eyes, his voice? Brad recalled the eerie feeling that he had felt when their hands had clasped. It had been a sensation that some sort of inexplicable force had streamed from *Abuelo's* touch.

Brad accepted food from his server and went through everything again as he ate in silence.

***

There were thousands of books. Every nook and corner of the popular bookstore was crammed to overflow. This was the perfect place to wait for Sid or Juanita to call. Brad ambled, moving from shelf to shelf, occasionally lifting a book to flip through its pages, getting a feel of its story and character. Brad loved bookstores simply because he loved books. Whether viewed as a means of escape or a window to the world, he had always found them to be treasured companions.

Checking his phone every few minutes, anxious to hear from Sid but desperate to hear from Juanita, Brad wandered the bookstore, his eyes skimming innumerable titles. When he saw the book, he immediately knew that it was exactly what he had unconsciously been seeking: *The Earth is Enough*, by Harry Middleton. Brad had first read the story years ago and had gone back to re-read certain passages several times since. He held the book, relishing the memory of the words of a master storyteller. The story was of a young boy growing up in the hills of Arkansas, where his grandfather uncle and an elderly Native American taught him the intertwining story of nature, the land and fly fishing. Elated with his find and knowing this was precisely what he needed, Brad made his purchase and stepped outside.

He checked his phone for the hundredth time. No calls or messages. Walking to his truck, he breathed a soft plea, "Please, Juanita. Come on, Sam, somebody help me out here."

Pulling on to Rio Grande Boulevard, Brad headed north, deciding to take a cruise through Corrales. The shaded streets and throwback lifestyle of this idyllic valley nestled along the Rio Grande River had somehow managed to escape modernized glitz. This struck Brad as just the right thing to do while he continued to wait. Just before he could make a westbound crossing over the Rio Grande, his phone finally rang.

Expecting the voice of Sid or Juanita, Brad was surprised when Sam's voice, brimming with excitement, burst into his ear. "Talk about timing or coincidence, I'm not sure which it is but opportunity may be knocking my friend."

"Really?"

"I made that call to Sid to tell him that you would like to meet and talk with him. But just as I called, he was receiving word from a small town, somewhere up in northern New Mexico, that Edmond Knapp had gotten himself arrested."

"You gotta be kidding me."

"No kidding on this one. Sid was busy getting the story sorted out so I had to wait on him for a while. That's why it took such a long time for me to get back to you."

"No problem. This is the kind of break that's worth waiting for. Do you know what's going on?"

"Yep, at least mostly. Sid was talking with an officer from this small town, let me see here, what the heck was the name of the place." Brad heard papers rustling. "Got it. It's in Union County, New Mexico. A town called Clayton. Sounds like it's up near the Colorado border. Ever hear of the place?"

"Oh yeah, I've heard of it and even been through it a few times but it's been a heck of a long time. As I remember, it's a very small town that's surrounded by big-ass ranches and a few farms. Not much there but lots of traffic passes through. It's in the pipeline for people traveling from Texas to Colorado, lots of folks looking for that Rocky Mountain High."

"Got ya but I don't think Edmond Knapp is a Texan and I sure don't picture him as the type to be out looking for mountains or streams. Know what I mean?"

"I understand and completely agree." Brad's reply was delivered in a laugh.

"Here is what I know and all that Sid Pruitt knows at the moment. Knapp was sitting at a traffic light in Clayton, driving the very Mercedes Benz that you saw in that photograph. He was just waiting at a red light, minding his own business, when some young cowboy and cowgirl come along in a pickup truck. It sounds like the cowgirl was playing with the cowboys weenie and a very distracted young man plows right into the rear end of Knapp's Mercedes Benz.

Brad couldn't help himself and began to laugh. "I love it that everybody wants to pass laws that prohibit talking on cell phones while driving. But, you know something, Sam? I haven't heard of a single state that wants to prohibit weenie playing while driving. Now, you tell me you old pervert, which would be more distracting to you as you cruise down the highway, a simple cell phone conversation or a lovely lady playing hide and seek with your pecker?"

It was just like the old days to Brad as Sam and he laughed out loud, delighting in their juvenile humor. Finally, Sam stopped laughing long enough to continue. "Well, I can't speak to the legality of what may have been happening in the cab of that pickup truck but I can tell you that when Edmond Knapp's Mercedes got smacked, the trunk of that luxury vehicle popped open like a dime store jack-in-the-box."

Sensing where Sam's story was headed, Brad let out a short chuckle, "I would so much rather be lucky than good."

"You nailed it, my friend. Edmond Knapp sits in a small New Mexico town, proud as hell of his Mercedes Benz and, the next thing he knows, whammo! He's clobbered by a young rodeo Romeo. There sits poor Edmond and the contents of his trunk are out there in plain sight for the whole world to see."

Sarcasm in his voice, Brad asked for what he already knew was coming. "And what in the world was it in the trunk of that fine man's car?"

"All kinds of Native American pottery and blankets. Apparently he had museum quality stuff along with broken pottery pieces and some other artifacts. I don't know exactly what all he had, but there was no way for him to hide it."

"Thank heaven for traffic accidents. But unless the stuff Knapp had in the trunk was stolen, what's the case?"

The case at the moment is flimsy but what saved the day was the fact that a loaded revolver and a nice big bag of marijuana were also in the trunk. Knapp claimed that the gun belonged to a friend but a stolen report was on file. The Clayton officer who responded to the traffic accident had his head on straight and made some calls to Albuquerque PD. Albuquerque is still trying to track down the owner of the gun and figure out the details of the theft. But anyway, there was enough to haul Knapp's ass to jail for possession of stolen property, and illegal drugs. The pottery, artifacts, gun and drugs are all impounded in Clayton."

"Wow, this could be a hell of a break. You agree."

"Absolutely, but Knapp has made contact with a hotshot attorney and is howling like a scalded skunk. The shitbird swears he's going to sue the entire world. Apparently he is one obnoxious SOB. The folks in Clayton aren't sure of how long they'll be able to hold him."

"God love those guys."

"Oh, hell yes. But here's the deal that you need to know right now. Sid Pruitt is heading up to Clayton at the crack of dawn tomorrow to try to talk with Knapp before his lawyer springs him. Once I told Sid about you and your interest in the case, he threw out an invitation for you to join him in the interview. Sid will just badge both of you in and you boys can take a crack at Knapp. Who the heck knows, you may learn a bunch more about what's going on."

"Put me in coach. I'll be there."

"In all probability, Knapp will tell you to cram it where the sun don't shine but at least you can get a look at him. Never can tell where this will end up going. Between drugs, a stolen gun and possible stolen property, something may shake loose."

Logistics spinning through his mind, Brad was quiet for a moment. "Okay, here's what I'm going to do. As soon as we hang up, my hairy ass is on the road back to Cimarron to find Lucy's diary. I'm pretty sure that whatever Lucy may have written, Sid should know about before he talks with Knapp. He may spot names or something that he recognizes and the entire nature of the interview may change. I think I'll stay the night in Cimarron and then shoot up to Clayton bright and early to meet Sid for the interview."

Sounds good. Sid will meet you at the Clayton jail at noon tomorrow. He has your cell and I'll text you his contact information as soon as we're off this call."

"Perfect. Thanks, Sam, this is hugely appreciated."

"No sweat but listen a second, you moron. The last couple of times you went off like this you ended up chasing some human trafficking goofball through a mountain canyon in the middle of a storm. Then, a few months later and lessons unlearned, you got you head bashed in by a white supremacist. How about being just a bit careful this time? You owe me money and beer. I intend to collect."

"Your concern for my safety is truly touching," Brad replied with a cynical snort, "But I hear you. All I'm going to do is take a drive and sit in a jailhouse while an Albuquerque bonehead lies about anything and everything he's ever done. No chases, no head bashings, I promise."

"I want my money and I want my beer. That's all I care about."

"Tell Sid I'll be there at noon sharp. He'll know it's me by my dashing good looks and suave demeanor." Brad was laughing as he ended the call without giving Sam an opportunity to respond.

Leaning back in his seat, Brad muttered under his breath, "Looks like no drive through Corrales and no dinner with Juanita." Disappointment worsened with each keystroke as he punched Juanita's number into his phone. It was her message recording again. He could barely stand it. Knowing that he would not be seeing her as he had so hoped, the sound of her voice delivered sheer torment. Brad offered a quick explanation that a break in the case may be imminent and that he was headed out of town to follow up on a lead. He promised to call soon and provide details. Brad realized that he held his phone in death-grip as he calculated what to say next. "I'm sorry Juanita. I wanted very much to see you tonight. I'll call as soon as I can." Brad took a breath. "I miss you. I'm missing you a lot."

After terminating the call, Brad took a few moments to sit quietly. He needed time to allow his heart to slow and his mind to settle. From where he sat in his truck, he had an unobstructed view of the Sandia Mountains. They now shimmered orange as the sinking sun settled over the desert. He wondered where in Albuquerque did Juanita live? From what perspective did she see a sunrise or sunset? He thought back to the evening they had shared on her ranch. The image of her face and skin in the fading light of those magical moments still enchanted his thoughts. Brad again heard the windmill's serenade. He thought of the cup of water they had shared, how it had tasted and how her eyes had held him as he drank. Brad breathed deeply. How long had it been since that evening and when he had last seen her? Three days, four days? Brad realized that he had lost track of time but however long it had been, it was too long and felt like forever.

***

Two more calls were necessary. Victoria was surprised but pleased to hear Brad's voice. She promised that she and Alphonso would wait up and Lucy's personal belongings would be ready for him to sort through.

A smile could not be suppressed when Louise answered the phone at the St. James Hotel. Upon learning that Brad would be back in Cimarron late that night, her response was bullet fast. "I've got it, I see the picture quite clearly. You can't live without me and you are returning so soon, desperate for my charm and another coffee conversation. Believe me, it happens all the time. What can I say? I am simply irresistible and you can't help yourself."

"Guilty as charged," Brad spoke with exaggerated humility. "But, what are the chances you could reserve a room for me tonight. It will be late but I'll show up, I promise."

With a flippant huff Louise replied. "If I had a nickel for every time a man has promised me something, I'd be a zillionaire. But yes, Mr. Brad Walker from Colorado, I will hold a room for you. Which do you prefer, haunted or non-haunted?"

"Hell's bells, give me the most haunted room you have. I'm feeling lonely. Some company will be appreciated."

"Ask and ye shall receive," Louise retorted. "I'm pulling an all-nighter so I'll look forward to seeing you stroll through the door. Heaven help us both, I might even buy you something better than coffee if you get here before the bar closes. You won't tell my boss if I happen to sneak a little nip while on duty will you?"

Loving this woman more by the minute, Brad Laughed, "Miss Louise, you have all the nips you want. Your secrets are safe with this old cowboy."

"I'll leave a light on for you. Travel safe, my dear and see you in a few hours."

****

Immensity of the night sky dwarfed the Hernandez house, its porch light scarcely able to penetrate the darkness. Brad pulled to a stop and stepped from his truck. In spite of the dim light, he spotted the old dog hobble from the house, making a slow approach to his truck. A wagging tail and lack of barking told Brad that the gentle canine remembered him and that they remained friends. After a few moments of rubbing the dog's scruffy ears and whispering words that only dogs and dog lovers understand, Brad walked toward the house. Just as he reached the front gate, the door to the house opened. Victoria and Alphonso stood together, arms about the others waist, silhouetted against the light inside their home. Alphonso held open the door for Brad to enter as Victoria offered a silent hug. Alphonso then shook Brad's hand, holding the gesture for several seconds, not a single word yet spoken.

Victoria broke the spell by pointing to the kitchen table where a plastic trash bag had been placed. She spoke softly and in a matter-of-fact tone. "Those are Lucy's things. You are welcome to look through them. In fact, you will be doing us a favor. We haven't been able to cross that bridge yet." Alphonso nodded his head in agreement.

Awkward silence descended as they all stood before the kitchen table, every eye focused upon the trash bag. There was a sense of haunted ceremony in the room, conveying a notion that the bag was something cursed or a forbidden relic not to be disturbed. Brad shuffled his feet, shifting weight from leg to leg, calculating how to do what had to be done with minimal pain to Victoria and Alphonso. He spoke softly. "What I think I would like to do is to take the bag into your living room. Let me go through her things. I'm looking for something very specific. When I'm finished, I'll put everything back into the bag and return it to Lucy's room. Then, I will come back here to talk and explain why I am here and what I have learned. Victoria and Alphonso held their eyes directly on Brad, never looking at each other. Simultaneously, they nodded agreement and, as if programmed, turned away as Brad lifted the bag and all that remained of their daughter.

The contents of the bag were just as Alphonso had described. Handling each item with reverence, Brad removed a few articles of clothing along with books, toiletries and typical things that a teen-aged girl would have. When he came to a blue dress of satin-like material, Brad knew it was what Alphonso had described as the dress Lucy had worn to her high school prom, Brad almost choked. Visions of his daughter, Meghan, flashed through his mind. Bitterness gathered in his throat and he had to swallow as he blinked in anger. He lifted the dress for examination. The silky blue material seemed weightless in his grasp, but yet Brad felt Lucy. The life and spirit of a young girl still lived within the fabric. As he draped the dress over the chair where he had so recently sat, Brad ran his fingers over the garment, allowing his fingers to feel, hear and listen. He dropped his head, feeling himself on the verge of explosion. Brad saw inside his own heart and realized that these past few seconds had been transformational; everything had changed once he touched Lucy's dress. Even though anger and frustration swelled, he also felt his mind clarify. Up until now, he had cared for Lucy, of course he had. And, he cared deeply for the sorrow of Victoria and Alphonso and the unspeakable pain that would be their burden for life. But, if Brad were to be brutally honest, he had to admit that until this moment everything he had done had been largely motivated by his feelings for Juanita. It was her plea for assistance and his feelings for her that had brought him thus far.

No longer.

Emotions boiling, Brad again lifted the cloth that had at one time embraced the skin of Lucy Hernandez. He brought it to his face, pressing the dress to his cheek. Closing his eyes, Brad intended to utter a prayer but the whispered words that left his mouth were not a prayer, they were an angry and determined vow: "*Abuelo*, perhaps you sent me here, I don't know. I have no idea what the hell to think. But I swear to you, *Abuelo*, or whoever out there might be listening, I'm going to crucify the son-of-a-bitch that hurt Lucy and took her life."

Removing the dress from his face, Brad again placed it over the chair. Sucking a breath of resolve, he turned to the bag that held remnants of Lucy's life. He opened it and looked inside. There it was, the last thing on the bottom, Lucy's diary.

***

Declining food or anything to drink, Brad sat with Victoria and Alphonso at their kitchen table. He spoke in a subdued tone, holding each of their eyes in his gaze. He told of visiting *Abuelo* and how the old man knew that Lucy had maintained a diary. He left out everything else that *Abuelo* had said to him as Brad felt that those words had been private and intended only for him. Besides, he would not have had the slightest idea how to relate the mysterious conversation anyway.

Realizing the intimacy of what Lucy's diary represented, Brad handed it to Victoria as he quietly asked for permission to take it, promising that it would someday be returned. She held the book in her hands for a few seconds before handing it to Alphonso. She made no attempt to open the diary or read anything that her daughter had written. Alphonso simply let the pages flip through his fingers before he looked to his wife. Their agreement was sad but firm as they nodded their heads together, pain filling their eyes. Alphonso lifted the diary as he spoke, "This is my daughter's life. Take it, please Brad, and use it to save the life of another person." He handed the diary to Brad.

After taking Lucy's diary, Brad also told of how he had learned the identity of the Mercedes Benz driver that had been in the photograph from Victoria's cell phone. He explained that the man had an extensive criminal record and was suspected to be involved in dealing in drugs and stolen property. Brad said nothing of bartering sex for property. He explained that he intended to meet this man, face-to-face in only a few hours in Clayton.

Alphonso spoke. "I know Clayton. I've been there a few times. It's in the middle of nowhere. What would he be doing there?"

"I have no idea, Alphonso. I hope to find out." Brad shrugged his shoulders. "Who knows, I may not learn anything at all but I'm going to try."

Victoria again offered Brad food or drink but he declined, saying it was late and everyone needed rest. Looking into the faces of Victoria and Alphonso, Brad felt it better left unsaid that Victoria's face looked drawn and that she had aged a decade in only the past day. Exhaustion in Alphonso's face and eyes clearly spoke that there had been little or no sleep since Brad had first appeared at their door. Brad knew that tonight's events would not change that.

Hugs and handshakes were exchanged in a silent farewell. Brad stooped to rub the old dog as he left; Victoria and Alphonso stood in the doorway until the lights of Brad's truck disappeared into the night.

***

Silence of late night hung in the St. James Hotel. Brad carried his overnight bag into the lobby and looked about as if it were his first time there. The chandelier that had caused so much fascination on his first visit seemed even brighter in the night's stillness. As he approached the registration desk, Louise magically appeared from a room behind the desk. "Well, look what the cat drug in from the alley. It's my favorite wayfaring stranger come to visit once again." Despite the late hour, Louise looked crisp and fresh in jeans, a western-cut white blouse and a squash blossom necklace of silver and turquoise about her neck. Her smile seemed even brighter than the glow of the chandelier. With a quick up and down evaluation of Brad, Louise offered her assessment. "And you're still not wearing red shorts, thank heaven!" Bringing her hands together in a single clap and with a laugh, she stepped from behind her desk. "I've been waiting all evening so get your skinny bones over here and give me a hug. If you play your cards just right, it's possible that I might treat you to whatever you would like from the haunted bar." Louise gave a nod and a point toward the bar on the far side of the lobby.

"That's the best offer I've had all day" Brad dropped his bag, placed both arms about Louise and gave a squeeze. "You are not allowed to ever leave here. Your charm is exactly what this spooky old place needs. I'll talk to management and tell them to triple your salary, effective last week."

"Fat chance on that one, my friend. You'd be better off trying to kiss a bear with honey on your lips." Louise grabbed Brad's arm and led him through the lobby into an empty bar and restaurant.

A lonely looking bartender, methodically wiping the bar in preparation to close for the evening, spotted his guests. Nodding his head in acknowledgement, he directed his greeting to Louise.

"Hey there, Louise, this here that skinny guy you've been telling me about? The one that promises to carry you off to Hollywood and make you famous?" The bartender's smart aleck remark was followed by a wink directed to Brad.

"Zip it, Bozo. I'm way too old and crusty to be taking guff from a little piss-ant runt like you. I'll have red wine and make it pronto." Louise turned to Brad. "And what about you?" Louise was contemplative for a moment. "Just so you know, I can tell the character of a man by what he drinks." Her eyes twinkled. "Let's see what you're made of,"

Throwing his arms into the air in a gesture of exasperation, Brad shook his head as he spoke. "I'm just a simple sort of guy. All I want is a cold Moosehead if you have it. Otherwise, a mug of anything that's cold and remotely resembling beer will be absolutely fine."

Poking Brad's shoulder, Louise laughed. "You done good by golly, Mr. Brad, you passed the test. If you had ordered a strawberry daiquiri or a Manhattan, poor Louise would have had to drink alone tonight. Shaking her head with determination, she spoke emphatically, "No red shorts and no daiquiri drinking cowboys for this lady." Louise pointed to a table where she could keep an eye on the lobby. "Right here, Mr. Brad. Sit a spell and tell me all about where you've been, where you're going and what you're up to." With a sly smile and jabbing at her chest with her thumb Louise made a proclamation. "Inside this hotel, other people's business becomes my business." Lowering her voice to little more than a whisper, she leaned across the table and spoke as if the empty restaurant were packed with eavesdropping patrons. "How else am I supposed to know if you are for real? You might be a tricky ghost of some sort with nefarious mischief up your sleeve. We already have too many of those guys in here and it's my job to see that no more sneak in." Louise looked at Brad expectantly. "Just doing my job."

Struggling for a response to match the cleverness of Louise, Brad welcomed the bartender's arrival with wine and a cold Moosehead. Accepting the bottle, he lifted it toward Louise in toast and as their glasses clinked, he spoke, "To nefarious ghosts and red shorts, may you be forever haunted."

Fingering her necklace, Louise's laugh carried through the bar. "Okay, Brad, I'm just teasing with you. Your business is your business and I'll stay out of it. But, let me tell you what I've already figured out." With her index finger, Louise tapped the side of her head. "Don't underestimate me, I'm pretty darned quick for an old broad. You aren't a tourist and you aren't a businessman. You aren't fat, you don't wear red shorts and you don't drink daiquiris." Louise shrugged. "That makes it easy, you're a cop of some sort. I can spot your kind a mile away." She gave Brad a genuine smile. "That means I like you and if this grey-haired lady can ever help you in any way, you just let me know." Her smile widened and eyes radiated expectancy. "Impressed aren't you?"

The grin on Brad's face acknowledged her spot-on perception. "Yes, I'm most impressed. All I ask for now is that you give me a little time. I'm not sure where some things are going but I intend to find out and I absolutely know that you are my friend. I will someday talk with you and tell you a heck of story." He lifted his Moosehead to offer another toast.

"Here's to someday," Louise raised her wine glass, "Someday soon, I hope."

"Do you really have to stay awake all night?" Brad leaned back in his chair. "Even with ghosts floating about, that would make for one long night."

"No, I manage some rest. There's a cot in the room just behind my desk. As soon as I get you tucked in all snug as a bug, I'm going to stretch out and sleep like a little baby. We have no other guests coming in so I should be free until time to fire up the coffee tomorrow morning." She gave a short laugh. "Heaven knows you cops gotta have your coffee or else Mr. Grumpy comes calling. Plus, I have a busy day planned for tomorrow with my grandchildren. I intend to be rested and ready to behave like a child all day long."

Draining his beer, Brad rose. "Come now, Miss Louise, let's get you to bed. I'm exhausted so give me a room key and I'll be kind and leave you to your slumber." With a stern look and commanding tone he concluded, "Just have that coffee hot and black, bright and early. Got it?"

After a snappy salute in response, Louise pulled a key from her pocket. "Here you go, upstairs, end of hall on right. Be quiet for heaven's sake. I don't need other guests or ghosts complaining about your racket. We'll do the paper work tomorrow over coffee." Louise gave Brad's forearm a squeeze. "Sleep tight up there." She paused and with a false look of desperation, increased her pressure on Brad's arm. "Tell me the truth now, you don't sleep in red shorts do you?"

Laughing as she waved goodnight, Louise walked away.

***

The room was small, a picture straight from the Old West. Tossing his bag on the floor, Brad placed a hand over his forehead and moaned. He had no idea for what reason but in the past few minutes he had developed a splitting headache. By the time he brushed his teeth and splashed water over his face, the pain was bringing him to near helplessness. Lights off, he eased himself onto a quilted blanket that covered the bed and gingerly lowered his head onto the pillow. Grimacing in pain, he placed both hands over his face in the darkness and silently mouthed, "What in the name of God is wrong?" Lying motionless, he could do nothing but endure the sudden and inexplicable ailment that had overcome him.

Finally and with mercy, some level of sleep descended but Brad remained fitful. In a state somewhere between sleep and consciousness, and still knowing exactly where he was, he felt as if he drifted through space. Friendly voices called out from unseen places as he drifted further, feeling himself enter into another world. He welcomed the fantasy, anything to escape the agony pounding within his head.

Then he was there, inside her cabin, just as before; recently assaulted and lying on a bed, subdued lantern light casting faint illumination. Where was Juanita? Everything was murky. He struggled, wanting to see her so badly but unable to find her. Brad felt another presence, someone was close by but Brad could not turn his head. The sense of another being coming closer was definite but Brad remained unable to see. Then the face appeared. Bending over to come close as he stood at the edge of Brad's bed, Moustache smiled. Just as before, Brad saw white teeth that were brilliant behind brown skin and a huge moustache. "Ah, *mi amigo*, we meet again." Moustache chuckled. "When I first met you, someone had tried to take your head. It seems we only talk when you get yourself into trouble." Moustache laughed softly and spoke as a parent to a child. "How do you manage to do these things again and again?"

It was exactly as before: the same smile and voice, the bushy moustache, black hair falling over his ears and a *sombrero*, suspended by a leather thong, across his shoulders. And just as before, Brad could not speak.

Moustache looked at Brad with compassion. "The first time I was sent to you, I placed you on a horse." He moved his head slowly. "That was a painful ride." He shook his head in sympathy. "I took you to Juanita, the sister of Manuel, so that she could help you heal and allow you to finish important work. Now, *compadre*, it is Manuel who needs you." Moustache was quiet, his eyes scrutinizing Brad for reaction.

Brad could only stare.

"Ah, *muchacho*, how sad, you have no memory. You have forgotten what I told you on that terrible night?" Moustache paused, waiting. "The name of Juanita's brother you have forgotten. Think, *mi amigo*, think." Moustache pointed to his head. "I told you that the sister of Manuel would heal you." Moustache smiled with kindly understanding.

Brad could not move or speak but his eyes widened in comprehension.

"*Bueno*, now you understand." Moustache leaned closer. "I must say to you again what I said to you on that night. "*Dios me ha mandado a ti*" (God has sent me to you). Moustache lowered his voice. "*Tienes mucho que hace.*" (You have much to do). Moustache looked directly into Brad's eyes. "*Si, mi amigo, tienes mucho que hacer*" (Yes, my friend, you have much to do). Moustache placed a hand on Brad's shoulder and gave a squeeze.

Brad blinked his eyes in acknowledgement.

Moustache then grinned, devilment in his brown eyes. "I am told that you care for Juanita." Lifting his eyebrows and smiling broadly he continued. "It makes me happy to know that when you were struck you did not go completely *loco in la cabeza*." Mustache laughed and again pointed to his head.

Brad could only blink but he hoped that his eyes answered appropriately.

The mysterious man leaned close and spoke softly. "Juanita is a good woman, *muchacho*." He moved his head as a grave expression shadowed his face. "Do not let her slip away." He was quiet before he spoke again, "Hold her tight, *mi amigo*. Do not let her slip away." With another squeeze to Brad's shoulder, Moustache stood and walked from Brad's sight. When he was gone, Juanita was there.

Brad's heart felt as if it would erupt from his chest. It was her! The simple brown material of her dress reached to the floor. Her ponytail draped over a shoulder and in the dim light of the cabin, he saw her smile, that beautiful smile. She held a clay pot as she came to him. Lifting his head to cradle it within her hands, Juanita spoke in English, "Hello my love. This is the special water that I bring to you. Drink now and be strong." Her smile glowed. "Our time is almost here." Their eyes never parting, she held the vase as he drank, the pain in his head simply dissolving with each swallow. She leaned close, her lips touching his, soft as a shadow, and then she too stood and walked away.

Brad awakened with a start and sat straight on the bed. Where the hell was he? It took seconds before he gathered his wits and memory that he was in a hotel in Cimarron. "Jesus Christ!" He dropped back to the bed, breathing hard and feeling his heart pound. Placing a hand over his forehead, Brad realized his headache had completely vanished. Raising his arm, he checked his watch; straight up two o'clock in the morning. He lay still for a few moments trying to wrap his head around what the hell had just happened. "God Almighty!" Brad rose and walked to the bathroom where he held his head under a stream of cold water, catching his breath as it dripped down his neck. After wiping his hair dry, he returned to his bed, whispering in a stream of soft swearing, still feeling absolutely no pain in his head, he again lay down.

Brad intended to lie and think, contemplating his dream. But it did not happen. He was asleep in only seconds.

***

In contrast to the late night before, people now milled about the lobby with energy and conversation. Having slept later than he intended, breakfast aromas from the dining room were tantalizing. Brad made his way to the coffee carafe near the registration desk. Louise was engaged with a couple, pointing out something on a map and apparently giving directions. She saw Brad from the corner of her eye and snapped her head in his direction. But it was not her usual smile that he saw. Instead, a stern expression came his way. Brad poured coffee and wandered the lobby as he waited for Louise to break free. Finally, the couple walked away and Brad hurriedly grabbed a space in front of the desk to offer good morning wishes and to learn the reason for her austere greeting. "Good morning, sunshine. Why the somber face?"

"No Miss Sunshine here this morning. I'm not a happy broad, not even a little bit."

Up close, Brad saw that Louise's face looked tired and no twinkle radiated from her eyes.

"Last night was crazy in here. Not hardly a wink of sleep and I'm too old for this idiocy. I've got myself grandbabies to love and I'm over this place!" She shook her head in disgust. "Pranksters or ghosts, I don't know and I don't care. Miss Louise ain't a happy woman this morning!" Her eyes drilled Brad.

"Good grief, what in the world happened, Louise?"

Rolling her eyes and blowing air from her lungs as if she could discharge whatever ailed her, Louise leaned over the counter and deftly snatched Brad's coffee from his hand. "Gimme that. I need more than coffee but if you'll share with me, I can make it till I get my aching old bones outta this goofy asylum." With that declaration, Louise took a long sip from Brad's coffee. Finally, a hint of the usual sparkle appeared in her eyes as she sighed with contentment, savoring Brad's coffee and giving no indication that she intended to return the cup that she had confiscated. "I knew I could count on you, Brad." She hoisted the coffee cup. "Not polluted with a pint of cream or twelve lumps of sugar." She widened her eyes. "Or, worse yet, a bunch of that powdered diet crap that people with red shorts pour into their coffee." She winked and took another sip.

"Jesus, Louise, how 'bout I take that coffee back to the bar and pour in a snort of bourbon for you?"

It was the Old Louise again as devilment radiated. With a starry-eyed gaze, she returned the stolen coffee and spoke with contrived adoration. "Tell me something, Brad, where were you when I was twenty-five? How come you waited until now to come riding into my life?"

"Give me a break, young lady, you're too much for me to handle right now. I can't imagine you at twenty-five." He placed a hand over his chest. "I'm feeling a heart attack coming on just thinking about it."

Louise let loose with a real laugh. "Okay, you win. The BS award for the year is presented to you and you alone. Now, do you want to hear my tale of woe about what happened during the night or not?"

With his own dream still fresh on his mind, Brad sipped coffee and nodded, "Yes, as a matter of fact I would love to know the reason for you being so contrary this morning."

Giving a dismissive wave, Louise lowered her voice as she spoke. "Well, after getting rid of you last night, I went to my little office and got all tucked in on my cot. I fell fast asleep and was doing just peaches when all of a sudden I was awakened by voices and all kinds of racket in the lobby. I jumped up and poked my head out to see what in the world was going on but there wasn't a soul to be seen. The place was empty and quiet as a church on Saturday night." Louise gave Brad a questioning look. "I would have sworn I heard voices but I just wrote it off that I must have been dreaming. I crawled back under my blanket and was just getting all comfy again when the night bell starts ringing like the dickens." Louise pointed to a bell on the registration desk. "I mean someone was pounding on it and making a heck of a racket. I was up and off my cot in a flash and came charging out here, ready to scalp some drunked up idiot." Louise was quiet and her face no longer smiled. "Not a soul, Brad, *nada*, nobody." She looked at Brad with an expression that defied him to explain the mystery.

Brad dropped his gaze for a moment and said nothing. When he looked up, he offered a look that said he sympathized with how she felt. "My first instinct is to accuse you of sneaking back into the bar after I went upstairs." He grinned and shook his head. "But I'm not going to do that. I believe every word of your story, and I won't even try to come up with some sophisticated explanation," He shook his head. "Cause I ain't got one."

Louise and Brad were quiet for moment, neither sure what to say next.

"Let me ask you something, Louise. Did you happen to notice the time when this happened?"

"Well, of course I noticed the time. You think I'm impaired or something?" Louise rolled her eyes. "It was two o'clock sharp. And, after that little incident, this lady slept not one more wink. I've been awake for hours, not like you up there in your featherbed, sucking your thumb and snoozing away in red shorts." Her look defied Brad to respond.

Without even trying to challenge the jab Louise had thrown, he turned and abruptly walked away. Speaking over his shoulder, Brad addressed her confused look. "I'll be right back. I need to make a call."

Stepping outside, Brad took a deep breath, hoping that the crisp air of a New Mexico morning might help bring clarity to what seemed a muddle of nonsense. He found a chair and sat, thinking of the dream that had again taken him to the surreal world that seemed never to completely leave him. He had seen and heard Moustache and then, the Juanita he could not explain had kissed him, jolting him from his dream.

It had happened at two o'clock.

***

Seconds passed. Brad reached for his phone and punched in a number. A sigh of relief escaped when Samantha's voice answered. He had no idea what he would have said if Raylene had been the person to answer. He simply didn't have it in him to deal with her again.

Brad managed a polite greeting before Samantha began laughing at the memory of his tortured experience with Raylene. After sharing her humor, Brad's voice became serious but he tried to sound casual. "I was just calling to check on Mr. Lujan. Can you please tell me how he's doing this morning?"

The split second hesitation in Samantha's response gave Brad the answer he had known he would hear before she even spoke. "I'm so sorry, Mr. Walker, Manuel Lujan passed away very early this morning." Samantha paused and her voice became subdued. "Two of our nurses were with him. They held his hand during his last moments. Manuel Lujan closed his eyes for the last time at two o'clock this morning."

Brad closed his eyes and held his breath.

Samantha continued, speaking softly. "I do have some good news for you Mr. Walker. First, Mr. Lujan died very peacefully. He did not suffer at all. Next, shortly after you left him yesterday, his daughter came in for a visit. When she left, she was crying but told a nurse that she was so glad she had come when she did. His daughter told the nurse she knew her father did not have much longer to live and that they may have shared their last words. It was a very emotional moment, Mr. Walker. His daughter told our nurse that Mr. Lujan had made a dying request of her and that she would make certain his wish was carried out." Samantha was quiet for a moment. "We don't know what that dying request was, but his daughter seemed determined to see that it happened." Samantha was silent and Brad knew that she had nothing more to say.

"Thank you, Samantha. You were very kind to me yesterday and now again this morning." Brad swallowed. "I suppose there is nothing more to say except that I appreciate you and thank you."

A moment of silence followed. "You are quite welcome, Mr. Walker."

Brad clicked off his phone and picked up his coffee, welcoming the warmth that seeped into his suddenly cold hand. He lost track of time, sitting in silence and staring into endless depths of a New Mexico turquoise sky. He knew that he could never express an explanation for what had happened, but Brad new perfectly well what had happened.

***

Squinting her eyes, Louise carefully watched as Brad walked back toward her desk. Concern on her face and in her voice she spoke quietly, "You okay?"

With no trace of a smile Brad answered. "Yes Louise, I'm fine and I hope to heck you are okay yourself." Louise and Brad looked at each other, letting their eyes do the talking. Brad reached for her hand and held it tightly. "I'm outta here, sweet lady. I've got stuff to do." He looked hard, straight into her eyes. "Get out of this place and go see those grandbabies of yours. They are more important than anything in this old hotel." He gave her hand a hard squeeze. I'm coming back soon and we are going to have a long talk." Taking a breath, he held her gaze. "But for now, give me my bill and let's promise to think of each other every day."

Returning the grip of his hand, Louise simply nodded.

***

A lonelier road was difficult to imagine as Brad headed east from the small town of Springer. He recalled driving this route in his youth and absolutely nothing had changed. In all directions, rangeland stretched to the doors of eternity. The country was unrelenting in its vastness, equally forlorn and beautiful. As miles slid beneath his truck, Brad drove with *Abuelo*'s letter tucked inside Lucy's diary, both on the seat beside him. Every few minutes, Brad reached to touch them, feeling the texture of Lucy's life and the mystery of *Abuelo*'s message. Brad felt that he was scarcely moving. Distance seemed frozen. Time crawled.

Well before reaching the town, Clayton's profile materialized as trees and buildings seemed to sprout from the horizon. Once he entered the small settlement, Brad was forced to slow as the highway narrowed and transformed into a street. Elm trees shaded modest houses and, with his window lowered, the hum of lawnmowers seemed to follow his progress. He cruised slowly, wondering what in the world had brought Edmond Knapp to this remote place.

The street made a broad swing and then up a slight grade to cross railroad tracks. At the elevated crossing, Brad had a bird's-eye view of what appeared to be the town's main street. It was no more than two or three blocks of stores and business fronts. Parked cars were sparsely scattered, leaving plenty of options from which Brad could choose. Grabbing one of the first parking spots he came to, Brad realized that he had stopped in front of an old movie theater. Thinking of what life would be like for a kid to grow up here, he left his truck and stepped into a gift shop next to the theater. A cheerful 'hello' acknowledged his presence as a woman walked forward to greet him. With clothing and jewelry that bore striking resemblance to that worn by Louise, she smiled brightly. "How may I help you today?"

Realizing that his question would sound a bit strange, Brad gave a self-conscious grin. "I'm trying to find your city jail. Any chance you could point me in the right direction?"

With a cheerful laugh but a curious look, she replied, "Not that I spend a bunch of time there but, yes, I can help you." Pointing as she spoke, "You're almost there. Go just over a block, right up that street and you will find it. It's a white building that houses the police department and the jail; Clayton's finest and Clayton's worst, all under one roof." The lady gave Brad a scrutinizing look. "You're not some sort of desperate criminal or something are you, surrendering yourself after a life of crime?" She continued to smile but obviously thought Brad's inquiry strange.

Brad thought a moment. "I don't think I'll answer that question until I check out their menu. If the food looks good, who knows what I may confess." They shared a good-natured chuckle as Brad thanked her and walked out. He looked up the street, seeing small mom-and-pop businesses, few people and almost no traffic. Diagonally across the street, a distinctive three-story structure of sand-colored stone rose above other buildings. Realizing that he looked at a hotel and saloon, he muttered softly, "Jesus, this place is right out of Gunsmoke." Standing and absorbing the feel of Clayton, a single thought persisted; what had brought Edmond Knapp to this isolated place? It made no sense. The town was in the middle of nowhere. Why would a person of Knapp's lifestyle have reason to be in such a small town? Brad began a slow walk to his truck. There had to be a reason. There was always a reason. As he drove the short distance to the jail, he felt the rumblings of inexplicable instinct developing within his gut; whatever Knapp's reason for being here, a tie to Lucy Hernandez existed. It may not be obvious but the connection was there.

Killing his engine, Brad removed *Abuelo*'s letter from Lucy's diary and tucked it into his pocket. Premonition, how many times had he experienced it? He sure as hell felt it now. He had no idea what he was about to encounter but every nerve in his body told him it was time to pay attention. With Lucy's diary in hand and *Abuelo's* letter in his pocket, Brad stepped into the Clayton Police Department.

***

Police Chief Robert Montoya's broad shoulders filled the shirt of his police uniform and his handshake told Brad that he was dealing with a man who could handle himself. His eyes, voice and confident manner conveyed a similar inner strength. Sid Pruitt had arrived just minutes ahead of Brad and was seated in the department's small interview room. Sid spoke in a soft Texas drawl, and a sense of humor sparkled within his eyes as he shook Brad's hand. "I'm told you aren't too bad for a Fed. Sam Trathen told me you even learned to tie your shoes before leaving high school." Brad shook his head with a grin and Montoya laughed with Sid as the men took seats in the cramped space.

Taking the lead, Montoya laid out an assortment of photographs over the desktop. "You gents already know pretty much what happened here. Our friend, Mr. Knapp, was waiting at a traffic light when whack, he gets rear-ended. Nobody is hurt but the impact pops open the trunk of Knapp's car and, lo and behold, there's all kinds of stuff in there that Mr. Knapp wishes to hell no one would ever have seen." Shoving the photographs closer to Sid and Brad, he continued. "This is what we found: all kinds of pottery, blankets and Native American relics that look to me like they belong in a museum somewhere. They were well packed in boxes with lots of protective material but the box tops were open. It was easy to see what he had." He pointed to a specific photograph. "Look at this one here. I'm guessing that vase is hundreds of years old." Montoya was quiet while Sid and Brad studied the assortment of photographs.

"Has anyone else seen these things?" Sid held a photograph up close before passing it to Brad.

"Yes, we wanted some verification so we called a man who runs a retail store here in town that specializes in antiques and pottery. He also teaches in our high school. The guy really knows his stuff. Kirby Cook is his name. Kirby came down to take a look and, boy, was he impressed. He wouldn't even touch the things except for the few we had already removed from their boxes. Most of what was in Knapp's trunk is still wrapped up. We're not taking any chances to screw with something that may be incredibly valuable. Kirby said the stuff probably ranged from fairly modern to possibly centuries old."

Sid and Brad acknowledged Montoya's assessment with a glance and silent nod as they continued to study the photographs.

"Of course we smelled a rat right away but there's nothing illegal about having pottery in the trunk of a car. Thanks to mighty sharp eyes of the responding officer, a handgun and a bag of dope was spotted, tucked nice and neat into a corner of the trunk. We locked Knapp's ass up and made a quick call to Albuquerque since that's where the car was registered and where the gun was stolen. The good Mr. Knapp has been a guest in our jail ever since."

Montoya handed more photographs to Sid and Brad. "That's a nice looking handgun, .38 caliber Smith & Wesson. It was stolen about six months ago in a burglary. It's legally registered to a guy in Albuquerque." Montoya looked to Sid. "You have that information already."

Sid shook his head. "Yeah, we're working on the gun angle and would love to learn how it ended up in Knapp's possession." Sid thought a moment before continuing. "We're looking at an unsolved murder in Albuquerque that just might have a connection here. I'll be very interested to learn how ballistics tests with this recovered gun might turn out."

Brad just moved his head in understanding.

Robert Montoya leaned back in his chair and placed both hands behind his head. With a smile that conveyed a mixture of sympathy and mischievousness, he spoke. "You boys are in for a treat when you meet Mr. Knapp." He looked to the ceiling, searching for just the right words to express his thoughts. Leaning forward and placing both arms on the desk, he looked at Sid and Brad. "Let's just say that Mr. Knapp has a way with words. His vocabulary is limited but I'm betting you'll find it, shall we say, expressive." Montoya grinned, "He's also a real sensitive type. My guess is that he spends a lot of time burning incense and reading poems, stuff like that. You guys are going to absolutely love him." Montoya stood up and laughed out loud. "Yep, you are gonna love this son-of-a-bitch like nobody you've ever met!"

Sid grinned. "Can't wait to have the pleasure. But, I can tell you for sure that the lawyer he called is one of Albuquerque's premier defense attorneys. He doesn't even answer his telephone without a bill for a thousand bucks. That makes it clear in my book that somebody with juice is behind the Knapp Man."

Montoya was pacing as he thought and shook his head in agreement. "I think we caught a break in that department. Apparently his big time lawyer is out of the country on a vacation in Tahiti, or some such place, and Knapp is having trouble tracking down the connections he needs to bail his ass out. But, I'm pretty sure he's speaking the truth when he says he will be out of here very quickly." He sat down again and leaned over his desk. "Knapp is a no good, lying asshole but I've got a feeling he's not blowing hot air when he tells me his lawyer will burn our little town to the ground to get him out of this jail."

With a sad laugh, Sid agreed. "Yep, that's probably true." Turning to Brad he asked, "Well, you ready to get this over with? Milk and cookies with Mr. Knapp?"

Lifting Lucy's diary, Brad replied. "I want you to take a look at something first. This little book is filled with information that might very well be your key to nailing Knapp."

Sid's face reflected surprise. "Really?"

Brad gave a quick summary of how he came to possess the diary. He simply stated that Lucy's parents had given it to him, choosing to leave out the part about *Abuelo*. "This could be evidence someday," Brad stated as he initialed and dated the inside cover of the diary before handing it to Sid.

Sid accepted the book with a questioning look to Brad.

"Now, please understand, I've not had a chance to study her diary in detail. In fact, I've only read a few pages and then barely skimmed over the rest. But, I've seen enough to realize that what's in there," he nodded to the diary, "is powerful stuff. The words of that young girl are remarkable." A rueful expression came over Brad. "As I read her words, it was like she became a real, live person to me. Knowing the tragic ending she met, I swear to God, I think Lucy was making a record with full knowledge that she would not be around too long." Brad leaned forward, elbows on his knees, staring at the floor. "Maybe I'm wrong but I think that poor girl somehow knew what lay ahead and was preparing for a future that she knew she would never inhabit." Brad looked up to Sid and Montoya. "After you've read it, tell me if you agree."

Giving Sid a chance to glance through the diary, no one spoke for a few seconds. Watching Sid's face as he grasped the significance of what Lucy had written, Brad offered another comment. "I'm thinking that her diary may change how you decide to handle this interview."

As Sid continued to turn pages, clearly captivated by what he read, Brad looked across the desk to Montoya. "You want to be in on this little talk or have you had enough of the guy?"

"Oh, that's an easy one," Montoya replied with a cynical snort. "There's enough hatred between the two of us to fill up this room three times. Trust me, if there is any hope at all for you to have a successful interview," he shook his head, "And I don't think that's going to happen, I can't be anywhere around. I want to kill the bastard and he wants to kill me. When you guys are finished, you'll understand what I mean." Lawrence Montoya smiled a smile that was not intended to convey humor.

Montoya and Brad watched in silence as Sid continued to flip through the diary, eyes opened wide in amazement. An occasional "holy shit" or "oh, my God" came as a whisper upon seeing the contents of a page. When only half way through the diary, Sid closed the small book, shut his eyes and rubbed the bridge of his nose with thumb and forefinger. Finally he spoke, disbelief and disgust in his voice. "It is exactly what we've been told by a source and what we suspected. That son-of-a-bitch is running a prostitution ring and about half the transactions involve some sort of a deal where artifacts, drugs or sex get swapped around like baseball cards."

A nod of agreement came from Brad. A look of astonishment came from Montoya.

Sid's eyes moved from Brad to Montoya and then back to the closed diary that he held in his hand. Seconds passed as he formulated his thoughts before speaking. "This changes everything."

Speaking slowly and his head acknowledging agreement, Brad replied. "Knapp thinks your interest is in the gun or drugs and probably simple curiosity about the artifacts. He has no idea that you have that type of information." Brad nodded to the diary.

"I agree completely and I think it needs to stay that way for now. What do you guys think of just asking some bullshit questions about the gun, let him give us whatever line he chooses to deliver and wrap it up? I need some time to go through this book slowly and methodically. A mountain of research needs to be handled to track down the names and information that are in here." Sid was quiet, moving his head in a gesture of disbelief. "God love that girl. Do you honestly think she understood the significance of the details she recorded?" Sid did not expect an answer and the room was silent.

"And, since Lucy Hernandez is deceased," Brad spoke softly, "her dairy will end up as evidence. It will take a bit of legal wrangling, but I'm sure it can be done." Gesturing his head toward the book that Sid continued to hold, "That diary will be Lucy's testimony. It will be her voice in the courtroom."

Montoya and Sid both nodded. "And what a voice. What incredible testimony that will be." Brad's voice scarcely carried across the tiny room.

The three men sat for a few moments, each dealing with their own private thoughts.

Brad broke the silence. "Also, before we leave today, I want you to have a ton of papers that Sam Trathen gave me. They came from that suicide case that started this entire thing. You should have them all so you can compare what's there with what you find in Lucy's diary."

Sid rose from his chair, "Yeah, Sam told me about how this all started. Thanks for bringing the stuff. Something tells me those papers from up in Gunnison and this diary," he lifted the small book, "are going to open a bunch of doors. The Gunnison investigators are keeping all of the originals for me." Brad and Montoya remained silent, their eyes on Sid who stood, obviously in deep thought. With a sigh that spoke of determination, Sid finally spoke. "Okay, let's rock and roll. You ready, Brad?"

"Ready."

They looked to Montoya who still seemed to be lost somewhere in contemplation of events that recent hours had brought into his life. Returning to the here and now, he also stood and glanced at his watch. "Tell you what, boys, lunch is just wrapping up for the jail. How about a ten minute break to let the good folks back there finish up? Then I'll bring his stinking sorry ass right to you. That sound okay?

Sid and Brad simultaneously agreed as Lawrence Montoya pointed the way to the men's room and water fountain. Sid headed down the hall as Brad stretched and worked kinks from his legs. "Too many hours in a car recently." Brad moaned as he did knee bends.

"Boy, do I understand how you feel. We spend some mighty long days in a patrol car and the old body pays a price." Walking across the room, Montoya directed Brad's attention to framed maps that hung in the entryway of the department. "Take a look at these and you'll get an idea of the territory we cover." Pointing as he spoke, Montoya explained, "This one is a street map of Clayton and the other is a map of Union County. Talk about lots of miles to drive. Look at the size of this county." He chuckled. "I'm glad my only responsibility is within the town, but we still end up helping the sheriff or state police with a zillion things that pop up all over the place." Tapping his finger on the county map, "We put in miles and long hours on those dirt roads. And in all kinds of weather."

Reaching for his reading glasses, Brad looked at the two maps. Montoya stepped close and pointed to Clayton. "Here we are, right here. We've got highways going in all directions so we're like a wheel with spokes. By far the busiest route is this one here." Montoya tapped his finger on the map, "Highway 87 is one busy-ass road. In the summer, Texans and folks from all over the south pour through here like ants running from fire. They're heading to the cooler mountains of Colorado. Then, fall comes around and it's a parade of Daniel Boone and Davy Crocket wannabe's off to hunt elk and deer. Right after that, snow bunnies by the thousands head to ski country. Holy cow, it never ends. Sometimes I wonder if there's anyone at all left who aren't out on the road and actually still work for a living."

"Oh, yeah, you've got that right. I've managed to keep a couple of trout streams a secret but it gets tougher each year." Brad turned to Montoya. "You have any thoughts on what brought Knapp to Clayton? I'm pretty damned certain that he isn't a fisherman, hunter or snow bunny."

Montoya assumed a thoughtful look and shook his head. "Nope, I've racked my brain over that very thing and I have no idea at all. You guys can ask him but I just don't think you'll get an answer." Montoya grinned, "Unless 'go fuck yourself' qualifies as an answer."

Both men were still laughing when Sid again joined them and Montoya glanced at his watch. "Okay boys, lunch should be all finished. Another round of mother's home cooking into the mouths of innocents." Montoya was still chuckling as he stepped through a doorway on his way to get Knapp. He turned for a last shot at Sid and Brad, his face in a tantalizing grin and moving his head in a gesture of sympathy, "You are going to really love this guy!" With that proclamation, he threw his head back and laughed out loud.

Taking seats again in the interview room, Sid drawled, "If this goes well today, I'm thinking maybe I'll invite Edmond Knapp over to the house for Christmas."

For some reason, Sid's remark struck Brad as the funniest thing he had ever heard. He was still swallowing laughter as the shapes of Montoya and Knapp filled the doorway of the interview room. Knapp was handcuffed with both hands behind his back. Taking no chances, Montoya steered his prisoner with a powerful hand that remained clamped about Knapp's right arm.

Still dressed in the clothes he had been wearing when arrested, Knapp's shirt was wrinkled and completely soaked from armpits to waistline. It occurred to Brad that Clayton's jail probably did not spend a bunch of money on air conditioning. The small interview room quickly turned sour and breathing an unpleasant necessity.

Knapp stood about six feet. He had a medium build with a well-developed paunch that drooped over his beltless trousers. Apparently not accustomed to being without shoes, he hobbled awkwardly in the thin socks that covered his feet. Hair that had seen too much sun and artificial dye hung in sweat-matted strings of burnt orange, reaching almost to his eyebrows. A perspiration-soaked bald spot glistened under lights of the interview room. Days-old whiskers sprouted about his cheeks and liver-colored splotches mottled his face. Brad thought to himself that Knapp looked like he had been dipped in wax.

Initially, it was the pallor of Knapp's skin that was most striking but that changed the instant Knapp looked directly at him; Brad had never seen such eyes. Perhaps it was the fluorescent lighting but Brad struggled to conceal both shock and repugnance. Like marbles burning within his skull, Knapp's eyes were tiny, somewhere between hazel and red, and all Brad could think of was that they appeared reptilian. *Abuelo's* warning of an evil serpent flashed through his mind.

Montoya escorted Knapp to a seat that kept Sid and Brad between his prisoner and the door. "Want me to leave him cuffed?"

After a moment of consideration, Sid answered. "Nah, it's okay. Make him comfortable, we might be here a while. Cuff one arm to the chair and that should do just fine."

Montoya clicked cuffs in place, securing Knapp's left arm to the chair in which he was seated and started to step away. Knapp's high-pitched voice grated through the air, shocking everyone to attention and halting Montoya. "Hold on to your burro for a second, Poncho Villa. You think I could at least have a Coke and a cigarette since I'm being so cooperative with you gents? Not to mention, I've been a model prisoner ever since you locked me up on a bunch of lies and bullshit fake evidence. That should count for something." An artificial smile twisted Knapp's face into a sneer that radiated hatred.

After a moment of icy contempt, Montoya replied, "Yeah, sure, anything at all. I'd be delighted to bring you a Coke and a smoke." With a mocking voice he continued. "But you be sure to wait right here, Mr. Knapp, don't you go anywhere at all. I'm coming right back."

Edmond Knapp leaned his head back and laughed. "What a marvelous day in New Mexico. Cops, cokes and smokes. My poor ole wilted pecker's getting hard just thinking about how wonderful life is here with all of you."

Neither Sid nor Brad spoke but sat in silence as they waited for Montoya to return. Within seconds, he came back through the doorway and approached the sneering Edmond Knapp. He placed a can of Coke and a package of Marlboro cigarettes on the desk before carelessly tossing a lighter in the general direction of Knapp's free hand. "Thanks for waiting. I was afraid you might have up and walked away." Montoya turned to Sid and Brad. "Okay, gentlemen, I'm right outside. Let me know if you need anything at all. Lemonade, ice cream, steak dinner or dancing girls, just give me a whistle." With a beaming smile, he left the room.

"Now there goes one stupid and greasy Spic. He wouldn't know lemonade if he pissed it and unless the dancing girl is fat and named Rosa, that dumb-ass Mexican wouldn't have brains to pork her." Knapp's upper lip curled.

Sid seemed not to have heard a word Knapp spoke as he calmly displayed his badge. "Mr. Knapp, my name is Sid Pruitt, from the Albuquerque Police Department. This is my partner, Brad Walker. We would appreciate a few minutes to talk with you."

Knapp turned to Brad with scrutinizing eyes. "What's the deal, you don't have a badge? My cell has a great big window, probably a full eight inches by eight inches, and I get to look at beautiful scenery all day long. I watched you pull up and park. Those Colorado tags gave you away. You sure as hell ain't no Albuquerque cop." Knapp snickered. "My guess is you must be one of them finely crafted plastic mountain men. You've probably been sharing a tent with other mountain men since your balls grew fuzz." Knapp's laugh sounded more like a wheeze. "I bet the two of you stir each other's pork and beans with your little weenies."

While Knapp enjoyed his laugh, Sid and Brad exchanged glances. With mere eye contact, they clearly mocked Knapp's antics.

"Oh-Kee-Dokee, gentlemen, let's go over this nice and slow. An Albuquerque cop and a Colorado mountain man, who ain't got no badge, would appreciate a few minutes to talk with a simple man like me. Hmmm, what a privilege. Now, what is it you want to talk about?" Knapp shook a cigarette from the pack, placed it between his lips and sparked the lighter. Inhaling deeply, he forced smoke through his nostrils in a long deliberate exhale before lifting the Coke can to his mouth.

"I'll be happy to tell you what we want to talk about." Sid's demeanor was totally unruffled. "It's about the gun and drugs that were found in the trunk of your car. But, there's something we have to do first. This isn't your first rodeo, Mr. Knapp, you know the routine." With that, Sid placed an Advice of Rights form on the desk. "Would you please read that and then I'll go over it with you. We want to be certain that you understand your rights before we speak."

"Oh, yes, absolutely, the gun. The one my lawyer is going to jam right up your sweet ass. That was an illegal search and I'm in this jail illegally. Just so you know, I'm going to own this chicken-farming town real soon." A fly dropped from the ceiling and walked across the tabletop before stopping to investigate a drop of spilled Coke. In a lightning quick strike with his free hand, Knapp slapped the table and held. As the echo subsided, he lifted his hand to examine the smashed fly. A smile turned his lips upward before he wiped the hand across his trousers.

"Sent that son-of-a-bitch to fly heaven."

Knapp looked at Sid and Brad for a few moments, obviously expecting a response. When he realized nothing was forthcoming, he leaned over the desk to examine the paper Sid had placed. He read for several seconds before looking up, his eyes locked onto Sid. "You want to know something?" Knapp pointed to his head. "I am one smart dude. I nailed you spot-on right away. You are a God-fearing Christian man, not a doubt about it. Here I sit in this lonely jail, eating Spic food three times a day and I'm plugged up tight as a whore in a Sunday revival. So help me Jesus, I've been wondering what in the world will I do when all them tamales and beans decide to come blowing out like a goddamned hurricane on Easter morning." With his free hand, Knapp lifted the paper. "And you, God love ya, you bring me toilet paper." Waving his arm to flutter the paper, Knapp spoke in cadence of a chant, "Hallelujah. Hal-le-fucking-luliah!"

Sid and Brad sat quietly. The complete lack of emotion or reaction of any manner from the two men seemed only to delight Knapp.

The breath of three men was stifling in the tiny room.

Knapp extended his body across the table as he brushed the Advice of Rights form off the table, letting it fall to the ground. With a curl of his lip he whispered, "Go stroke your dicks till your blisters bleed." Another drag on his cigarette, a slow expulsion of smoke and a glare of sheer hatred brought silence to the room.

Sid evaluated Edmond Knapp with no indication of being perturbed in the least. "Okay, no problem at all. I'll have Mr. Montoya come and take you back to your cell."

"Mr. Montoya?" Knapp's voice reflected disbelief. "Mr. Montoya! Is that what you call that greasy, chili-shitting Mexican?" Knapp's eyes appeared on the verge of spontaneous combustion. "You know what I think? I think there might be one really good thing about this stinking town. With so many Mr. Montoya types around, it must be crawling with little Mexican girls." Knapp's entire face smiled. "You know, them beautiful little brown pussies just beginning to itch." Knapp leaned forward, his voice straining with hatred. "You listen closely. I've got news for you." His eyes narrowed even more and Brad swore within his mind that the man was part snake. "Since you are probably secretly recording everything I say anyway, be sure you understand me. I'm not confessing to a goddamned thing. But there's a guy back there in the cell block." Knapp pointed. "I'm just going to tell you what he told me." A sneer contorted his face. "He told me that there ain't nothing better in this whole world than soaking a hard dick in some little Injun girl that's just sprouting her feathers or a little greaser just as her chili starts to ripen." Knapp's smile widened. "He told me you can hear them little bitches squealing for a mile." Knapp leaned back in his chair, his teeth fully exposed. "Now, that's just what that jailbird back there told me. You understand, I'm only repeating what he said." Knapp plunged his cigarette into the can of Coke with a startling hiss. *The hiss of Satan* was all that Brad could think of.

Tapping his fingers on the completely blank tablet in his lap, Sid remained silent. Finally, Brad spoke. "Well, like the old country song says, I guess that about does it, now don't it."

Sid stood. "Yep, that wraps up this conversation, nice and neat, pretty as can be." He stood, opened the door and called to

Robert Montoya. "We are finished with Mr. Knapp. Would you please take him back to his cell? Wouldn't want him to miss afternoon story and nap time."

Montoya unlocked the cuff that secured Knapp to his chair. With slightly more force than necessary, he pulled Knapp's arms behind his back and ratcheted the cuffs until he felt them pinch Knapp's skin. Without a word, he escorted Edmond Knapp from the room.

Exhaling hard and shoulders sagging, Brad sat for a moment. He stood up, walked past Sid to the door. "I can't sit in this room for one more second. Let's find another place to talk. I don't even want to breathe air that's passed through the lungs of that shithead."

"I'm with you." Sid followed Brad out of the room. Both men remained quiet, not yet ready to talk

Montoya stepped into the room and, with a glance at their somber expressions, understood immediately what had transpired in the interview room. "Okay, gentlemen, coffee or something cold sound like a good idea? Maybe a slice of pie to go along with it?"

Sid looked as though he had just been handed a gift and Brad chuckled as he answered, "You have a deal. And to make it even better, our good friend here," pointing at Sid, "has told me that he's flush and offers to buy."

Montoya grinned, "Follow me, I have just the place to help you purge your heads of that miserable asshole. Let's walk, be good for all of us." With that, he opened the door to the outside and Brad unconsciously gulped, sucking sunshine and fresh air as if he had been drowning.

***

Robert Montoya began the process of diluting Edmond Knapp's repugnance as they walked the few blocks from the jail to the Eklund Hotel; the very one Brad had spotted earlier in the day. Montoya seemed to know everyone in town and his exchange of greetings, often blended with friendly insults, offered a much-needed dose of humor. He explained to Sid and Brad that he had been raised in Clayton, played high school basketball here and intended to raise his family and die in his home town. "It's a different kind of world and I love it. The people here are wonderful. They are my friends and my home. I feel lucky to be in this place."

Brad looked at Montoya with both understanding and approval. "I hear what you say and certainly do not disagree. After the time we just spent with Knapp, I feel like I want to move as far away from a city as I can get."

The breeze of oscillating fans that hung from the ceiling of the saloon felt like breath from heaven. After ordering apple pie and iced tea, Brad looked about the saloon to find that he was completely taken by the beauty of mirrored walls and polished wood that adorned the bar. It was difficult to comprehend that what he saw were remnants of raucous elegance that had thrived when Clayton was a frontier settlement.

Photographs of the Old West were everywhere. Still needing to stretch, Brad stood to walk about and take a closer look. He soon came upon a collection of photographs that stopped him in his tracks. In disbelief, Brad scrutinized the images that lined the saloon's wall. He saw somber men, dressed in black suits and western hats, clearly go-to-church attire. But where the men stood was hardly a church. A hangman's scaffold was the primary focus of the photographs, with an obviously condemned man standing in the center. Like a movie in slow motion, the photographs told the doomed man's story: hands tied behind his back, hair perfectly combed and moustache drooping, he stared without expression, looking directly into the camera. A noose was placed about his neck and then a black hood forced over his head, obscuring the face. Brad was mesmerized. He looked again at each photograph. Brad could practically hear the hot gasps that would have been sucked beneath that hood. He could feel how pulse would have thundered as the rope cinched about his neck and the quivering that must have stricken the knees, with the brink of eternity only seconds away.

"Jesus!" No one heard Brad's whisper.

The next photograph defied imagination. Instead of the expected image of a dangling man whose life had just been snapped from his body, the camera portrayed a headless human torso with blood pouring onto the ground. Several paces distant lay the hooded head, now a macabre, inanimate object wrenched from its body.

"Jesus H Christ." Brad breathed a bit louder.

Next to the photographs, Brad spotted a framed news article written by an observing reporter from the Albuquerque Journal-Democrat. Still struggling to comprehend the photographs and the story they told, Brad read the reporters account of the 1901 hanging:

Clayton, N.M., April 26 – Thomas Edward Ketchum, alias "Black Jack," the notorious outlaw who terrorized the Southwest for the past fifteen years, was hanged here this afternoon for the last of his many crimes and his head was severed from his body as if by a guillotine. The headless trunk pitched forward towards the spectators and blood spurted upon those nearest the scaffold. The execution took place in a side stockade built for the occasion.

The enclosure was crowded, 150 witnesses having been admitted. When Ketchum mounted the scaffold at 1:17 p.m. his face was pale, but he showed no fear. A priest stood at his side as the rope was being put around his neck. The condemned man consented to this at the last moment. Ketchum decided not to make a statement. He muttered "Goodbye" and then said, "Please dig my grave very deep," and as the cap was drawn over his head shouted, "Let her go." His legs trembled but his nerve did not fail.

At 1:21 the trap was sprung, and his body shot through the air, his head being torn from the trunk by the tremendous jerk. His head remained in the sack and fell into the pit, while the body dropped to the ground, quivering and bleeding.

Some men groaned, and others turned away, unable to endure the sight. For a few seconds the body was allowed to be there, half doubled up on the right side, with blood issuing in an intermittent stream from the severed arteries as the heart kept on with its mechanical beating. Then with cries of consternation the officers rushed down from the scaffold and lifted the body from the ground....

"Holy shit," Brad whispered as he again looked at the photographs. He turned to the table where Sid and Montoya were seated and found that they both watched him intently. Sid grinned widely and Montoya was on the verge of outright laughter. Brad sauntered back to the table, shaking his head, unable to disguise the sheepish expression that consumed his face. As he took his seat, he looked to Montoya, "Good Lord have mercy, I've never seen anything quite like that."

Loving the moment, Montoya now openly laughed. "Welcome to Clayton. The Chamber of Commerce hopes you enjoy your stay but warns not to steal horses or rob trains."

Lifting his arms in surrender, Brad joined in the laughter as he spoke, "You've made a believer out of me. Hell's bells, just to stay on the safe side, I'm going to double my tip for this pie when the bill comes."

Sid stood and looked to the photographs, "Guess I better see what all the excitement is about." Casting a glance of conspiracy to Montoya, he exaggerated his Texas drawl as he spoke.

"Heaven knows I can't trust whatever story this darned greenhorn might tell me. My friend in Colorado tells me Alice in Wonderland is his role model."

Pointing to the photographs, Brad fired back, "Go ahead. Take your time, shitbird. I'm feeling pretty hungry so no rush. I hope you enjoy a good hanging while I partake of your apple pie."

***

Inside the police department once again, Montoya made copies of the papers recovered from the crashed Ferrari in Colorado. Sid glanced through them, rubbing his chin as he spoke. "The minute I'm back in Albuquerque, I'll analyze everything here and match up what I can with what's in Lucy's diary. There's a ton of information here but it's going to take some work to sort it out and understand what we have." Sid looked to Montoya. "Can you let me know when the world's biggest asshole manages to get released? I want to keep up with him while I figure this out."

"You got it. We have a judge here who is tough but fair. A mighty steep bond has been set but, if someone posts the money, Knapp Man will be outta here and there's nothing I can do. His jail time won't last nearly long enough to make me happy but I'll keep you posted."

Sid turned to Brad. "What's next for you, headed home to Colorado?"

Calculating his response, Brad knew he could never talk about his conversation with *Abuelo* or the letter that was now tucked into his pocket. After an extended silence and a glance to the ceiling, he sighed before he spoke. "Oh, I'm not sure. I need to think about things. I'm hoping something comes of Lucy's diary and the paper work from the Ferrari." Looking to both Sid and Robert Montoya, Brad gave a shrug. "You guys are the ones that have to make this come together. I'm no longer a player in these games." Brad's reticence spoke loudly. "Let me know as things unfold. After being in the home of Lucy's parents and getting to know them," he shook his head sadly, "and after spending time with that despicable shithead," pointing toward the cellblock area, "I won't be thinking of much else until I hear from you. This one is breaking my heart."

The room felt heavy. Montoya pressed hands over his face before looking at Brad. "My friend, you will be the first person I call if anything breaks. My wife and I will both say a prayer tonight. We will pray for Lucy and her parents." He took a breath. "And we will pray for you too."

Understanding the sincerity of Montoya's words, Brad was again reminded of the incredible bond shared by people in law enforcement. "Thank you, Robert. I appreciate that more than you know."

Sid stood. There was nothing more to be said. With a round of handshakes among the three new friends, the men parted.

***

Having no plan in mind, Brad drove aimlessly, retracing the route he had followed into Clayton earlier in the day. Reaching the west edge of town and with no idea where to go, he made a right turn onto a side street and slowly cruised. In only a few blocks, he came to a church. Its steeple seemed to puncture the sky. Brad marveled at how the town abruptly ended at the church and, to the west, there was absolutely nothing except the vastness of New Mexico. This sense of openness and freedom was exactly what he sought after being confined with Knapp in the tiny interview room. Parking his truck, Brad walked around the church, gathering peace as he strolled. Did his peace come from being in the shadow of a building considered to be sacred or was it the expanse of the land and the sense of freedom it imparted? He didn't know or care. This was exactly what he sought.

Wind blew, not hard but just enough to remind Brad that it was there. Where the winds began, heaven only knew. But he was aware that they would almost always blow in this place. He lifted his face to mid-afternoon sun, seeking its warmth and the feel of breeze. He thought of Lucy. *Abuelo's* face and his toothless smile came to him. Were Lucy and *Abuelo* together again? Brad liked that thought and decided to keep it in his mind, it delivered a bit of peace. Yes, Lucy and *Abuelo* would be together, laughing as wind carried them over vast open spaces.

Behind the church and looking to the west, Brad dropped to the ground. He sat with his arms about his knees gazing to the horizon and feeling that he occupied the edge of infinity. Perhaps that was the reason a church had been erected here. He could not imagine a more divine setting.

Taking *Abuelo's* letter from his pocket, Brad held it as he thought about the day with Edmond Knapp. The man's sour smell and jeering face had been sheer repugnance. Both still fouled Brad's nostrils and memory.

The beauty of Lucy Hernandez filled his mind but then Brad had to recall the pain in the eyes of Victoria and Alphonso. *Abuelo's* face materialized. He could recall every wrinkle that lined the old man's face. Brad smiled to himself as he envisioned *Abuelo's* laughter as he took delight in the beauty of a woman's breasts.

Brad drifted his gaze over the horizon and the immeasurable distance that stretched before him. There was no sound except the rush of air sweeping in from over the prairie. Brad looked at the envelope in his hand. He remained perfectly still, listening, feeling the wind. After moments had passed, Brad replaced the document without opening it and stood, speaking softly into the emptiness. "*Abuelo*, I have absolutely no idea what the hell you are talking about."

In a thoughtful stroll, Brad returned to his truck. Only one idea had managed come to him during his introspection and it seemed far-fetched and absolutely crazy. Climbing into his truck and mumbling to himself, he reached for his cell phone. "Brad, this may very well be the dumbest damned thing you've ever done." He pulled up the Internet and searched for the word *Pajarito*.

Minutes later Brad was driving west, headed for Taos, and he had a plan.

***

Brad was now reversing his morning's drive. He would pass through Cimarron as he made his way to Taos. With nothing but time and miles for the next few hours, he decided to give himself the luxury of thinking about Juanita. The day had transpired with a level of such intensity that Juanita had crossed his mind in only quick whispers. But now the image of her face and sound of her voice were soothing companions as miles passed. He wondered if and when the time would come that he would be able to speak freely with her about his dreams. Had she experienced anything remotely similar? He tried to be analytical. To have had such dreams after being clobbered on the head was one thing, but last night's journey back into the Twilight Zone with Moustache and another encounter with the mystical Juanita was too much to blow off as happenstance. He couldn't explain it, and he sure as hell couldn't talk about it. But deep inside Brad felt, that in some manner, everything was real.

Longing for Juanita, he unconsciously pressed his rig hard and the speedometer quickly passed the one hundred mark. The power surge brought memories of when he had been a pilot. Jamming his foot onto the accelerator, the sound of a roaring engine and thrill of unleashed speed felt marvelous. How he yearned to fly again. The outside prairie passed in a blur. For a few moments fantasy seemed attainable. His mind raced as he thought in terms of a miracle, the empty highway now his runway. He had the speed, could he actually make it happen? Simply pull back on the wheel, he told himself. Surely his truck would float and, in the exhilaration of flight, he would set a heading straight to Albuquerque and soar to Juanita. Brad eased back on the accelerator. A rueful smile acknowledged his juvenile folly but his heart still pounded with the fantasy. Brad slowed his truck. Once again traveling at a sane speed, Brad accepted that only the thought of Juanita was the best he could do for the present.

The moment the town of Springer came into sight and his cell phone indicated service, Brad pulled over. With heart still not completely settled, he punched her number. When her voicemail greeted him instead of her actual voice, his shoulders sagged but at least it was Juanita and, for a moment, they shared the same space. He left a message with a brief synopsis of the day and that he was driving to Taos. Brad reluctantly placed his cell on the seat beside him, knowing there would be very little service until he reached Taos. Disappointment seeped through his chest as he threw his truck into gear, pulled back onto the highway and continued.

For what seemed like the thousandth time in only hours, he passed through Cimarron. But this time there would be no Victoria or Alphonso. There was not time for the St. James Hotel or coffee with Louise. Brad pushed on through the town and entered Cimarron Canyon. The trout stream that held so many memories and that he had grown to love sadly beckoned as he passed. Climbing out of Cimarron Canyon, the sun had dipped behind Wheeler Peak and reflective light caused the Moreno

Valley to shimmer as if illuminated by subterranean fire. By the time he made Taos, the first stars speckled in the heavens.

"Jesus, I'm hungry," Brad whispered as he passed through the Plaza. Taos and its plaza was a place that he could never again visit without thinking of the white supremacist who had tried to murder him. That memory quickly led Brad to the world of dreams, Moustache and Juanita's cabin. Now here he was, back in Taos having come full circle. But this time, there was a real Juanita in his life.

***

The image of a skeleton adorned in a sombrero and sporting a drooping moustache was what he looked for. Brad spotted the familiar sign and breathed a sigh of relief upon seeing that his favorite Taos restaurant was still open. The late hour worked to his advantage as the usual summer crowd was mostly gone and he was seated immediately in the outdoor patio. He knew from dozens of meals in this tiny place that Moosehead was not on their list of beers but Santa Fe Pale Ale, brewed only an hour away, suited him perfectly. With chips, guacamole and salsa delivered and his standard blue corn enchilada with green chili on order, Brad nervously hit the key to listen to Juanita's message. He had seen it as soon as he reached Taos and realized that it had been left sometime while he was out of cell service. Pressing the phone to his ear, he held his breath. "Oh, my gosh, Brad, I'm dying. Why can we never connect?" She paused. "Any hope for a plea deal in this senseless case fell apart today, so I am definitely going to be tied up in a trial for the next few days." Another pause. "I'm still working with witnesses tonight and then the trial begins tomorrow." Brad heard her gulp a hard breath. "I can hardly concentrate, Brad. I'm thinking constantly about you and our day on my parent's ranch. Didn't we have a marvelous evening?" Extended silence followed and Brad shut his eyes so tightly the pressure hurt his brain. Juanita sighed, "I suppose this will all work out, but right now time is crawling. Please stay in touch. The suspense of what you are getting into is unbearable. I will be impossible to reach until this trial ends. Just leave a message when you can." Her next silence was short, but a change in tone was noticeable when she continued. "I can't explain this, but I'm getting bad feelings about whatever it is you're doing. Some little voice inside is talking and making me nervous. Please be careful. I'm missing you terribly." Another pause followed that Brad intuitively knew was going to end her message. "Good night, Brad, good night."

Taking a long draw of Santa Fe Pale Ale, Brad leaned back in his chair, closed his eyes and listened to her message again. When finished, he gently placed his cell on the table, gazed at the sky and sat in contemplation. A handful of patrons remained in the courtyard, their laughter and conversation blending with sounds of dwindling late-night traffic and a distant siren. The sky shimmered.

There was something that Juanita had not said, and Brad felt a nagging emptiness from her unspoken words. With his eyes on the stars above the courtyard and thinking of his time with Juanita beside the windmill, a sense of peace began to settle. He knew perfectly well what had been on the tip of Juanita's tongue. He could feel her words just as clearly as if they had been spoken. Savoring this realization, a weight seemed to lift from his shoulders and he spoke to Juanita in his mind. "I'm in love with you too. Juanita, I am absolutely in love with you."

***

Outside of his motel, Brad was once again reminded that he loved Taos mornings like no other. Partly, it was the radiant blue sky, so vivid that Brad felt he could reach up and feel it. But it was more than that. For over one thousand years Taos Mountain to the north had silently watched a sleepy world awaken, smoke from mud ovens lifting aromas of life to the heavens. He looked to the mountain, sensing the war, peace and centuries of humanity shrouded within its shadowed canyons. He brought it all into his lungs. Walking slowly along Paseo Del Norte, Brad enjoyed the energy of morning's bustling traffic. In the freshness of a new day, yesterday's encounter with Edmond Knapp seemed galaxies away. How could such beauty and such repugnance co-exist, only hours apart? Looking to the mountain, Brad shrugged as he walked. "Who the hell has an answer?"

Taking a seat on the stone fence that encircled the boundary of Kit Carson Park and crossing his fingers, he rang Juanita. Elation jolted when he heard her voice, bursting with energy. "Oh, my heavens, I can't believe we finally are talking. I've been dying. Where are you? Are you okay? What are you doing? I miss you. Come to Albuquerque this very moment and carry me away. I'll walk away from this crazy trial and we shall never be found again!"

After having thought of her practically non-stop for days and wanting desperately to speak with her, Brad found himself mortified in that he could think of absolutely nothing to say. Racking his brain for some sort of clever response, he managed a reply. "Who is speaking please? I'm calling the Chamber of Commerce in Cheyenne, Wyoming for information on current beach conditions."

Juanita's magical laugh told Brad that she was either very kind or very easily entertained. "This is driving me insane. I'm supposed to be in court five minutes ago. Tell me fast, I want to know everything that you've been doing, what have you learned and when will you be finished." She gave a split second pause. "If you can't do that, tell me what I really want to hear. Tell me you miss me as badly as I miss you."

Firing back with auctioneer speed, Brad answered, "I'm in Taos. All is fine. I'm still working on things. Don't know when I'll finish but if I don't see you soon, I'm going to explode into a million fragments of a heartbroken Brad Walker." After his own blink of a pause that gave Juanita no time to respond, he slowed his pace. "Okay, young lady, how did I do?"

In Brad's mind, Juanita's laughter literally sparkled. "You did marvelous, absolutely marvelous. You have no idea how much this call means to me. Now, I'll be able to make it through the coming hours of this trial. Can you call me tonight so we can really catch up, nice and slow?"

He had not thought through how to get around explaining his plans for the evening so he had no choice but to be direct. "Tonight will be impossible. I'm going to be where there's no chance for cell service. How about tomorrow morning?"

"Okay, let's try. I have witness interviews and testimony preparation that I must handle very early before jury selection and the trial begins. But, please call me if you can. I'll be on pins and needles hoping we can sneak a few seconds to talk." Juanita's voice dropped as she spoke her next words. "You have no idea how badly I'm missing you."

They were silent. Just as when he had listened to her voice last night, Brad could feel what Juanita wanted to say and he ached to say the words to her in return. But he swallowed the impulse. Such a declaration should only be made when he could see her face, look at her eyes and wrap his arms about her. It would be a mockery of his feelings to say what he wanted to say in a rushed phone conversation.

Their silence lingered until Brad spoke softly. "I'm thinking of you constantly and am absolutely desperate to see you." Brad took a breath and held it for a moment before speaking again. "But, you are doing something that has to be done and I'm trying to make sense of what you asked me to do. We're going to get through this."

Juanita's sigh was gentle but failed to disguise her frustration. "I'm thinking of you also." She hesitated. "Yes, we are going to get through this. But you need to know that I have been worrying. Being a prosecutor sharpens instincts, Brad, and I'm having bad feelings. I can't explain why I'm so worried but I can tell you that in the past when I've had such feelings, my instincts almost always turn out to be accurate." She held her voice. "Don't take what I'm saying lightly, please. I need you, Brad. I need you to be safe." Juanita's plea was earnest and somber.

Unsure how to respond, Brad simply replied, "I need you too and I will be safe."

After a second of quiet followed by a delicate "Goodbye," Juanita was gone.

***

The bakery and café that had occupied a corner of Paseo del Norte for decades brimmed with locals and tourists alike. Brewing coffee and aromas both sweet and spicy delivered sensory overload as Brad stepped inside. Once seated at a corner table, coffee poured and huevos rancheros with *sopaipillas* on the way, Brad leaned back, looked about his surroundings and enjoyed a few moments of reflection. Elizabeth and he had loved this place. Heaven only knew how many times had they dined here.

Sipping coffee and thinking, it took a few minutes to get a grip on all that churned inside. The intimate exchange he had just shared with Juanita followed by such vivid memories of Elizabeth and him inside this restaurant brought the now familiar surge of conflicting emotions. He could see Elizabeth's smile as they enjoyed breakfast and planned their adventures for the day. His conversation with Sam Trathen at the suicide scene played again and Sam's words of wisdom echoed. Brad closed his eyes, living again his dream in the St. James Hotel. The face and voice of Moustache seemed to be with him in the midst of this morning's café crowd. The admonition of Moustache was clear, "Don't let her slip away."

His breakfast on the table, Brad ate in solitude and reflection.

***

The list of what he needed was inside his head. It wouldn't be much. He already had two of everything at home in Colorado but that did him no good now. Brad inwardly chuckled at the irony and continued with his planning. The weather was forecast to be perfect, so for once he would be a minimalist and pack lightly. Leaving the café, Brad headed for the plaza and a mountaineering store he knew was located there. He strolled past galleries, some with manicured gardens and hollyhocks on the brink of blooming. With a cut onto Bent Street and then a left turn, he passed the bookstore that had served Taos for as long as he could recall. It was always tough for Brad to pass up a chance to browse a bookstore and this one in particular had been a friend for years. How could it not be with a name like Moby Dickens? He knew some of the staff and longed to stop in for a quick hello. But today was not the right time and he walked with purpose, continuing to the plaza.

After purchasing a daypack and supplies, Brad walked back to his motel to make telephone calls. A few arrangements were necessary for what he would be doing later in the evening and into the night. After fueling his rig, Brad reluctantly said farewell to the peacefulness of his Taos morning and headed south. To his west, the Rio Grande Gorge paralleled his route, carrying Colorado snowmelt to ever-thirsty desert cities far from

Colorado's mountains. Piñon covered hills and rocky arroyos painted the east. New Mexico's enchantment filled the day.

There was no need to rush. He had tons of time. Making a turn to the east, he followed the Embudo Valley to Dixon. The boutique winery in this tiny settlement was unlike any other in Brad's mind. Its Spanish name, *La Chiripada*, meaning 'a stroke of luck,' had always prompted tantalizing looks and seductive intimations when Elizabeth and he had shared a bottle. Because they had introduced the vineyard's wine to so many of their friends, it was now nothing less than fundamental obligation for Brad to deliver the winery's precious nectar to half of his Colorado hometown after a New Mexico visit.

Out of his truck and stretching, he decided to meander a bit before going inside. Dazzling flowerbeds blending with the delicate perfume of grapes, hand-cultivated a mile above the sea, were nothing short of euphoric to Brad. "God, I love it here," he spoke softly looking to the sky. The same feelings that he had felt earlier in the breakfast café once again began to gnaw at his heart. Elizabeth had loved it here also. They had strolled these grounds in all seasons of the year. But while driving, Brad had reached resolution. He drew a deep, contented breath, confident that he finally understood what was happening. Someday he would be here with Juanita. They would visit the same places and do some of the same things that Elizabeth and he had done. These things were the crux of who he was and what made him Brad Walker. Not only would it be impossible to deny such reality, it would also be wrong.

Elizabeth understood. She knew Brad's heart and how he struggled with what was happening. He could now be at ease. When the time came, Elizabeth would smile.

***

With his credit card in serious trouble and the back of his rig stacked with cases of wine, Brad made his way back to the main highway. Southbound again, he drove through the clutter of Espanola's sprawl. A Native American gaming casino served as a jolting reminder of how this had all started and the tragedy of Rapid Ray.

Once clear of Espanola, Highway 502 became his westbound route. The land here was wide-open, classic New Mexico canyon and mesa country. Within minutes Brad spotted what he wanted to see. Pulling his vehicle off the road to park, he stepped out, seeking time to stretch and to contemplate the land. A dense stand of cottonwood trees to the north signified water and, for those who knew, San Ildefonso Pueblo, the childhood home of *Abuelo*. Beyond the cottonwoods, the rugged profile of Black Mesa rose as protector over the pueblo, intimidating, beautiful and powerful in a single image. Brad had been here before but had never taken time to really see or feel this land. The pueblo was primarily known for its artists who produced magnificent black pottery that was recognized as fine art by sophisticated collectors and marketed in posh galleries. To Brad, those refined collectors and exclusive galleries seemed another world from the raw beauty of where he now stood.

Thinking of *Abuelo*, Brad tried to imagine life here. He thought of the shifting seasons, relentless winds, floods, drought and the grind of daily life beneath the watchful presence of Black Mesa. He could only imagine the power of nature in this valley and how sunsets would consume entire horizons. Looking to Black Mesa, feeling small and insignificant within the immensity of this incredible land and sky, Brad took a deep breath. He held it, not wanting this moment to pass.

***

Passing road signs for Los Alamos, Brad was once again struck by the enigma of New Mexico, the incongruity of cliff dwellings from past civilizations that had somehow managed to keep their cultures alive, while the shadow of Los Alamos and the atomic age hovered.

Since first reading *Abuelo*'s letter, Brad had turned his brain inside out to make sense of the meaning of *Abuelo*'s words. This kind of stuff was way out of his league, but he had come to a couple of conclusions. When referring to the ancients and the Parajito, *Abuelo* had to have meant the early inhabitants of Bandelier in the Parajito Plateau. His childhood home, San Ildefonso Pueblo, and the ruins of Bandelier were neighbors. *Abuelo* had grown up with the people of the Parajito; they were his ancestors. But the real key for Brad was *Abuelo*'s line about water that always flowed. After searching the Internet, his memory had been jogged. Brad recalled that when Elizabeth and he had brought their children to Bandelier years earlier, they had learned that the very reason Bandelier was settled had been because Frijoles Creek was a reliable source for year-round water. Natural caves for shelter and easily accessible water had led to centuries-long civilization of cliff dwellers within Bandelier. Brad smiled to himself. It had required a refresher course on the Internet to open his mind to something hundreds of years in the past.

The more Brad had thought about it, the more convinced he became that he was on the right track. So, here he was with a plan to do something that only a week ago he would have ridiculed as completely crazy. With an inward jab at his own fickleness, an unconscious smile filled his face as he continued his drive. He was going to go through with this come hell or high water. Brad had absolutely no idea what to expect and he sure as heck had no idea or plan about what he might do after tonight.

***

The switchbacks of Highway 4 plunged Brad into Frijoles Canyon. Afternoon's lengthening shadows accentuated the effect of the descent, and Brad had the sensation that he and his truck were being swallowed by an ancient world. Upon reaching the canyon floor, the terrain softened into a giant meadow, lush with vegetation and rimmed by sand-colored cliffs that basked in late afternoon light.

After parking in an area reserved for overnight hikers, Brad gathered gear into his newly-purchased pack, hefted it onto his back and listened to his truck's chirp as he remotely locked its doors. There were no people to hear but Brad still needed to voice his strong feelings so he mumbled to no one as he walked toward the visitor's center. "Take my truck, my fishing gear or that marvelous wine, and I'll track your ass down and burn you alive."

Because he had made the necessary reservation before leaving Taos, Brad had his backcountry pass for overnight camping in minutes. When he stepped from the visitor center, the sun was within minutes of sinking below the canyon's rim. Realizing he had little time before night would be upon him, Brad began his hike into Frijoles Canyon, the home of Bandelier National Monument. The beauty was startling. It had been years since he had been here and he welcomed the opportunity. Regardless of whether or not his whim of a plan made sense, this was going to be his home for the night and he looked forward to the experience.

Brad had no agenda as he followed a well-marked and traveled trail that led up the canyon. A sheer cliff rose on his right. Caves dotted the wall, their mouths yawning open to expose blackened ceilings that told of the fires that once burned within. Brad remembered the fascination of his family the day they had explored those caves, touching and feeling the life that had once thrived here. He stood in awe of the circular housing complex of Tyuonyi. With hundreds of rooms constructed of stone and mud, this had once been the center of social and religious life for residents of the canyon.

Cooling temperature and shifting light patterns of late afternoon were serene. Day tourists were rapidly disappearing from the trail as they headed back to the visitor center. Finding that he was now alone, Brad thought a quick prayer of thanks for how lucky he was to experience such wonder in solitude. Standing still, he closed his eyes and listened to evening's silence. Brad looked up at the cliff with its multitude of caves that had at one time housed hundreds. He surveyed the breadth of the entire valley. In awe, he viewed remnants of so much life, so much death. Century after century, the cycle of life had transpired in this canyon, right where he stood. Suddenly, Brad felt uncomfortable. A feeling of unease, that he was an intruder, crept through his senses. Even worse than an intruder, he felt himself a voyeur who peered through windows onto the private world of ancient Frijoles Canyon. He continued to listen but not even a bird made a sound. The canyon seemed to hold its breath and Brad began to reconsider what he felt. Was he really the voyeur? Maybe it was just the opposite. Perhaps it was the spirits who watched him. The longer he stood in the canyon's hush, the more he felt himself an object of scrutiny, that unseen eyes were watching as he made his solitary trespass into a world where he did not belong.

Recognizing that his feelings were mind games and hoping for the moment to pass, Brad waited. But it did not happen. His uneasiness lingered and he drew a long breath, not sure what to do. He looked back up to the cliff. The lattice of shadowy caves now appeared as countless faces with hollow eyes, all focused on him. Brad felt his skin prickle. He wondered if *Abuelo* had visited here. Had he ever stood within the depths of Frijoles Canyon and experienced such transcendental moments? It really was not a question. Brad knew the answer to that one. *Abuelo* had not written about this place by pure chance. There had been a reason. There was no doubt in his mind. *Abuelo* knew exactly what happened in this canyon at night.

With his mind and heart unsettled, Brad began his way down, moving away from the cliff and closer to Frijoles Creek. As he hiked he tried to sort his emotions. Was it because he had never done anything like this before? Was fear nipping at his imagination? Continuing to move toward the valley floor, he steadily came to grips with his decision to come here. There could be no turning back. Darkness was rapidly approaching and whatever Frijoles Canyon and the coming night held, Brad vowed that he would be a part of it.

After reaching the bottom of the canyon, Brad knew he needed to hustle to get settled before nightfall. He found a comfortable patch of ground beneath a cottonwood with the trickle of Frijoles Creek only a few feet away. His pack beside him, Brad nestled against the trunk of the tree that would be his companion for the night and settled in to await darkness. He had anticipated that he would have some time to kill so he had come prepared. Reaching into his pack, he found the book he had purchased in Albuquerque, *The Earth is Enough.* If it were possible to take the edge from his jittery nerves, this would be the ticket. Brad had read the book at least three times and considered it a masterpiece. In his view, Middleton not only was a master of the written word but he wrote of things that were close to Brad's heart. So powerful were the messages of the story, Brad liked to think the pages had been written especially for him.

The story was one of warmth and grace, of lessons learned by a young boy named Harry and three elderly men who taught him and shaped his life. Brad scanned the book's back cover and the excerpt that described the story: *Seeking strength and purpose from life, Harry learns from his uncle, grandfather and their crazy Sioux neighbor, Elias Wonder, that the very pulse of life beats from within the deep constancy of the earth, and from one's devotion to it. Amidst the rhythm of an ancient cadence, Harry discovers his home: a farm, a forest, a mountain stream, and the eye of a trout rising.*

Brad half laughed and half spoke out loud, "What a perfect book for this evening." When he had selected the book in Albuquerque, it was simply because he had wished to again read the story. How could he have possibly foreseen the symbiosis of the book and what he now encountered as night fell in Frijoles Canyon? The ancient ones had lived here, their very existence in harmony with earth's rotation, what she gave and what she withheld. What were the odds that simple chance had led him to a story in which a grandfather and a Native American led a young person into life? Tonight, it was a Native American grandfather who was somehow responsible for Brad's presence in the canyon.

With a sense of comfort that he had selected this particular book for a reason that was beyond random serendipity, Brad shifted to become more comfortable and began to read. His familiarity with the story allowed him to skip and skim, seeking his favorite passages. Once located, Brad devoured the masterfully crafted lines. Through stories of fly-fishing and life lived outdoors, the author spoke of the power of nature and landscape in shaping the human spirit, how one learns what really matters in life. Brad had long recognized that the words of *The Earth is Enough* were as close to gospel as he would ever find:

> "In the gentle morning sunlight that came off the water, the fly cast a subtle glow, the way soft light sometimes does a woman's hair."

> "Each morning, even before he put the coffee on or began the biscuits, Albert would stand on the back porch and listen to the purling of the creek, the rush of water over stones. It was as if he needed to hear the creek, that sound of life ever on the move."

> "To say that it was just a matter of catching fish would be like saying that astronomy is nothing more than noticing the stars."

Page after page, Brad smiled, sometimes laughing out loud and sometimes dropping his head in contemplative thought. With each passage, he became more and more convinced that Harry Middleton had written *The Earth is Enough* with people just like him in mind. And for an evening such as this, when uncertainty roiled his mind, Brad felt he had found his own version of the Twenty-Third Psalm.

He read on and close to the end of the story came to one of the most profound pages of the book. Middleton had included a quote from Chief Seattle, his words spoken in 1854. Brad had read the passage before, but given where he was at the moment and the circumstances that had brought him into Bandelier, the words seemed to echo through Frijoles Canyon.

"And when the last Red Man shall have perished, and the memory of my tribe shall have become a myth among the white Men, these shores will swarm with the invisible dead of my tribe, and when your children's children think themselves alone in the field, the store, the shop, upon the highway, or in the silence of the pathless woods, they will not be alone. At night when the streets of your cities and villages are silent and you think them deserted, they will throng with the returning hosts that once filled and still love this beautiful land. The White Man will never be alone. Let him be just and deal kindly with my people, for the dead are not powerless. Dead did I say? There is no death, only a change of worlds."

"Jesus." Brad spoke under his breath. He read the line again. *There is no death, only a change of worlds.* With his earlier premonition that spirits of Frijoles Canyon watched his every move and now the haunting words of Chief Seattle, Brad admitted to himself that something inexplicable existed in this chasm of volcanic stone and its ever-flowing stream. There was an undeniable energy, a resonance of the people who had lived and died within this canyon. Brad closed the book.

Images of Moustache and Juanita in her simple cabin returned to his mind. He whispered the words of Chief Seattle, *"There is no death, only a change of worlds."* Looking to the sky, his barely spoken words were muffled by the sound of Frijoles Creek, swallowed by the caves and swept away by a breeze that now rippled through the canyon.

Brad pulled a jacket from his pack to use as a pillow. He settled against the cottonwood. There was nothing to do but wait.

Brad looked about his surroundings. He was surprised to observe that while engrossed in his reading, he had failed to notice the dramatic change that impending darkness was bringing to the canyon. The cottonwoods formed a sweeping canopy over the creek, giving the sense of an arching cathedral. The water that had earlier reflected ever-changing light and shadow was now dark, almost invisible, but the melody of its trickle remained unchanged. Brad scanned the cliff. Evening light gave it the blush of a fading ember. Earlier, Brad had paid little attention to the multitude of fissures that fractured the precipice wall. But now in dimming light, the jagged fingers became vivid. The cliff was webbed in a myriad of design, as if it were a giant sign proclaiming a message. Sheer magnificence was all that Brad could conjure in his mind.

These fading seconds of light were exactly how he remembered the light in Juanita's cabin as she cared for him. Candlelight on her face, her hair shimmering as she leaned close to give him water and broth. Brad held his breath, savoring the taste of her memory. He opened his mind, fantasizing how it would feel when finally he truly would hold her. Memory and anticipation drifted through his mind, each as enchanting as the flow of Frijoles Creek.

When absolute night darkened the canyon, Brad opened a granola bar, slipped his jacket on and extracted a flashlight. He didn't want to use it but, just in case, he would keep it handy. Innumerable stars filled the heavens but did nothing to diminish the intense blackness of the night. Brad had never been able to identify any constellation beyond the Big Dipper and thought that people who conjured such images in the sky were probably suffering from too much fun stuff in their youth. But no one had loved night skies more than Elizabeth and he when raising their children. How many times had they slept under the stars, talking and storytelling until heavy breathing told them their children were asleep? Cody was now a Navy medic, based at Camp Lejeune. Michael was working computer miracles in Silicon Valley and Meghan was in law school. Forever in love with her music, she still sang for him each time she visited. Where had the years gone?

A cool dampness seeped from the ground as night deepened. Brad zipped his jacket closed, recalling the cold nights he had camped above ten thousand feet with his boys. Those skies had been just as dark as tonight, the stars just as spectacular.

Everything was so quiet and still, the whisper of Frijoles Creek the only sound.

The music of Enya had always struck Brad as remarkable, and at this moment, her lyrics fit perfectly.

Suddenly before my eyes
Hues of indigo arise
With them how my spirit sighs
Paint the sky with stars

Brad knew that sometime later in the night the moon would rise. With so much running around in the past days, he had lost track of exactly when he should expect its appearance. He sighed as he gazed upward. Even though he found the beauty marvelous, he remained restless. His reason for coming here was not to experience a nature trip. "This may be a long-ass night," he muttered. "How the hell could I ever explain this nonsense to Sam Trathen?" Brad could not help but to see humor in what he was doing. If it were true that *Abuelo* had in some manner directed him here tonight, the old man had probably become distracted and was now busy chasing hot-bodied angels around the galaxy while dumb-ass Brad sat in the middle of nowhere, freezing his skinny ass off.

Questioning his sanity, Brad again looked to the sky and contemplated *Abuelo*'s message. He inwardly admitted that he would have dismissed the letter as undecipherable hocus-pocus but for his most recent dream of Moustache and Juanita. Brad had become so convinced that the dreams were somehow intertwined with reality and his relationship with Juanita that he simply could not ignore that Moustache had specifically mentioned *Abuelo*. Saying to hell with attempts to be analytical or rational, Brad had made his decision to come here. If he were wrong, what the hell, nobody would ever have to know a thing about his flirtation with such mysticism.

If there was a riddle to be solved, then this had to be the right place. This canyon was the only thing that made sense. And if ancient spirits existed, of course they would be angry that relics of their people were being used as barter for prostitution. Brad laughed to himself. The repugnancy of Edmond Knapp was so great that Egyptian Pharaohs, dead as fence posts in their fancy pyramids, may very well wake up pissed off and demand some sort of vengeance.

The night's chill seeped into his bones. Brad stood to stretch his legs that had become cold and stiff. He downed another granola bar as he walked in place and twisted his frame from side to side. Realizing that he had become thirsty, a part of *Abuelo*'s message popped into his head, the words about water he had tasted before and that he should drink again. Brad had packed a water bottle but shrugged and muttered, "What the hell." Inching a way through the darkness, Brad moved to the edge of Frijoles Creek. He dropped to his knees and dipped his fingers into the water, feeling its depth and force. "Jesus, that's cold." Able to see just enough that he could lean to the water's surface, Brad pressed his lips into the water and drew long gulps. With each swallow, icy shock jolted his throat.

Standing again, Brad questioned how his mind was working. The water was exactly what he had tasted in his dreams with Juanita and again when they had been beneath her windmill. Wondering to himself if his imagination was running wild, he had no answer. It was crazy as hell but he knew what he remembered and he knew what he had just tasted.

Once again nestled against the cottonwood, Brad looked in the direction of the cliff. It was scarcely visible in the night, its shadowy hulk camouflaged within darkness. Brad realized that during the entire evening, silence had been nothing short of remarkable. He could not recall a single instance of hearing a bird, coyote or other night creature. He had plenty of outdoor experience to realize this was extremely unusual. As he thought more about it, he realized that even though he had spent a great deal of time looking at the sky, he had not seen or heard a single airplane overhead. Were it not for the trickle of Frijoles Creek, there was absolutely no hint of life within the canyon or in the sky above.

The chill Brad had felt earlier suddenly seemed to simply go away and he inexplicably felt totally at ease within the canyon. Once again, his thoughts turned to Juanita. It was so easy to simply let his mind go and allow her to come to him. He felt his body relaxing and Juanita seemed to glide through his mind, carrying him away. In the dim light of her cabin, her face only inches from his, she offered water while the aroma and warmth of her body wrapped about him. Brad heard the windmill on her ranch and felt the evening breeze, just as he had felt it when they talked. Her fingertips touched his cheek. Brad's brain no longer cared about what was real. Any efforts to comprehend reality evaporated. Swaddled in the euphoria of Juanita, a narcotic serenity dissolved consciousness into a seductive blur. Juanita's lips brushed his.

***

Smoke! A taste of ash in his mouth and a singe in his nostrils sounded the alarm. Brad tried but could not awaken. Then it was dogs. Yapping and howling, it sounded as though packs of the animals surrounded him. How many? But mostly it was the smoke that signaled danger. He had to awaken, become alert. If only he could open his eyes but they remained sealed, refusing all commands. Were those voices he now heard? The presence of smoke became stronger. What type of music was he hearing? Why could he not open his eyes? With the sensation that he was drowning and feeling his lungs on fire, Brad finally broke through. He opened his eyes and blinked, squeezing his eyelids tightly before opening them again. Haze shrouded his vision. Again he blinked, desperate to clear his mind and comprehend what was happening. Panic threatened and his heart accelerated, chasing the grogginess that clouded his mind.

Brad leaned forward. His body felt as if it was filled with sand and his mouth and throat so parched he could not swallow. He shook his head from side to side, still blinking and unable to comprehend what he thought he was seeing. On the face of the cliff, fires burned inside the caves. Their glow was unmistakable as shadows danced on walls in flickering light. Smoke wafted from the mouths of the caves as if they exhaled. He looked across Frijoles Creek, through the trees in the direction of Tyuonyi. Just as in the caves, campfires illuminated the forest in subdued glow. With not even a hint of breeze, smoke from the fires settled onto the canyon's floor and ash collected on his clothing. The voices he thought he had heard were now unmistakable, their cadence rising, falling, and sometimes laughing. Dogs barked in all directions and Brad thought he could discern some sort of music, but from where it came, he could not be sure.

Regardless of his determination to be awake and his desire to observe and understand, Brad felt himself slipping again, unable to keep his eyes open. Voices faded and dogs no longer barked. The glow of fires within the caves retreated into blackness.

***

Shivering and inwardly cursing for not having packed a heavier jacket, Brad awakened. Blinking his eyes, he saw that moonlight now filled the canyon. The cliff appeared chalky white and orifices of the caves created a pattern of black lace across the stone. A breeze now stirred and puffs of clouds speckled the sky. Moonlight dominated the heavens and only the brightest of stars remained to be viewed.

Remnants of his dream lingered but cold penetrating his body startled him into full awareness. "Jesus, what a crazy dream," he muttered as he looked to the caves to reassure himself that no fires burned within. With aching and stiff legs, Brad stood to twist his body and flex his knees. A glance at his watch showed 3:30 in the morning. Moonlight flooded the canyon with brilliance that rivaled that of day and the entire palisade shimmered in silver beauty. Fissures sliced across the precipice as bolts of jagged, black lightning.

Sitting down again he stared at the cliff in stunned amazement. "Holy Jesus!" How many times had he stared right at it since entering the canyon? Brad slowly moved his head. Had he not looked in just the right manner or had he been blind? It had taken the moon, that gorgeous moon, to open his eyes.

Brad tried to assess how to interpret what he saw. Was this sheer coincidence or had his brush with *Abuelo* taken him over the edge of common sense. Unless he had completely lost his marbles, this was astounding. The cliff of Bandelier had transformed into a courier that delivered the answer that Brad had sought. Across a moonlit billboard of ancient stone, stretching at least seventy-five feet up and across, the fissures on the cliff created a near-perfect replica of the map he had seen while with Robert Montoya in the Clayton Police department. Stone fracturing over centuries solved *Abuelo*'s riddle, absolute and spectacular.

"Good God Almighty," Brad breathed. Standing beneath the cottonwood, he remained still for a few moments, needing time to listen and gather his thoughts. In surreal awe, Brad memorized the cliff and its fissures, a near-perfect road map inscribed in the stone of Bandelier.

With the exception of his crazy dream, for the first time in the long, night since entering the canyon, Brad heard the sound of another living creature. From across the creek, near the base of the cliff, an owl hooted.

***

The rim of Frijoles Canyon glowed pink in dawn's light as Brad reached his truck. He tossed his pack into the passenger seat, turned the key and drove away. Within seconds, he became aware of something that he had not noticed up to this point; his clothing and pack carried the unmistakable smell of campfire smoke.

***

Back in the same motel room he had vacated less than twenty-four hours earlier, Brad collapsed across the bed and stared at the ceiling. As he waited for sleep to come, he reflected back to when he had left his home in Colorado. Had he ever miscalculated the magnitude of what he was getting into! He had anticipated a quick trip to Gunnison for a visit with Sam Trathen to gather a few facts and then report his findings to

Juanita. He had thought it was going to be neat, clean and no big deal. Brad contemplated the ceiling fan that spun over his bed and realized he was not even certain how long he had been gone. His exhausted mind could scarcely recall the miles driven and all that had happened. He closed his eyes and stood with Sam, visualizing the suicide scene where all of this had begun. He recalled Victoria and Alphonso, their home and the heartbreak in their eyes. He felt the dress of Lucy Hernandez against his face. He walked halls of the nursing home, to *Abuelo* and saw the old man's toothless smile as his shoulders quaked in humor. Brad again heard *Abuelo*'s premonition and warning. He missed Louise and her razor wit.

Drowsy breeze carried thoughts of the night he had just experienced in Frijoles Canyon. The ceiling fan whirled and Brad slept.

***

It was well past noon when Brad stepped out of the shower. Feeling refreshed a million times over, he threw on gym pants and his least dirty tee shirt. When he had left home he certainly had not packed to be away for such a long time and everything he had was well past the ripe stage. He knew about a laundry from past fishing trips so he decided to get things cleaned up. While waiting, he would use the time to make some calls and hopefully figure out what the hell to do next.

As badly as he wished to talk with Juanita, he had no idea what he would say if she happened to answer. In some ways he was relieved when her voicemail responded. He left his message, keeping it short and vague. What could he possibly say about last night? His heart hurt to see her.

Surprisingly, Sid Pruitt did answer. Brad inquired if Sid still intended to invite Edmond Knapp for Christmas and soon both were laughing as they envisioned introducing Knapp to their families. Brad compared Edmond Knapp to Cousin Eddie in National Lampoon's *Christmas Vacation*. Laughter always made Brad feel better when things were bothering him and this time was no different. With a few hours sleep, a shower and some humor, he felt his battery charging by the second. "What can you tell me about good ole Cousin Eddie, is he still in jail or is he out and having dinner with Aunt Bethany?"

Still laughing, Sid Pruitt thought for second before replying. "Yeah, he's out of jail but he said he loves Clayton so much he wanted to stay a while, you know, make it his home. Now, you remember how much Robert Montoya thinks of Eddie? I mean those guys are tight. Montoya told me that the city hired Knapp on as a full time sewer pumper. They gave him an enema syringe and put him to work for two bits a day. Knapp is happy and Montoya is ecstatic as hell. In fact, Montoya told me that he intends to invite Knapp to his house for Christmas. So, I guess that means I'm clean out of luck." Sid's dry, Texas drawl in telling his story brought tears to Brad's eyes in another round of laughter.

When it was time to get serious, Sid's tone changed. "I'm sad to say that Knapp is indeed out of jail and free as a bird. Montoya called me the morning after we left Clayton. Money was wired to get his sorry ass out of the slammer. All the stuff that was in his trunk is still being held for further investigation, but Mr. Knapp is in the wind."

"I was afraid that would be the story. Any idea where the shitbird is headed?"

"Montoya thinks he was headed back to Albuquerque but doesn't know for sure. From where I sit, there ain't no telling what that crazy guy might do. But, I have a few bits of information I can pass on, for what they're worth."

"Thanks, Sid. I'll take anything I can get." Brad was aware that Sid was being deliberate and diplomatic in his avoidance of asking Brad anything at all about what his intentions were in regard to Knapp.

Sid's voice reflected frustration as he continued. "Just as I expected, going through Lucy's diary has been a tedious process. Much of what she recorded simply offers no solid or verifiable lead information. But when she did write down a name, phone number or address, something that we can follow up on, by golly it's a gold mine and doors are starting to open. We are looking at quite a network of people moving stolen artifacts to fund a prostitution operation, mostly of young girls."

"I sure hope some doors open quickly, Sid. I can't tell you how it affected me to spend time in Lucy's house and meet her parents. That's what really gave me a feel for her life and the heartbreak of this whole scenario. Of course, after our time with Knapp every suspicion and hatred I have for him and his ilk was magnified a million times."

"I'm with you on that one. Look, Brad, I think we have good news and bad news here. I wish to hell things could move faster but I honestly feel good about things in general. I'm absolutely positive we're going to put this together, it's just going to take a little more time and a little more digging. The downside is I think we have a ticking time bomb on our hands. I have no doubt at all that a bunch more victims are out there that are just like Lucy Hernandez. Until we crack this thing, bad stuff is gonna keep happening. You can go to the bank on it, my friend."

"You are absolutely right. Ain't no doubt about it in my mind either." Brad's voice carried his concern.

"That's why I'm feeling so damned much pressure to make progress." Sid took a breath. "Here's what I can tell you right now. We've done work with Knapp's credit cards and that son-of-a-bitch is no stranger to Clayton. You remember that hotel and café, the one with all the photographs that showed the hanging of that poor train robber who got his head popped off?"

"Of course I remember." Brad chuckled softly.

"Edmond Knapp is there regularly, for Christ's sake! He's got all kinds of charges in the dining room. That bastard has probably eaten at the very table where we sat. Once I found out about this, I called Montoya and he went over there with a photo. The wait staff and management all recognized him. Sometimes he shows up alone and sometimes he has other people with him but he's a regular there."

"Jesus! Does he stay in the hotel?"

"Nope, he just eats and runs. But, we may have a lead on what takes him there and this is where things get really interesting. From Lucy's diary, we found that Knapp used more than one cell phone. We're still going through a ton of records. The guy must make a hundred calls every day. But, right away a name popped up that got our attention. Knapp made bunch of calls to a real dirt bag that we've had our eye on for years. He's a clown named Sylvester Hurley and he squirted out of his mother's womb as a first rate home burglar and stolen property fence." Pruitt paused. "Now, honestly, Brad, if you had a name like Sylvester hanging over your head since you was a tiny baby, what kind of total, back-asswards mess would you be? Maybe the guy never had a chance."

Brad started laughing again. "Sounds to me like Sylvester may be a perfect match for your sister, Myrtle."

"You FBI shits are all alike. My sister's name is Gertrude and she sports the most beautiful fuzz moustache you ever did see. She's way too classy for our boy, Sylvester."

Sid's country style delivery had Brad laughing again. "Jesus, quit making me laugh, my whole body hurts. Get back to police work and tell me about Sylvester."

"Okay, okay. When I saw Sylvester's name on Knapp's phone records, I knew we had something because everybody from El Paso to Santa Fe has been trying to nail this bastard for years. I made a call to the Bernalillo County folks because I knew they have been working him really hard. And, bingo, they came through in grand fashion. Sylvester, the cat burglar, had walked right into a trap just a few days ago. He tried to sell a ton of stolen property to an undercover guy so they snagged his ass, pretty as you please. He's been in jail ever since." Sid chuckled. "And even the dumb turd that he is, Sylvester knows he's facing some serious jail time."

"Perfect."

"You bet it was perfect. I took a drive last night down to the jailhouse to see the poor boy. I even missed my supper just to get down there and have a chat with Mr. Sylvester." Another short laugh came from Pruitt. "I gotta tell you, Brad, it was like going to Aunt Sally's house for biscuits and apple butter compared to our interview with Knapp. Sylvester knows that he finally fucked up big time and he is scared shitless. He is dying to talk to anybody with a badge that might be able to help his scrawny ass out, even a little bit."

"So, does this mean that Sylvester did not want to use your Advice of Rights form as toilet paper like your pal, Knapp?"

"You nailed it. Sylvester acted like I had given him a page out of the Bible." Sid stopped speaking and Brad could smell another joke coming. "You know, Brad, I think you and Sylvester could become friends, maybe even soul mates. I'm pretty sure you should ask Sylvester and Knapp both for Christmas. You guys could be great pals."

It was difficult for Brad not to start laughing again but he was dying to hear what Sid had to say. "Maybe when this stuff is over, we can all go camping together. I'll bet you a wooden nickel that Knapp and Sylvester are the kind that love to toast marshmallows and sing campfire songs."

"It's on my calendar and this old cop is looking forward to the day we make it happen." Sid snorted in disgust before continuing. "Well, anyway, what Sylvester had to say was pretty darned interesting. He admits to working for Knapp and burglarizing homes and cars. His targets were usually places that Knapp had identified and directed him to hit. Sylvester says most places he burgled were pretty high end and he came up with all kinds of good stuff. But mostly Knapp was interested in old pottery, blankets, jewelry, anything Native American."

"No surprise there."

"Yeah but this is where the story becomes really sad and concerning. This is why I'm running non-stop with this case." Sid inhaled loudly enough that Brad could hear his concern through the phone. "Sylvester also delivered a bunch of stolen goods to other cities and states, usually with some drugs included in the shipments." Sid's voice lowered and his tone changed. "And, get ready for this, just in case you didn't already expect it. Knapp paid Sylvester in cash but a large part of his payment was sex with young girls that Knapp provided to him."

"Jesus H! Exactly what we figured."

"Yep, yep, yep. Knapp is a one in a million for sure. Every time I think about that sorry bastard and how he sat there grinning like a mangy old alley mutt that had just fucked Lassie, I get a knot in my stomach."

"No shit. But you said you had something that explained Knapp going to Clayton. What the hell is it that's been taking that pervert up to such a remote part of the world?"

"I think I can give part of the answer to that one. Sylvester says that there is some land up there that belongs to Knapp's uncle. This uncle sounds to be cut from the same bolt of cloth as Knapp, you know, they both crap in the same pot. Sylvester says this land is a ranch, farm or something like that but the only thing it's used for is to entertain the people that Knapp and his uncle want to keep happy. During certain times of the year, they let rich shits use the land for hunting. But year round, Knapp and his uncle keep the place running like the damned Mustang Ranch in Nevada. It's free girls and whatever else their pals want for a few days of fun and relaxation. Sylvester is certain about the ranch but he's never been there so can't describe it or anything. He says he's heard Knapp on the phone, arranging trips and girls for people that he's in business with."

"I guess I'm not really surprised except for the part that this is all happening near Clayton. I just never associated a small little place like that with Knapp and this kind of sick shit. It all fits Edmond Knapp to perfection but I didn't see the Clayton connection coming."

"Don't feel like the Lone Ranger cause it sure as heck surprised me too. But, there's more you need to know. Sylvester says the property is also used as something of a headquarters or clearinghouse for stolen property and artifacts. Knapp meets people there and makes all kinds of deals while they all get high on his dope and have sex with his girls."

"Good God. But you're telling me Sylvester can't give any help at all about where this pleasure palace is located?"

"Nope. All he knows is that he's heard Knapp tell people to stop in Clayton if they need anything cause the ranch, or whatever you want to call it, is out in the sticks and not close to anything." Sid gave a tired sigh. "We're working like fools to find anything in Knapp's cell records that might help us but nothing comes back to that area of the country. Sylvester doesn't know the uncle's name so we can't check property records."

"Anything in Lucy's diary to help?"

"Nothing to give a specific location but she sure as hell corroborates the story. Right at the very end of her diary, so it had to be shortly before she took her life, she entered almost an entire page about being driven for a few hours to a ranch house. She wrote about being abused by several men." Sid paused. "I'm telling you, Brad, the girl's pain is in every line of that diary."

"Holy Jesus."

"It's a goddamned heartbreak but thank heaven for that girl. If it weren't for her diary, we probably would never have found all those different cell numbers Knapp uses, not to mention a ton of other names and numbers we're still working on."

"I hear you. Anything more on this ranch?"

"Well, she wrote something that sure might be valuable at some point down the road, but we gotta do more work to bring all this together. Lucy described the road leading to the ranch house as being lined with large boulders on both sides. She mentioned a barn that looked like it was about to fall down and a bunkhouse, just behind the main home. That's where the boys enjoyed their sport with girls."

"Holy Christ. All this is a start but something more specific has to come up before anyone can do anything with this."

"Unfortunately, you are right. But Lucy did write one more thing, and if we ever find this place, it could be critical. Lucy described the main room of the house as having huge windows on two sides and a wall completely made of stone. She said right in the middle of this wall was a fireplace. And," Sid took a breath, "she described two elk heads that were mounted on either side of the fireplace. Now, FBI man, what do you think sits underneath the two elk heads?"

"I have no idea."

"Two wall safes, my friend, wall safes where she saw Knapp placing pottery, jewelry and what she thinks were packets of cocaine."

"Holy Christ, now that's specific."

"You bet your FBI ass it's specific. Remember how we talked about how Lucy's diary might someday become evidence?"

"Oh, my goodness, yes I remember. If you can find this ranch house, with everything else you have, a search warrant could get you inside those safes and in the bunkhouse in a flash."

"You are spot on." Sid sighed a discouraged sigh. "But that was a big 'if' you mentioned. We have to find the ranch house and, at this point, I have no idea where to start other than northeastern New Mexico." Sid's tone became sarcastic. "I'm guessing a tiny little area, something like maybe a couple thousand square miles. I've called Montoya, up in Clayton, but he ain't magic and sure as hell can't pinpoint anything for us."

Brad spoke softly. "I'm not sure what to make of this, but I'll definitely do some thinking." What was rolling within his mind was something he simply could not talk about with Sid: his experience in Frijoles Canyon and the image of Clayton's network of highways displayed across the face of a cliff. That was something that would have to stay just with him. "Okay, Sid thanks a million. If I have an epiphany, I'll give you a shout. If you develop anything new, I sure would appreciate a jingle."

"You've got my word. We are not going to let this one go, Brad. Every minute of police experience I have tells me that Knapp and whoever the hell else he associates with are going to keep on finding themselves a Lucy Hernandez until somebody stops them."

Once again, Brad appreciated Sid's diplomacy to not ask about his intentions. Brad knew that Sid was way too sharp to think Brad was sitting on his duff and doing nothing. "Okay, Sid. Thanks for your time and info. I'll let you go for now but don't forget about that camping trip we have planned. You bring marshmallows and I'll bring rat poison. We'll give Sylvester and Uncle Eddie the camping trip of their lives."

"I love the way you think, Brad. I may go marshmallow shopping this very afternoon. When this damned case breaks, I wanna be ready to rock and roll!"

Both men were laughing as they clicked off.

***

Clouds towered but then collapsed, creating nothing more than shadows across the mid-afternoon sky. Brad had watched as they tried to gather into something that could produce rain, certain all along that they would fail. He loved this road, Highway 522, north out of Taos and only forty-five minutes to one of his all-time favorite trout streams. On his right, the Sangre de Cristo Mountains bulged out of the desert while an eternity of open vista stretched on the left. This was classic New Mexico and exactly what he had been seeking when he decided on this afternoon's trip. His conversation with Sid had been disconcerting in that it was clear young girls remained at risk as long as Edmond Knapp was free and conducting business as usual. But with only a short time before darkness, Brad knew there was nothing to do but wait until the next day before taking his next step. Even though he was dying to get started on his plan and even though his gear was buried beneath cases of New Mexico wine, his fly rod was calling. A few hours on Costilla Creek and another plate of enchiladas were precisely what he needed to face whatever the next day held.

Making a turn at the village of Costilla, Brad headed east toward the mountains. This slice of New Mexico was special to Brad. He had been here several times with his brother, Matthew, and their friend Alton. Each time he traveled the dirt road along Costilla Creek, Brad marveled not only at the beauty of the land, but also the quiet, subdued history embedded within the cliffs and forests that defined the valley. For hundreds of years, Native Americans and Spanish settlers had cultivated and loved the soil, fresh water and stunning beauty of this region. Driving alone, Brad now wished for Matthew and Alton. Their company would have been wonderful as he drove his rig up stream. Savoring solitude, but with hints of loneliness nipping, he made it as far as he could before a locked gate blocked all vehicles. Access into much of the valley was denied until July in order to allow the local elk herd freedom from intrusion for their calving season.

Out of his vehicle and enjoying a vista of the valley and creek, Brad inhaled deeply. He held the breath and then forced it out as a way to begin his cleansing process. What an enchanting place! With thoughts of Juanita and *Abuelo* bringing solace to his mind, Brad assembled his rod and pulled on waders and boots. Except for memories, he was totally alone.

As anticipated, the moment he stepped into the creek he felt the grime of his talk with Edmond Knapp wash away. The river was alive just as Bandelier and Frijoles Canyon had been alive. Brad believed that the spirits that inhabit such magical places usually hold their secrets close, but to those who take time to listen, stories can be heard.

His selected flies were small as were the Rainbows and native Rio Grande Cutthroat that populated the stream. The wary creatures usually ignored his drifting imitations but occasionally a deceived fish rose to the surface and sipped his fly. The feel of a trout on his rod was as close to divine as anything Brad could imagine. It was the feel of his own heart and the heart of the trout coming together. As far as he was concerned, the brief moments before releasing a trout, the precious seconds in which he could admire its colors, hold it in his hand and feel the pulse of its life was like nothing else.

When the sun's angle created more shadow than reflection, he knew it was time to go. Back at his truck, rod and waders packed away, he took a last look at the stream, etching its beauty in his mind. Brad whispered into evening breeze that drifted through the valley, "I needed this."

The return drive to Taos did not disappoint. Looking to the west, the hills of Tres Piedres and San Antonio Mountain provided the backdrop for another New Mexico sunset. Thoughts of Juanita and their recent conversations were his companions as he drove. He prolonged the experience by stopping several times to get out of his truck and breathe, tasting the air and saturating his senses with memory of a trout stream, Juanita and the hush of evening.

Blue corn enchiladas and beer awaited him. Brad had no idea what to expect after this evening, but whatever it might be, the short time he had just experienced on Costilla Creek had been perfect preparation.

***

Morning diners gradually filled the patio café. Sipping coffee and savoring the decadence of a giant cinnamon roll, Brad felt perfectly at home as the shops of Bent Street came to life about him. He had shared this very table with Matthew and Alton on their last fishing trip. On that day, they had talked of trout and the streams they planned to visit. Today was a bit different. Brad had already closed his map, no longer needing it to decipher or contemplate what he must do next. It had been relatively easy to identify where to go. What the heck would unfold once he got there was another matter entirely. All he knew to do was to enjoy his coffee and the big fat cinnamon roll. Next, he would leave a message for Juanita and then head back to Clayton. Beyond that, he would just have to figure it out on the fly.

For a moment he thought about calling Robert Montoya. On one hand, Brad longed to talk things over with a man like Montoya but the pointless nature of such a conversation quickly obliterated any real consideration of making the call. What in the name of heaven could he say? Could he relate his experience with *Abuelo* and then tell of his night in Frijoles Canyon? He finished his coffee, left money on the table and walked away. He had a smile on his face as he thought of Sam and Sid. He could only imagine what their reaction would be if he should tell them of *Abuelo* or how he saw cracks in a cliff as a sign of what he should do. Montoya would probably lock him up.

Brad made a final stroll from Bent Street to his motel. He loaded his truck, checked out and left a message for Juanita. Feeling like a boomerang, he began another drive to Clayton. He had no idea what was about to happen but every instinct in his body told him that he would be far away from the peace of Taos when the story of Lucy Hernandez and Edmond Knapp came to an end.

***

It was just past noon when he made Clayton. A stop for lunch was nothing more than an excuse to get one more look inside the Eklund hotel and saloon. While waiting for iced tea and a sandwich, Brad walked through the hotel's lobby to limber his legs. He again admired the woodwork and architecture of the saloon and, when he walked past the photographs depicting the hanging of Black Jack Ketchum, he thought of Sid and Montoya.

He recalled how they had laughed at his reaction to the gruesome images and a grin unconsciously crossed his face.

Following his scrutiny of the barroom, Brad guessed that today's crowd was mostly local since no one seemed to be paying any attention at all to photographs of the decapitated outlaw. The second clue that cinched his judgment was that cowboy hats, jeans and boots were definitely the wardrobe of choice, not a single pair of red shorts or sandals were in sight. Already grinning, Brad's face broke into full smile as he thought of Louise. It seemed a year ago that they had laughed together. Now that some time had passed, he wondered what she was thinking about her late night experience with voices and ringing bells. Did she doubt her own senses or would she have come to accept that some things occasionally happen for which there simply is no logical explanation? He had known Louise only briefly but Brad felt certain of the answer; Louise would never say a word to anyone, but she knew damn well what she had heard and that someone had visited her in the hotel's lobby. Brad took comfort in the memory of Louise. Even if they never saw each other again, Louise and he shared a special secret.

***

Leaving Clayton, an arching bridge elevated the highway, taking drivers over a railroad track. In a panoramic moment, the road offered a glimpse of the immensity of the land and the geological power that had shaped this corner of New Mexico. Yawning canyons fractured the rangeland and Brad felt small. This was land where one could be blown away or simply swallowed by the earth.

Once his elevated perspective was lost and the road leveled, Brad locked his speed at seventy but still felt he was scarcely moving. Within such emptiness, isolation gripped like blight and highway markings became hypnotic. He felt loneliness and thoughts of Juanita hung heavy. She seemed so far away and he realized how desperate he was simply to hear her voice. For the first time since leaving Taos, a wave of self-doubt descended and hit hard. What in the name of hell was he doing in this forsaken section of nowhere when Juanita was in Albuquerque? Why was he so intent on following an instinct that defied rational thought to the point he was embarrassed to even tell anyone where he was going? If he told Juanita about Frijoles Canyon and where he was now heading, would the enchanting woman of his dreams quietly roll her eyes and tell him to seek professional counsel?

"This is fucking insanity." Brad spoke out loud as he jammed his brakes and careened from the pavement onto a dirt road. With dust billowing and neglected ruts jolting every bone in his body, Brad scarcely noticed the obscure road sign that identified his newly arrived destination as Mt. Dora.

Bringing his truck to a skidding halt beside a clump of nearly dead trees, Brad sat in frustrated silence. The dust cloud he had created hung in animated suspension directly over his truck, refusing to move. "Jesus H, what am I doing here?" With his swear, he threw open his door and stepped through the swirls of grit, the taste of dirt instantly in his mouth and nose. Silent curses firing in his head, he walked away, spat and cleared his lungs with a deep exhale.

"Be a frigging miracle if a cell phone works from here." Brad practically forced his fingers through the case of his phone as he punched the pad for Juanita. It was her voice mail but at least it was her voice. He held his eyes shut as he listened, bringing her inside his head. When a beep signaled that it was time for him to speak, Brad looked up to the sky. "This is crazy, Juanita. I have a million things to tell you but I can't say them to a goofy machine. I'm thinking of you a hundred times a day and hoping everything is going okay for you in your trial." He lowered his eyes from the sky and stared at the ground. "I sure do need to see you and talk with you," Brad concluded in a gentle tone. "Bye for now. Hopefully we will talk soon."

Pocketing his phone and his insides in turmoil, Brad began to walk. He needed to get his head straight. All he wanted to think about was Juanita, but that would do no good. If he was going to continue with the business of Lucy Hernandez and Edmond Knapp, some decisions about what the hell he should do had to be made right now. Had gone he completely nuts? Had his night in Bandelier and Frijoles Canyon really meant anything or had he become delusional? Eyes on the ground and absently kicking at the dirt, Brad moved slowly.

"Holy Jesus. If I told anybody this they would think I'm looney as a shithouse rat!" Brad tried to analyze the workings of his mind. Until only a few minutes ago, he had felt some level of confidence in what he was doing. What had caused him to suddenly be filled with doubt? Was it something in this land? He could see forever but the sense of isolation was borderline strangling. He surveyed the landscape. He did not have to be a geologist to intuitively understand that nothing here had changed for a million years. And, if he could return to this very place in another million, not a thing would have changed.

Brad shook his head, wondering at his own actions and behavior. Why had he suddenly felt compelled to stop here? Why had he not experienced such misgivings before now? He contemplated but no answers came.

Brad again walked. Thinking of the final lines in *Abuelo's* letter, he sauntered with his eyes locked on the ground. He had already met the serpent, he was certain of that. Edmond Knapp was despicable, a man to be hated. *Abuelo's* words about the serpent living near the fire were the part he wasn't sure about.

After his night in Frijoles Canyon and seeing what appeared to be a map on the canyon wall, along with Sid Pruitt's information about Knapp utilizing a ranch near Clayton, Brad had made a decision as best he could. He was going to the only place that made sense. That's where he had been heading when this bout of skepticism struck.

The earsplitting scream slammed his body with the force of an explosion. Brad felt the marrow within his bones curdle as the freight train, horn blaring, thundered past, missing him by only inches. The ground beneath his feet trembled like an earthquake as tons of steel practically brushed his body. Feeling that he moved in slow motion, Brad teetered before leaping backwards, giving his body safe space as the thundering rail cars roared by.

A hammering heart continued to pound within his head after the final car rumbled into the distance. In a stunned daze, he listened to the train's metallic dissonance fade. Gathering his thoughts, what had happened began to settle in a chilling realization. He had been so completely absorbed in thoughts of what the hell he was going to do, he had not recognized that he had walked to within inches of a railway track; a railway track with a freight train coming at full speed! "Jesus." Even though he spoke in a faint whisper, his voice cracked.

After a few seconds, and in spite of being shaken to this core, Brad couldn't help but grin as he wondered who had been the most surprised. Was it the fool named Brad who had been in a brain-dead trance when the train's whistle had shrieked or had it been the poor engineer on the train. What must have gone through that poor man's mind when in the middle of this vast emptiness, he saw some idiot about to step right into his path?

Breath coming more normally, Brad now took notice of the immediate surroundings he had previously ignored. A clump of trees displayed meager signs of life, their gnarled trunks standing among a thriving forest of weeds. Not until he stepped into the weeds and looked closely at the surface beneath, did Brad recognize that he stood within the remnants of a crumbling foundation, the only remains of what looked to have been a house. As he more closely examined his discovery, he was astonished at how close the building would have been to the railroad tracks. "Jesus, only a few feet," Brad whispered in amazement. Thinking of the noise and unspeakable clamor he had just endured in his near miss with the freight train, Brad stood in awe as he contemplated what it must have been like when the steel giants roared past this home.

Glancing up for a larger view of the area, he saw other similar stands of trees and mounds of weeds along the tracks. He vaguely recalled the road sign labeling this place as Mt. Dora and Brad realized that he was standing in what had at one time been a village of sorts, probably existing solely to support the railroad. Once again in absolute silence, he felt as if he were in a museum of imagination. What life and labor had transpired here? Brad looked about in a sweeping circle. Had a family lived here? Had children played in these trees? Was it possible that the sound their voices could still be heard somewhere in the unrelenting winds?

In a contemplative walk, Brad returned to his truck. Aside from concern that with his near miss with a freight train a full decade of his life had been frightened right out of his body, he now felt fine. He didn't know if it was the screaming train or the bleached skeleton of an abandoned Mt. Dora that was responsible, but Brad once again felt confidence in where he was headed. As he opened the door of his rig and in a final glance at Mt. Dora, he spoke into the emptiness, "Let's get this over with."

Brad fired his truck and made his way back to the highway. He knew where he was going.

***

After leaving Mt. Dora, the terrain and character of the land quickly changed. Ridgelines of black volcanic rock appeared. Trees crowded into gullies where water from rare downpours cut sharply into the earth. In the distance Brad spotted the distinctive profile of a substantial mountain. He knew from studying his map that he looked at Sierra Grande, an incredible mound of volcanic debris that towered over endless prairies. He also saw that grey storm clouds were gathering behind the landmark mountain. He also somberly recognized that these boys had real shoulders. They were building with a strength that meant a New Mexico squall lurked behind Sierra Grande, an ambush in waiting.

Passing through Des Moines, a ranch and rail settlement desperately clinging to life, Brad pressed his accelerator a bit harder. He had to get there ahead of whatever storms might be brewing. In minutes, he slowed for his turn.

A sign beside the highway identified Brad's intended destination, CAPULIN NATIONAL MONUMENT, and a directional arrow marked the way. He thought to himself that the sign certainly wasn't necessary as he was face-to-face with a cone-shaped mountain, practically perfect in its symmetrical ascent to over eight thousand feet. Approaching the ancient tower of ash that had once spewed fire and molten rocks for hundreds of miles, he again felt a sense of insignificance within this staggering landscape. The volcano had been sleeping for centuries but Brad still felt its power. Surely this was it. This had to be the big fire of *Abuelo*'s message. "I hope to hell this is the right place." Brad's mutter was lost to the sound of his engine and gravel striking the underside of his truck.

With no idea of what else to do, Brad paid his fee at the visitor's center. Then, following a narrow road that encircled the frame of Capulin Mountain, he spiraled upward. Upon reaching the summit and parking in a designated lot, Brad left his truck and stood in quiet awe.

Reading from the brochure he had been given at the visitor's center, Brad learned that he stood on a volcanic cone about sixty thousand years old. It took a few moments to grasp the incredible nature of this formation. The mountain was practically hollow. Standing on the rim, Brad looked down, peering into what looked to be the throat of a prehistoric beast. The crater descended hundreds of feet, burrowing into the very bowels of the earth. "Lord have mercy," Brad spoke reverently as he imagined the unimaginable forces that had billowed fire, smoke and stone into the sky.

Reluctant to remove his eyes from the ominous subterranean shaft that seemed to glower back at him, fearful that it may roar back to life at any second, Brad turned to observe the surrounding country from this sky-high perspective. What he viewed challenged his imagination and sense of comprehension. Molten stone had flowed in rivers that now lay in frozen, catatonic limbo. Their courses, twisting and turning in the manner that all rivers flow, had created an alluvial plain of solidified lava. Suspended in time and holding cataclysmic power if ever the cryogenic state should awaken, the land lay in eerie stillness. Wind was the only sound.

Brad felt that he stood on the cusp of creation. He attempted to fathom the eons of time. He remembered the crumbled remains of Mt. Dora and contemplated the lives that had been lived beneath the shadow of this slumbering mountain of fire. In a mere blink, those lives had passed. Did they now sleep just as Capulin Mountain slept? Brad thought of Elizabeth and their children, how quickly life passes and how decades become lifetimes that meld into centuries. Brad took a deep breath.

Juanita filled his thoughts. He knew that she would love to see this.

His trance may have lasted indefinitely but for a flash of lightning that ripped the sky near Sierra Grande. It was miles away and the ensuing rumbles were distant and non-threatening but Brad knew that could change in a heartbeat. With a sigh of resignation, he forced his mind back to the mission at hand. He looked about hopelessly. He had made it here but what now? The diary of Lucy Hernandez and Sid Pruitt's investigation spoke of a remote ranch site used by Edmond Knapp. Brad scanned the vista surrounding Capulin Mountain. Its enormity was intimidating. "I'm probably looking at the damned place but how the hell am I supposed to know?" He kicked at a stone as he mumbled.

Returning to his rig, Brad retrieved the binoculars he always carried and, sensing a weather change, he grabbed his windbreaker. The temperature was chilling noticeably and the smell of a storm hung in the air. Finding support by leaning against a wood sign in the parking lot, he meticulously scoured the landscape. With the aid of binoculars, it was a whole new perspective. In magnified detail, he studied the spiny fingers of lava flows that webbed from Capulin Mountain. Fascinated at the handiwork of the violence that had once occurred here, Brad traced the ridges and troughs beyond the mountain's base to where they ultimately fused into flattened terrain. In these distant miles, chalky soil of ranch roads sliced the land in precise, razor-like etchings.

Lowering his binoculars, Brad realized that depending on the direction he gazed, his view extended well beyond New Mexico. Oklahoma, Texas or Colorado became the distant horizons. "Good Lord, this makes the old needle in a haystack a piece of cake." Brad scanned the entire panorama. Glancing again to building storm clouds in the west, he squatted to the ground, found a rock to sit on and closed his eyes. He forced his mind into a re-run of everything that had transpired to bring him to stand on this spire of cinders. What was he missing? With an ocean of land, space and time surrounding Capulin Mountain, there had to be something. A starting point was all he needed. Surely there was a clue of some sort.

Wind now blew harder across his face and thunder rolled like an angry voice coming from the sky. Something clicked. It had taken hours and the arrival of a full moon for Brad to wake up in Frijoles Canyon, open his eyes and see the obvious design of cracks in a cliff right before his eyes. Now, in the wake of thunder over Capulin Mountain, Brad realized that just as in Bandelier, he was looking but was not seeing.

Purging his lungs with rapidly cooling air, he thought he knew what to look for but he had to do it fast. Zipping his jacket to the throat, Brad began walking the rim, his eyes once again looking down the mountain's side. But this time he did not want the benefit of binoculars. It wasn't up-close detail he should be looking for but the large, all-encompassing picture. He wished to be a bird or to have an airplane. That was the perspective he needed.

"Look to the south and east first," Brad mumbled to himself, his heart pounding with anticipation. That was the direction back to Clayton and the restaurant that Edmond Knapp frequented. He needed more elevation. Brad raced to his rig and wheeled it into a position that offered the best view to the southeast. Jumping out, he noticed that the impending storm had frightened all other visitors and their vehicles out the parking area and off the mountain. Brad was alone. "Screw it, I have to get this done." Every few seconds lightning now sizzled between Capulin Mountain and Sierra Grande. Thunder jolted the air in shock waves that penetrated to Brad's core. The beautiful afternoon of only an hour ago was now frigid and wind ripped at his light jacket.

"Please, Jesus, don't fry my ass with lightning. I just need a few seconds." Grabbing the rack mounted to the roof of his rig, Brad hoisted and kicked his body onto the truck's roof. For a split second he lay prone over his vehicle, breath now in gasps in what had developed into an all-out gale. Scarcely able to maintain balance, Brad gulped as he stood and stretched his six foot-three inch frame as far as he could possibly manage. Praying that he would remain alive for a few more seconds, he braced his body in a wide stance and, fighting panic, scanned his eyes over the edge of Capulin Mountain.

It was so easy. It was absolutely easy and so incredibly obvious. Brad's breath sucked even as he tried to speak out loud. Streaking the mountain's side from its midpoint, three jagged flows of petrified lava carved a twisting path. They came together at the base to form a single river of black stone that flowed arrow straight into the rangeland beyond the mountain. Terrified as he was, Brad laughed out loud. As the giant lava flow dissolved into flat land, it took no more imagination to see it than it had to see a map etched across the cliff in Bandelier; randomly scattered boulders formed a near-perfect compass needle that pointed to the southeast.

He had what he needed. Dropping to the prone position and with a quick roll, Brad was off his truck and back on solid ground. Now that he knew where to look, it would be easy. Wind howled and lightning was incessant. "Son-of-a bitch, it's cold!" Grabbing his binoculars again, he focused on what lay beyond the mountain, exactly where the tip of the needle pointed. Once again, easy as pie, the ranch house was exactly where the arrow said it would be. With his naked eye he would never have spotted it, but the binoculars easily picked up boulders lining a long drive from the primary ranch road. There was everything else Lucy had described in her diary: a crumbling barn and a bunkhouse just off the rear of the main house. Brad lowered the binoculars. "Holy Jesus, I found it." In the howling wind, his words were in Oklahoma before he finished speaking. Gales clawed at Brad's jacket. Granules of hurled debris stung his face.

He thought he could remember, but he sketched it out just to be sure. It would be easy enough to track back to the main road and follow the pattern of dirt roads to the ranch. The place looked deserted but from this distance, it was impossible to be certain. Brad found his hand trembling as he moved his pen over paper. He lied to himself saying it was because of the cold. A racing heart told the true story.

All he need was ten seconds to peek through a window. He had no doubt that he would see a wall constructed of stone, a fireplace, two elk heads and two safes. That's all he needed, ten lousy seconds and he could give Sid Pruitt and Robert Montoya everything they needed for a search warrant.

From what Brad had seen through binoculars, he didn't think any vehicles were around the ranch but he couldn't be sure. He whispered a prayer that his initial instinct was correct but, either way, what he intended to do remained the same. No way in hell was he waiting around, sneaking like a secret squirrel, just to try and spy on the damned place. Ten lousy seconds, that's all he would need!

He started his engine and blew warm breath into his hand with a muttered swear. "God Almighty, it turned cold." Brad turned his truck and began the drive from Capulin Mountain.

Once off of the mountain and back on flat land, Brad drove from his memory of the ranch roads he had seen from Capulin's summit. He kept the rough map he had sketched on the seat beside him for an occasional glance but he never doubted where he was in relation to the ranch house.

The first hailstone bounced harmlessly from the hood of his truck, followed by sporadic bursts. Pellets of ice not much larger than peas pinged and ricocheted from hood to windshield. Within the truck's cab, the noise was nothing more than a loud popping, much like heating popcorn.

Brad was only yards away from the turn that would put him on the boulder-lined drive to Edmond Knapp's ranch when the gates of a frozen hell opened in unmitigated fury. Within seconds, the small peas transformed into huge balls of ice that bombarded from the sky. Battering his truck in ear-crushing explosions, the storm's ferocity stunned Brad. He had seen plenty of hailstorms but nothing like this. His vehicle shuddered as tires suddenly were mired in frozen muck. Chunks of ice, catapulted from the heavens, assaulted the body of his truck. Sensing that he was literally under an artillery attack of ice, Brad swallowed hard and engaged four-wheel drive. He feared that his windows would shatter or that his roof might fail, leaving him vulnerable to death by bludgeoning and burial in a trash heap of ice. Slowing to a crawl and in stark fear, Brad repeatedly mumbled the only words that seemed remotely appropriate, "Holy shit, holy shit!"

Submerged in a world of white and without intending to do so, Brad sucked his breath hard and held until his lungs burned. Feeling as if he was drowning and, after another repetitious stream of "holy shit" exclamations, he gave up cursing for silent but desperate prayers that he was steering his truck in a straight line. Seeking the delicate balance on the accelerator to avoid a spin but not become mired in the slush, he inched forward, his heart thundering. He moved forward totally blind to any visual reference and with full knowledge that disorientation was worsening by the second. He dared not stop for fear that he would be unable to regain momentum. "Please, God, don't let me screw this up." Brad crept forward. The noise had become so deafening his instinct was to bury his head and curl into a ball until the nightmare ended. Not an option. He kept moving. Palms sticky with sweat, Brad held his gaze straight as he strained not to deviate from where he prayed the road should be.

Almost as quickly as it had begun, the hail miraculously stopped. Straggling marbles of ice continued to bounce across his ice-covered hood in whimpering thuds but the sudden silence seemed eerily louder than the terror that had just passed. Able to see again, Brad eased his foot from the accelerator, coasting to a halt in inches of muck. He saw that he had barely managed to remain on the road; his front right tire was only a hair from striking one of the boulders that lined the drive. He thought a quick prayer of thanks, realizing that another second and he would have collided into the stone with no knowledge of how to back up and correct his course.

With the clearing sky, a starkly changed world greeted Brad. Winter white now startled the landscape and his senses. Brad felt he had been transported to a frozen desert on a distant planet. "Good God!" Brad sat with both hands still in a death-grip on his wheel, allowing his breath to settle and heart to recover.

He was still a good quarter mile from the ranch house. Not a hint of life could be spotted. Brad sensed that he was alone but knew he couldn't count on it. Gathering his wits, the purpose of why he had come here began to again emerge within his mind. Taking deep breaths and forcing his emotions to settle, he was back in focus. "Ten seconds, Lord, just give me ten seconds to get a look inside that house."

Still in four-wheel drive, Brad coaxed his truck back to the center of the road and continued. The sky remained obscured enough that if anyone were home, lights should have been turned on within the ranch house. The dwelling remained dark. "Jesus, this is weird. It feels like January." As he had always done when in threatening situations, Brad talked to himself. Even if whispered, the sound of his voice brought some level of relief. Hoping a dark house was a good sign that he was alone Brad drove closer. Even though he knew the storm could have knocked out power, the dark house just exuded an empty look. Things were feeling right. "I'm going to catch a break here. Ten seconds. Ten seconds."

Once he made it to the front of the premises, he saw that an expansive circular drive separated the house from the barn. Ample parking space existed with room for ranch equipment and multiple vehicles. Brad turned his rig for a straight shot back to the road in case he needed to make a quick retreat.

Then it started. It was down in his gut; apprehension for sure, maybe a twinge of guilt for trespassing. But outright fear was rapidly creeping into the mix. All of a sudden his earlier optimism that this was going to be quick and easy began to slip away. He recognized the sensation of cotton filling his mouth. None of these feelings were new. He had felt them plenty of times but things were different now. He had no badge and no authority. He was completely on his own. "Ten seconds, Lord. Give me ten little seconds."

In a quick survey, he determined that house was nothing extraordinary. Brad estimated three bedrooms, sprawled on one level with the bunkhouse in the rear.

So far so good, still no sign of life. Stepping from his truck, his running shoes were instantly soaked. His feet submerged in slush and hail covered the tops as water saturated his socks. Icy cold seeped between his toes and each step squished. It was like walking in freezing mud. His nerves electrified and his eyes riveted for any hint of life, Brad made his way to the side of the ranch house, the logical place to find the windows that Lucy had described. "Please God, don't let there be curtains drawn."

Brad may as well have been wading in a river. His feet were soaked and cold was beginning to sting in spite of his fear. There was the window. No curtains! "Come on, come on, just a few more seconds." With a sharp inhale, he cupped his hands beside his eyes and pressed his face to the glass. It was all there. Brad saw exactly what he had hoped to see, what he expected to see: the wall of stone, a fireplace, two elk heads and, most importantly, two monstrous safes.

"Thank you God, thank you!"

Brad had no idea of the sequence. Did he hear the violent crack before the pain of a shock wave registered in his ear or was it the other way around? Exactly when did the window shatter? Then he knew. A second rifle shot passed over his head so close he felt its wind blow his hair. Now on his stomach, hands clawing and legs kicking as a novice swimmer, Brad rolled, crawled and kicked through frozen muck. Desperate for the protection of his truck, he flailed. Another shot. In a sickening thud, the bullet impacted just beneath his writhing torso.

With panic now coming in wheezing gasps, Brad made it to the rear of his truck and crouched behind a tire. Not that he had stopped to look around, but in the terrifying seconds of his scramble for cover Brad had seen what he needed to see: a pickup truck stopped on the road about seventy-five yards from the ranch house. A man stood beside the truck, rifle in hand, intent on killing the person he had caught peering into the window of the ranch house. Even though he had seen the man for less than a blink, Brad knew without a doubt that the man who stalked him was Edmond Knapp.

Every breath felt like fire and seared his lungs. But craving oxygen, Brad continued to suck in desperation. While crawling through the slush, globs of ice had become trapped under his shirt, jacket and jeans. Even in a state of fear, it flashed through his brain that he was completely soaked and debilitating cold was only minutes away.

He was safe only for the moment. Brad had to think clearly if he was going to survive. It was surely a ranch truck that Knapp drove and practically all ranchers kept rifles in their trucks. That part was easy. Did he have a handgun? That was a tougher question. Knapp had just been released from jail. A gun had been confiscated. Would he risk being caught again with a concealed weapon? It was fifty-fifty.

A roaring engine and the whine of tires spinning through inches-deep hail sounded like an approaching jet. Knapp was coming to him and coming fast. Brad was a sitting duck. Where to go? His mind threatened to blur but he forced clarity. If a rifle were Knapp's only weapon, close quarters would be the best environment. A handgun meant trouble under any circumstances. Knapp was almost upon him. At least he couldn't shoot a rifle while driving. Holding his breath and now relying on sheer instinct, Brad left the protection of his truck and sprinted to the dilapidated barn.

Doors hung open wide and their gaping hole offered the only source of light. Dashing inside and making a turn, Brad removed his silhouette from the doorway but the sudden darkness stopped him instantly. Blinking violently, he tried to adjust. He heard the truck come to a halt just outside the barn.

Jesus, he couldn't see. The truck's door opened. Brad felt something hard under his foot. The truck door slammed shut. He reached to the floor. It felt like an ax handle. He had a weapon.

"If it ain't my good friend from the jail house." Knapp had not yet entered the barn but his shouting was easily heard. "I recognized that piece-of-shit truck of yours and was happy as all hell. You have no idea how much I love having guests like you on my ranch." Knapp howled in laughter. He still had not set foot inside the barn. "Where's that fucking partner of yours? He get tired of the taste of your dick and run off looking for some fresh sausage?"

Brad's eyes had adjusted enough to see he had crappy options. The barn was a wide-open layout with no place for decent cover. A hayloft hung precariously with no visible way to access it. Knapp's Mercedes sat in the middle of the barn's floor.

"I'm getting this special gun of mine all loaded up. You got nowhere to go and your scrawny ass is gonna look like Swiss cheese when I get finished."

It was so damned dark! Brad squinted. In the back corner was a staircase leading down. An underground storage room, it had to be. There was no other option. It would buy him time and possibly a better place for a confrontation. This was it. Praying that he would not trip over some piece of unseen junk and fall flat, Brad made his move. Calculating that Knapp would not know if the Mercedes was being used for concealment, Brad tried to maintain silence as he headed toward the staircase but the squishing of his shoes sounded like a percussion orchestra.

"Any last wishes? Let me know. I'm really a nice guy. I like to make my friends happy."

Brad stood on the brink of the steps. God, it was even darker going down. He counted five steps down and then barely made out the outline of a door, half hanging on hinges. Hopefully it would be confining and Knapp's rifle would be awkward as he came through the door. Brad would be ready with the ax handle.

"You and that truck of yours are going to have a nice long sleep at the bottom of a big-ass lake we have on the ranch. Maybe some exploring Boy Scouts will find your bones someday, in about two hundred years." Knapp howled. It was more of a shriek.

Inching, Brad took the steps one at a time. His heart pounded so violently, he feared Knapp would hear. Standing on the last step, he reached to touch the door.

Knapp was inside the barn, making no effort at stealth, his boots clamored on the barn's floor.

Fingertips on the door, Brad felt it give. The wood was dry and splintering. If the door opened at all, it would surely squeak but what the hell. He pressed harder. The door swung open in absolute silence. It took a second for Brad to gain a glimmer of bearings of what faced him. He squeezed his eyes to bring things into focus. Light came from somewhere but was obscured, dusky and indistinct. The room was just a hole dug into the dirt. About eight feet square with dirt walls, crumbling and bleached from decades of no sun, the room's size was perfect advantage to Brad if Knapp tried to use a rifle.

"Okay you son-of-a-bitch get ready to meet that God of yours." Knapp was walking with purpose, straight for the corner and the steps.

He had to move. Brad saw the source of the murky light. A window well, several feet below the ground's surface allowed nebulous haze into the room. He lifted one foot at a time, easing his body into what felt like an earthen crypt. He sidestepped right, toward the window well, pressing his back against a dirt wall. Cold breath of entombed soil brushed against his spine and crumbling soil trickled down his neck. Brad shuddered, crouched his body and gripped the ax handle.

Knapp had stopped walking. Brad held his breath, straining to hear. The taste of fear flooded his saliva glands. He fought the urge to spit.

Knapp was not moving. Where the hell was he?

Holding breath deep in his lungs, Brad closed his eyes and listened with everything he had. The sound was almost imperceptible but its frequency registered in the hairs of his neck. It was that of rustling leaves, a sound he had heard as a kid when wind blew through an old garage on a fall day and leaves rustled without stopping. Something was terribly wrong. He squinted, slowly discerning something his brain desperately wished to deny. The floor was moving! A terror more sickening than anything he had ever known cycled in electric pulses through his spine and into his marrow. His tongue became numb. Disbelief became nauseating reality. The dirt floor was a mass of writhing rattlesnakes.

Slithering and entwined, their bodies found traction against one another in sluggish but perpetual motion to create the sound he was hearing. In an unconscious flash, Brad realized the snakes had taken refuge from the hailstorm in the cellar. They moved slowly because of the cold. His legs quivered, threatening to collapse. He craved unconsciousness. Vomit coagulated in his throat.

"You are one dumb-ass son-of-a-bitch." Knapp's shouting now seemed distant, as practically the only thing Brad's brain could discern was the mass of serpents about his feet. Knapp barked a sharp laugh. "What are you, a fucking Boy Scout? I don't think you were prepared for today. Isn't that your motto, always be prepared? Probably some fat, faggot Scout leader was more interested in ramming his dick up your ass than teaching you that important lesson." Knapp's feet moved across the barn's floor. "You didn't want to face me straight on, did you? Nope, no balls for that. You thought you could sneak around when I wasn't here." More steps across the floor. "I sure as hell surprised a few Boy Scout turds right out of you when I fired that first shot." Knapp laughed as if in a comedy routine. "I wish I had a movie of you crawling and hopping over that ice, trying to get away." Knapp's laughter sounded hysterical. "You looked like a goddamned worm trying to fuck a cockroach."

Laughter subsiding, Knapp lowered his voice. "Now look at you. You've gone and trapped your little weenie in the old cellar. In case you haven't figured it out yet, you have no way out, you dumb ass, no way out but through the door you just entered and I'm standing right here. You are all fucking mine."

Knapp ceased speaking leaving only the sound of snakes.

"This is just a little bit different from when I was handcuffed in that jailhouse, ain't it dick breath? Oh yeah, things are a whole lot different today!"

Brad's mind moved in a daze. Initially, he had not feared a physical struggle with Knapp. But hand-to-hand combat in a rattlesnake den was not what he had planned. If Knapp made it through the door and they fought over his rifle, they would both go down. If Knapp recklessly charged into the room, he would go straight into the snakes. But, if he approached cautiously, as he almost certainly would, there would be no second chance to take him out. With both hands, Brad tightened his grip about the ax handle.

"I could just set this old barn on fire and roast you alive. That would sure as hell be a kick in the ass." Knapp's voice was shrill. "But let me tell you something, every once in a while the boys and I still use this barn. Yes we do. I want this barn just as it is and I want you dead. I'm going to kill your ass straight up and use you to feed my catfish. Right here in my own lake." Brad wasn't sure which was more hideous, Knapp's laughter or standing in a pit that teemed with serpents.

The snakes seemed to be becoming more active, probably because of the screaming from just above. Brad didn't know how much longer his legs could support him. His clothing was drenched and felt himself going numb with either cold or fear. Then something registered, something in his periphery. He either had initially missed it in the poor light or it had just appeared; a solitary rattler lay fully stretched along the dirt sill of the window well. Dry spit settled like sand in his mouth. Knees quaking, Brad tried to think. The snake was only a couple of feet from his face, at eye level, lying perfectly still. If Knapp should do anything to startle the lethargic creature, a coil and strike could happen in a blink.

Knapp was on the steps, his footsteps banging and loud. Brad was sure that the lack of light was all that kept him from charging into the room.

"Say your prayers you asshole. After I blow your kneecaps off, I'll do you the favor of a bullet in your brain."

The snakes sensed danger. What had been the sound of rustling leaves became a static-like hum. The floor appeared to levitate as the serpents twisted en-mass, elevating their heads to better evaluate the approaching predator. The snake beside Brad's face slithered just enough to curl, the first step of a full coil.

His decision was pure guttural instinct. With a twist of his body, Brad slammed the ax handle onto the rattler's body and, in an act of lightning-fast courage he never imagined possible, he grasped the stunned snake just behind its diamond shaped head. Like raw electricity, jolts of sheer terror pulsed. He felt detached from his body, as if he observed from an elevated perspective.

Brad's dazed brain translated events in slow motion. He saw his arm lift the snake, its rippling muscles writhing in astonishing strength. Like a tattered rag in a storm, the snake flailed in mid-air before whipping into a coil about his forearm.

An explosion reverberated within the tiny room in bone crushing waves. Back to reality, Brad held the rattler at arm's length, realizing that Knapp had fired into the room, not with a rifle, but a shotgun. The snakes were no longer sluggish. The pit erupted into the sound of a high voltage power line. The floor boiled.

Within Brad's hand, the enraged serpent again flailed, lunging with herculean strength. Brad felt the surging body inch through his grip with each thrust. Another explosion from the shotgun. No more time.

Edmond Knapp and Brad practically collided as Knapp stepped into the cellar with an immediate pivot, his shotgun seeking Brad. Defying his paralysis of fear, Brad stepped directly into Knapp. The shotgun's barrel slid beneath his arm, brushing past his ribs until it lodged beneath his armpit. The weapon discharged again in a blinding flash and ear-shattering concussion. For a millionth of a second, time within the serpent-infested cellar froze. Edmond Knapp and Brad breathed into each other's face, exchanged body heat. Time resumed. The rattlesnake's fury found its target; snapping its body about Knapp's neck, fangs buried into soft cheek tissue, just below an eye that was now wide with terror.

With a violent shove into Knapp's back, knocking him onto the cellar floor, Brad leapt up the steps. Pitiful sounds bubbled from his mouth in ragged, wheezing gasps. In a stupor, Brad staggered toward the light of the barn's entrance.

On his knees, hands grasping the bumper of his truck, vomit finally came. Spasm after spasm, his insides erupted in repulsion. When finished, he held to his vehicle as if it were his savior. Too weak to lift his body or even raise his head, Brad simply held on. Mucus stung within his nostrils and streaks of gore dangled from his mouth. Closing his eyes and holding a deep breath, he listened. The shrieks that had been coming from within the barn had gone silent.

Utilizing his truck for support, Brad pulled himself from the ground. The hail had settled and was rapidly becoming a glacier-like mass of compacted ice. He was soaked and freezing. He still shivered but knew this time it was borderline hypothermia, not a den of snakes. Just that simple realization warmed him a bit.

Looking around, Brad assessed his circumstances. Within hours, the hail would vanish and not a clue of his presence would remain. No tracks in the road. Nothing. Even his vomit would dissolve into the earth. He surveyed the ranch house and then looked to the barn. The opened doors yawned wide as if they dared one to enter. Standing still, Brad listened to cathedral silence that came from within its darkened void. Gathering himself and releasing his support from the truck, he stepped toward the driver's door. Giving his head a sad shake, his whisper was scarcely audible even to his own ears, "Hunting accident."

Starting his engine and with a quick check to be sure four-wheel drive was still engaged, he eased his rig through slush. With distance growing between him and what he had just experienced, Brad cast a glance into his rearview mirror. The ranch house of Edmond Knapp and its crumbling barn faded; grey light of a stormy sky enveloped the barn in a cold shadow.

In less than a mile there was not a trace of hail. There was ample evidence that torrential rain had ravaged the ever-thirsty land but the winter scape was gone. He was almost to the highway when he jammed his brakes hard. In a panic, Brad jumped from his rig and felt through the material of his saturated jeans. Thank God! Juanita's pendant was still there. He could not imagine if he had somehow lost it while crawling through ice, water and mud. He knew that it would be impossible to go back to the ranch and search; his daily dose of courage was all used up. Brad pulled her pendant from his pocket, more than ever he yearned to feel its warmth.

The angry sky of such a short time ago was now clearing. Brad stood by his truck, terror of the past minutes still roiling inside. He looked around and realized that now that he was safely removed from the ranch, the best thing he could do was to take a few minutes and give himself time to calm down.

He allowed time to pass and gave his shivering body an opportunity to settle. With no sense of time or how long he stood, Brad finally realized what was happening in the sky. He was stunned by the majesty. To the west, the sun hung low, just touching the horizon. Clouds that had earlier attacked with monstrous power now tumbled in harmless billows, scattering like giant dandelions across the vast New Mexico sky. Shafts of light pierced through the dispersing vapors, appearing as ethereal beams straight from God himself. Brad stood in awe at the display of cosmic wonder. The sky was literally unfolding before his eyes.

He shifted his gaze not wanting any aspect of this marvelous spectacle to escape unseen. But when the profile of Capulin Mountain came into view, Brad froze. Every light in heaven appeared to shine directly down onto the conical spire. As if fire burned from within, the mountain glowed in hues of orange, radiating upward into the sky. Wisps of clouds drifted over the rim, casting an illusion that the mountain yet breathed fire from a bubbling inferno. "Oh, my God. Oh, my God, this is so beautiful." Standing beneath the illuminated mountain, Brad remained motionless, marveling at what he witnessed and comprehending the magnitude of the forces that had sculpted this land.

But something more than being witness to natural beauty was happening here. What was it? Gradual realization made Brad smile. Savoring the moment, he breathed deep, not wanting to let go of this special moment but understanding that it was not his decision to make. Brad had no choice. Looking directly to Capulin Mountain as it glowed like an ember, Brad felt a sad reticence. Was this *Abuelo*'s way of saying farewell? Light faded and Capulin lost its glow.

Back in his truck, Juanita's pendant in hand, Brad drove. How long had it been since he left his house to talk with Sam Trathen? It felt like a thousand years. All that had transpired melded into a single, blurred event. What he had just done in Edmond Knapp's barn seemed from another world.

Foremost on his mind was when would he be able to talk with Juanita? When could he hold her? When could they talk? When could he ask if she too had experienced premonitions that they had known each other before in a twilight world that lay somewhere between reality and fantasy?

Reaching the highway, he made a right turn and headed toward Colorado. His mind feeling like a carrousel, Brad knew only one thing with certainty: on this evening, he was going home.

Chapter Five

A week passed. Conversations with Sid and Juanita had been his only interaction with other people. Brad was having some luck in blocking events of his day in the barn. He struggled not to let those terrible images foul his mind. He had managed a couple of workouts at the gym and each day he found that he was not quite as jittery as the day before.

Nights were still pretty rough.

***

Alone in his home, Brad didn't just hold the fly rod; it was more of a caress. It was always with reluctance that Brad disassembled the treasure. Before the necessary breakdown in preparation to place it in a nickel-coated tube, he admired its beauty for the millionth time. When not in use, the rod hung on a wall, the centerpiece of his library. But for now, the rod would go into his truck and be a travel companion for a few days.

A gift from his brother, Matthew, it was like no other fly rod Brad had ever owned. It was a masterpiece. Nine feet long when its four pieces were assembled, the high modulus graphite was a wonder of precision. A handle of select cork, interspersed with Copano exotic burl fit perfectly in his hand. The reel seat of nickel silver and black ash insert gave the rod its heft. Gold-plated titanium guides gave it strength while inlays of Jungle Cock and Kingfisher graced the rod with delicate beauty. Above the grip, skin of a diamond back rattlesnake and windings of chestnut with metallic copper trim commanded respect from any person who saw or touched the extraordinary work of art.

Matthew had commissioned the rod to be built by their friend, Alton. Craftsmanship of a virtuoso now rested in Brad's hand. Matthew had presented the rod with a personal letter, offering sage advice of how one should live a life of significance, offering service to others, but never underestimating or neglecting the life-shaping power of a river. Holding the rod and thinking of his brother and Alton, Brad felt an earned confidence. He knew that Matthew, Alton and he were part of a small fraternity. They were some of the very few whom genuinely understood that the vision of a fly rod is the arc it inscribes between a fisherman and a trout.

Sliding the rod into its tube and placing it beside the rest of his gear, he walked through his house in a final check. Lord, it felt empty. Since returning, his loneliness had been unbearable, even borderline haunting. That was why he arranged this trip. He wanted a day of fishing on the Gunnison River. The Gunnison was more than a creek, it had real heft and held trout that didn't suffer fools or mess around when snagged. That was precisely what Matthew's special rod had been designed to handle.

Most importantly, Brad needed some solitude and to feel the strength of a river.

Gear loaded, Brad headed west. It was impossible not to think of how much had happened and changed since the last time he set off for Gunnison. Mid-day sunshine highlighted the dents that speckled his truck's hood; a perpetual reminder of the hailstorm he had endured on the road to meet Edmond Knapp.

After fishing the Gunnison he would follow his nose. Bottles of New Mexico wine were in the back. These would be presents for Louise, Victoria and Alphonso. He needed to see them all again, hear their voices and look into their eyes. Since his encounter with Edmond Knapp, a taste of repugnance occasionally surged in his throat. This trip would purge that, Brad was certain.

Sid Pruitt had been fantastic. His voice had remained perfectly flat when telling Brad of an anonymous call made to the Albuquerque Police department. Sid offered no hint that anyone had a clue as to the identity of the caller. He explained that from the jail interview of Sylvester Hurley and Lucy's diary information, along with detailed information provided by the anonymous caller, a search warrant had been obtained for the house on Knapp's ranch. Sid told Brad it would take some time to decipher the artifacts and paper records that he and Robert Montoya had recovered from Knapp's ranch house. Sid's voice had cracked with emotion when he spoke of the stacks of pornographic photographs within the house that told heart-shattering stories of depravity.

Sid said not a single word about the living room window being shot out. He never mentioned the barn.

Brad grinned to himself. Perhaps it would be best if he steered clear of Albuquerque on this trip. There was no need to push the courtesy Sid was extending. Some other time and after all of this had become history, he would drop in for a visit with Sid Pruitt and buy the man one hell of a steak dinner.

Miles passed. Brad had always loved this trip. He had driven it a hundred times. The scenery was spectacular and every mile held a memory. But today, he paid no attention. His thoughts remained far away and he drove robotically. Could he stand it without her another four days? He wasn't sure. Her trial had concluded the day of his encounter in Knapp's barn. They had spoken the next morning, frustration and urgency simmering in each of their voices. He had planned to drive to Albuquerque the next day and finally they would be together. She had called back an hour later, choking on tears and anger. An attorney in her office was slated to attend a prosecutor's conference in Los Angeles. That person had become ill and Juanita would be the attendee. She had no choice. She would be leaving in twenty-four hours and away for almost a week.

Brad lost track of the hours that he spent in his house with no workouts, no shower and barely eating. He spoke with Sid but that was it. If it couldn't be Juanita, he had no desire to see or talk with anyone. Finally, one morning he opened his fridge, downed a peanut butter sandwich and Moosehead for breakfast before heading to the gym. The next day, after another sandwich and another workout, he made his decision to fish and visit Cimarron. Instantly feeling better, he went home to pack.

South Park passed unnoticed. Salida and Monarch Pass disappeared in indistinguishable mists. Four days until she would join him on the horse trip that had been scheduled for months. Sam Trathen would be there, along with Kurt Riddle, a deputy sheriff friend for years. His brothers, Patrick and Matthew would join him. It was their annual horse and fly-fishing trip into the Flat Tops Wilderness. It had been a tradition for years. The sheer beauty and solitude of the lake where they camped was straight from paradise, not to mention that the icy water brimmed with trout.

However, a big difference was taking place this year, a huge difference in fact. This year wives had been invited. For better or worse, the guys had given in to unrelenting pressure that a female presence would enhance, not distract from the magic of the trip. Serious doubt lingered in their minds about the wisdom of their decision but it was way too late to change course now.

When Brad had invited Juanita, she practically jumped through the phone. She wouldn't miss it. The environment of horses and camping was not exactly how Brad had envisioned his next rendezvous with her but it sure beat not seeing her at all.

Four more days. Four more days without Juanita.

***

As happened every time he fished, Brad left the Gunnison River a different man than when he had stepped in. The horror of Edmond Knapp's barn was somewhere miles downstream and would soon be a mere drop in the Pacific Ocean. Rivers have such power if given a chance.

When he asked for Louise in the St. James Hotel, a young man behind the desk told him that she had resigned without notice. "She just walked into the manager's office and said it was time to take care of the things in life that really mattered." The clerk shook his head with a smile. "That woman is a pisser. I'll miss the heck out of her. She promised to drop by and see us from time to time but, so far, no Louise." Brad went into the restaurant for a glass of iced tea and, while there, wrote a letter to Louise. He left it with the clerk, thanking him for his promise to hold it until she visited.

***

His visit with Victoria and Alphonso lasted for hours. They bounced over rugged terrain in Alphonso's aging pickup truck. Their old dog, ecstatic to be included, rode in the back, tongue hanging and wind in his face. Brad helped Alphonso repair a downed fence while Victoria sliced apples and cheese.

Seated on the tailgate of the truck, New Mexico blue above, crows and magpies holding court, Brad told the story of how Lucy's diary had been the key to bringing an end to Edmond Knapp. Many details were omitted but Brad told enough that he hoped Victoria and Alphonso could realize some sense of peace.

After eating, Victoria took Brad's hand and with a mysterious smile she spoke. "Come Brad, we have something to show you." Brad looked to Alphonso who shared Victoria's strange expression and nodded that Brad should follow Victoria. The three walked in silence, the dog happily trotting beside. Coming to a clearing surrounded by boulders, deep red in color,

Victoria stopped. Without speaking, she simply pointed to the stone formations. Brad's breath stopped when he saw what she intended him to see. A small, white cross stood within a rectangle of rocks. Freshly planted flowers cast a delicate beauty that added to the sense of reverence of the scene.

Brad was unable to move or speak. He knew exactly what he was looking at. With a gentle tug on Brad's hand, Victoria urged Brad to step closer. When finally he stood before the cross, Alphonso looked to Brad and smiled. "*Abuelo's* final resting place, my friend. He shall live on forever right here in this land that he loved."

Without conscious thought, Brad dropped to his knees before the cross. "*Abuelo*" was the single word inscribed on the cross. His heart racing and mind spinning, Brad lived again in a flash his moments with *Abuelo* and the night in Bandelier. He stood on the crest of Capulin Mountain and felt the horror of Edmond Knapp's barn. Then he saw Capulin Mountain once again, glowing in a setting sun and drifting clouds.

Alphonso was absolutely correct. *Abuelo* would live here forever. *Abuelo* would never be gone.

Brad dropped his head and closed his eyes in a prayer. Making the sign of the cross as he stood, he looked to Victoria and Alphonso for explanation. Alphonso simply smiled, waiting for his wife to speak. Victoria came close to Brad, looking into his face as she spoke. "*Abuelo's* daughter went to see him shortly before he died. It was his dying wish that he be buried here, on our land, the land where he and Lucy use to walk and talk." Victoria gave Brad some time to grasp what she had said. "We had a ceremony right here. Practically everyone in Cimarron came. His daughter came and planted the flowers." Victoria smiled, "*Abuelo* was happy on that day. Victoria paused and looked to the cross. Returning her gaze to Brad she spoke softly, "He is happy today that you have come to visit."

In fading light of afternoon, Brad stood once again at the door of Victoria and Alphonso. They had laughed and cried. Now it was time to say goodbye. With warm tamales as a gift, a hug from Alphonso and *Vaya Con Dios* whispered by Victoria, Brad drove away.

***

Just as before, Brad made Taos in the nick of time to beat closing time and be seated in his favorite outdoor patio. Santa Fe Pale Ale and thoughts of Juanita were his company as he waited for blue corn enchiladas.

His luck in finding the casita available during the mid-summer tourist rush was incredible. As soon as he switched on the lights, he knew that not a thing had changed. It was just as he remembered it from the last enchanted stay he and Elizabeth had enjoyed here. This casita had been their private Taos Shangri-La. Brad moved slowly. The wood floor, warped and irregular, exuded familiarity and the adobe walls felt like welcoming arms. Everywhere he looked, Elizabeth returned his gaze. Her smile was in every corner and her laughter would forever echo within the walls.

After tossing his overnight kit on the bed, Brad splashed cold water over his face and stepped outside. He wanted to see the night. Hollyhocks, now in full bloom, rose in shadowed silhouette within the tiny courtyard. Historic LeDoux Street slept in silence. Brad lifted his face to the sky, black darker than black and so many stars. He thought of the night they had sat in this courtyard with a single candle and pizza from Stella's, just up the street. Of course, they had shared a bottle of *La Chiripada* wine. That night had been every bit this dark and the sky every bit as wondrous.

Brad walked. The night was still as Taos slept. He stood before the darkened R.C. Gorman Gallery where they had purchased art for their home. A dog barked in the distance. He walked further. Ed Sandoval's Gallery held enough light to allow window peeping. A rusting iron sculpture of Sandoval's signature "El Viejo" would forever remain in Brad's flower garden.

He headed back to the casita. With hands in pockets he sauntered, his mind in another world, another time. Once again in the courtyard, he stood still. There was no other way. Tonight had been something he had to do, a step that had to be taken. With a hard breath and one more look at the stars, he felt her. Elizabeth was there. She knew that he was going to Juanita and everything was fine.

The sky was so vast, so dark.

Chapter Six

Groceries and ice chests filled nooks and crannies of every vehicle when Brad and the guys met with the wranglers. After a transfer of gear and a couple of hours to pack horses, the real cowboys rode away to set up camp for the city slickers and wives who would be riding in the following morning. This was a special arrangement that had been decided upon to make the trip as perfect as possible. Everything would be ready and waiting when the campers arrived before lunch the next day.

Before the experiment with female companionship altered their established traditions in ways yet unimagined, the guys gathered in a restaurant for their tradition of Mexican food, beer and jokes. Wives were on the way. After a night in a motel, they would all make the ride into the Flat Tops Wilderness.

Juanita would be leaving Albuquerque at an ungodly hour to join the group by morning. Brad smiled when he recalled her reaction to having no choice but to make a difficult drive. "What's wrong with you?" she had laughed. "Am I riding with a bunch of drug store cowboys? I've been getting up early all my life. I'll be there and ready to go while you sissies are still taking your morning vitamins!"

It was now down to hours. He was going to make it.

***

During the sleepless night before her arrival, Brad realized that he had failed to think through what it would be like to see her again in the presence of so many people. His friends, brothers and their wives were thrilled for Brad. But an aura of uncertainty and caution persisted as they obviously wondered about the mystery woman who had so suddenly entered their closed world. Tossing and worrying through a long and miserable night, no brilliant ideas materialized.

When morning mercifully arrived, it appeared that a small convention was underway with so many vehicles and people milling about outside the motel. Laughter and private jokes among people who had spent years sharing life was the easy banter as they awaited Juanita's arrival. She had called and was only minutes away. It crossed Brad's mind that he hadn't been quite this nervous in the hailstorm on Edmond Knapp's road.

She arrived. Juanita wheeled her small Jeep into the motel parking lot, beeped her horn and waved. Brad had never considered what she might drive. It was perfect. She and her vehicle fit each other perfectly.

Watching her profile as she parked, he walked toward Juanita. Brad suddenly felt on center stage with nothing to say. He heard the group fall silent as he moved to greet her. The weight of so many eyes pressed hard as he came close. Juanita stepped out of her Jeep. She glanced at Brad with a smile but her eyes clearly registered alarm at the audience who so obviously scrutinized her. Walking straight to Juanita with his back to the group, Brad focused his eyes directly on her face. Wrapping his arms around her and pulling her close, he whispered, "Screw 'em!" Brad felt her laugh as she returned his embrace.

Under the dissecting gaze of dozens of eyes, Juanita and Brad held each other. He could wait no longer. The time had come and it was right now. Brad pressed his lips to her cheek as the words he had held so long now gushed in a desperate whisper. "I love you, Juanita. Oh, my God, I love you!"

Their embrace tightened and bodies swayed. "I love you too," was her return whisper before she pressed away to look into Brad's face. With their eyes locked, time froze and countless unspoken words flowed. Finally, with a scarcely perceptible movement of her head, Juanita spoke. "You have no idea how long I have waited for you. Our time has finally come."

There was nothing to say. Brad swallowed and held her eyes.

Brad did not know who started it, but within seconds the entire group erupted in a chorus of whistles and catcalls. Turning to face his so-called friends and with a self-conscious grin across his face, Brad placed his arm about Juanita's waist and walked her to the gauntlet.

Awkwardness quickly subsided as introductions were made and a parade of vehicles made tracks to the trailhead. Morning sun and perfect weather seemed to applaud as a single file caravan of horses began their trek. Hooves in rhythmic melody with creaking leather and excited voices came together in a chorus that filled the pristine valley. Brad seldom took his eyes from Juanita. Words that her father, Harv, had spoken echoed in Brad's mind, *"You should see her on a horse. It's like she was born with reins in her hands and a saddle beneath her."* Juanita rode with the women, several horses ahead. Harv had been spot on. She was obviously as comfortable on her mount as are most people in their living room chairs.

Wildflowers exploded across the valley. At water crossings, the horses drank and riders shifted in their saddles. Only the wranglers and Juanita seemed unfazed by the rigors of the ride. The trail became steep and the alpine valley evolved into dense forest. Anticipation among man and beast increased. The trail's end could be smelled by the horses and was longed for by the humans. When the lake came into view, a collective gasp rippled along the chain of riders. This was what they had ridden for. This was the beauty they had anticipated for so many months.

Camp looked as luxurious as a five star resort when the group finally dismounted. With cramped legs and agonizing rear ends, the riders offered prayers of gratitude. It had been decided ahead of time that the women would occupy one tent and the men another. The women had no interest in putting up with what men do on camping trips and then laughing hysterically like ten-year old boys. Women went about the business of arranging the pre-set camp to their liking while the guys assembled fly rods and fishing gear. Through it all, each person marveled at the beauty in which they were to spend the next few days.

A campfire and lunch came quickly. They all agreed that food had never tasted so wonderful. Rising from his seat beside the fire and looking at no one, Brad spoke. "I'm heading to the lake." That was all he said as he grabbed two blankets, two pillows and walked away.

The water was perfectly calm, like glass, except for the ripple of an occasional rising trout. He heard her approaching. When her footsteps were directly behind him, Brad turned and, with no words spoken, Juanita fell into his arms. They simply held each other. The slight movement in their embrace spoke of so much that had been unsaid and how long they had waited. It was as if their entire lives had transpired in anticipation of this precise moment.

Juanita pushed away and looked into Brad's face with her smile. The whispered words that followed echoed from another world, the words Brad had heard while lying in her cabin. "*Hemos esperado tanto tiempo*" (We have waited so long). Juanita softly kissed Brad's mouth. Her next words, "*Nuestro tiempo finalmente ha llegado*" (Our time has finally come) were spoken by the woman Brad held in his arms.

Passion stirred in the next kiss.

***

"My love, my love, my love." Juanita moved her head from Brad's shoulder and rolled her body until she lay on top of him.

Hair tumbling about his face and into his mouth, she brushed her lips over his eyes.

"I don't want you to leave."

Moving her head in mock sympathy, she smiled her Juanita smile. "Poor bambino. I will never leave you." With a short laugh she rolled onto the blanket, elbow and arm supporting her head. "However, Mr. Brad, since I fully intend to spend the entire night right here with you, beneath a magnificent star-filled sky, I sure would like to sneak back to camp before darkness. My sleeping bag and jacket will come in handy before dawn. Whatcha think about that, Daniel Boone?"

Brad laughed out loud. "I think that is just fine as frog's hair. You go on up there, all by your lonesome, and face that motley crowd after being here with me the entire afternoon." His laugh became a soft chuckle as he spoke. "Want me to go with you?"

Hopping to her feet, Juanita deftly pulled on jeans and a shirt before giving Brad a gentle kick in his butt. "Nope, I do not want you with me. I plan to walk into that camp, smiling like the ecstatic woman I am, grab my things, and march right back here to you. As you said to me earlier today at the motel," Juanita bent low over Brad and spoke emphatically, "screw 'em."

"I love it!" Brad smiled as he locked his hands behind his head and looked up to Juanita. "When you come back, I'll go up there and just stroll through camp like it's any old day. Once I'm sure they're all looking at me, with a big fat smirk on their nosy faces, I'll casually ask if anyone has any idea where in the heck Juanita might be."

"Triple dog dare you!" Juanita laughed as she walked away.

Brad lay on the ground listening to her footsteps fade. The sun had dropped behind the mountains and evening's light was turning the lake into fiery rose. He breathed. Brad could see into the darkening cosmos. He could hear the trout as their bodies moved within the lake.

The first star of evening appeared.

The taste of Juanita remained on his tongue: her body, horses, and campfire smoke. No perfume or feminine fantasy. It was the taste of her pure humanness.

The second star of evening joined the first.

CPSIA information can be obtained
at www.ICGtesting.com
Printed in the USA
FSOW02n0456300817
38035FS